Stone Baby

Joolz Denby

W F HOWES LTD

This large print edition published in 2003 by
W F Howes Ltd
Units 6/7, Victoria Mills, Fowke Street
Rothley, Leicester LE7 7PJ

1 3 5 7 9 10 8 6 4 2

First published in 2000 by HarperCollins

A CIP catalogue record for this book is available
from the British Library

ISBN 1 84197 656 3

Typeset by Palimpsest Book Production Limited,
Polmont, Stirlingshire
Printed and bound in Great Britain
by Antony Rowe Ltd, Chippenham, Wilts.

Dedicated to Justin Sullivan and Warren Hogg

ACKNOWLEDGEMENTS

I would like to thank the following for their help and support: Steve Pottinger the poet, for his careful reading of the manuscript, advice and kindness. Tessa Grant for taking the time to make much needed corrections. Andrew Taylor and Janet Lawrence of the Crime Writers' Association, and the judges of the New Crime Writer Award 1998 – all of whom were willing to bet on a dark horse. Gregory and Radice, my agents – shooting from the hip as ever. Julia Wisdom and Karen Godfrey, my editors at HarperCollins, for having belief and wrestling unflaggingly with my manuscript, plus all the excellent Harper's Crew. Ian Rivers of Bradford Shooting Supplies for unstinting technical advice about the Desert Eagle. Inspector David Wormald of the West Yorkshire Police for being so courteous, helpful and generous with his time. My lawyer, Nicholas Burnett, for doing the legals and being a gent. Ben and Vic Stone for much needed moral support. Justin, Warren, Finn and Screamer for being there and being the very best friends anyone could ever wish for. And my respect and thanks to the Goddess, as ever.

A woman who died aged ninety-two had been carrying her dead baby – long since calcified – for sixty years. The foetus was discovered after she went to a Viennese hospital suffering from senile dementia and pneumonia. She had a large abdominal mass extending from the pelvis to the right upper abdomen. Radiography showed 'lithopaedion' (a stone child). The woman died a week later and an autopsy revealed that the baby had reached thirty-one weeks gestation. The woman's son said she had become pregnant for the fourth time at thirty-two, developed abdominal pain and then recovered. Her menstrual periods resumed. She had no subsequent serious illness, apart from infertility.

The earliest documented case of a stone child comes from a 1200 BC grave in the United States. The complication of extra-uterine pregnancy is very rare because ectopic gestation escapes surgical treatment less frequently than before. Stone children now occur once in every 250,000 pregnancies. The body forms calcium on dead tissue too large to be absorbed. This latest case was probably the longest time a woman had carried a calcified foetus.

Report by Doctors Paul Speiser and Konrad Brezina of the University of Vienna Medical School, in the *Lancet*, 8th March 1995.

Courtesy of the *Fortean Times*

BOOK I

CHAPTER 1

I don't care what anyone says, I know how much it cost her to walk out on that stage night after night in those horrible clubs. I watched her from wherever I could – at the back being elbowed by students so sozzled they would unzip their jeans and piss in a corner – or side-stage if there was one, where watching the faces of the punters was a game in itself. I must have seen her a thousand times.

She always said, *What'ya think, Lil?* And I always told her the truth, even if it was bad news. She was much taller, bigger than me. Somehow it upset me more than if she was small, to see her slump into herself when things went badly. To my mind, you see, what she was doing wasn't just comedy. Really, it was more like teaching than anything else. She talked about things no one else would. It wasn't to be outrageous like some of 'em – she just talked about life and death and how things really are for people. And, man, she was funny! She couldn't half get 'em going, and then, quiet and slow as a serpent, she would have them in tears with the truth of what she said. Oh, she was just brilliant . . . But she was too much, far too much for the people

3

that make you famous; she told too much truth, with too much passion, and she was too intense and too big and . . . see what I mean? But she put 1000 per cent into it, every night, without fail. She would go out there, out into that lion's den – the mouth of hell, she used to call it – and just talk to them. Sounds so easy, doesn't it? Just pop out there, dear, and chat to the audience . . . But she never wrote anything down beforehand, never had a plan. Not *improvisation*, which as we all know is really a total put-up job, but honestly – just *talking* to them.

She looked so relaxed up there, too, so careless, as if nothing could ever faze her. Even that night in Middlesborough when the lighting truss collapsed behind her, she just smiled and made some crack about God not approving of her. Sounds stupid when you come to write it down, but at the time, well . . . Still, she didn't care what happened on stage, she said, because that was her home, where she felt in control, even if there were disasters. She said she liked herself, out there.

But I was there that night; that fucking awful, awful night. Man, I tell you I shall never forget it, not as long as I live, I swear. And not just me, either. Even Ricky, who never liked her – well, that's not fair, I suppose. He never knew how to treat her, he's crap with women. Anyhow, even he was white with fury and disgust. Me, I wanted to faint, or throw up, or both. We stood there, Ricky an' me, and I'm not kidding, he took hold of my

4

hand as we watched and just said, *bastards*, over and over under his breath like a prayer.

Oh, I'd pleaded with her not to do the gig, it was right in the middle of things. She said it was booked six months ago and it'd be OK, she was second on the bill, no one would pay much attention to her except her 'faithful following'. The FC, we called them.

'Lily, girl, they'll forgive me, they understand me, they know . . .' she said with that twitchy half-smile. 'They're my Football Club . . .'

'Forgive what, what should they fucking forgive?' I said, tugging crossly at a tuft of my new short haircut, which I still hadn't gotten used to. 'You've fucking done nothing, there's nothing to forgive. Nothing.'

'Come on,' she said, 'the publicity and stuff. Me being with *him* when – you know. They'll forgive me, I know it, man. It'll be cool, it'll be OK, no sweat, I'll be on an' off an' that'll be an end of it. Come on, it's gotta be done, you know it. Contracts, all that crap.'

I wasn't happy, not one little bit, but I rang the promoter and he seemed fine, if a bit harassed. How could I have been so *stupid*? Of course he was fine, and of course he was tense; he'd double-sold the gig on the strength of Jamie's notoriety. We didn't know, how could we? We didn't live in London but in the frozen bloody godforsaken Northlands. And to be honest, we'd been a bit – well – fucked-up, to say the least.

5

But Christ, we – no *I* – should have been more together, should have been extra, extra on the ball considering everything. But we weren't, either of us. God Almighty – how could we have been, after what had happened? But it was that terrible desire we both had to be normal, to have everything be *normal* again, it was like an obsession, it made us blind.

We only discovered when we got to the fucking gig that the promoter had pasted banners over all the posters with '*Did She Or Didn't She? Find Out At Club X-L-NT, Exclusive!!!!!*' on them. He'd given an interview to *Time Out* about whether he was morally justified in putting such a person as Jamie on, 'under the circumstances'. He said the public had a right to know and to see for themselves, and he felt almost an obligation to go ahead with the show if for no other reason than to defy the Nanny State Moral Majority attitudes he was disgusted to see appearing in the Alternative Comedy Scene, etc., etc. Also, not that he mentioned it, he'd arranged for Vauxhall TV to film that night for a whacking fee and was negotiating to sell his story of what would happen to the highest bidder.

We knew nothing of this until we drove into London and saw the posters. I wanted to turn round then and there but she said no. No, if we don't carry on as normal, nothing will ever be normal again. She thought people would be on her side, you see. That they'd realize what was going on, disregard the lies in the press, the sensationalism. She was a real old punk rocker at heart. She thought that the punters were intelligent, decent types who only needed to be treated nicely and they'd come to a rational decision. What we got was bread and circuses. Enter the Gladiator. Abandon hope, all ye who enter here. We who are about to die, fucking salute thee.

The first six rows of tight-packed chairs (no dinky little cabaret-style tables with candles on tonight) was solidly the gutter press. We didn't realize at first, not having been trained to spot a *Sun* reporter at fifty paces. Next there was row after row of loud, weird people in expensive clothes. I mean, they looked weird to us, but now I know they were your lower-end ad/media/ mag Londonfolk out for a bit of a slummy thrill. The men were trying to look jaded and experienced, the women attempting sad versions of Uma Thurman in *Pulp Fiction*; they were already drunk. Squashed up the back were a handful of real punters. I recognized a few of the hardcore FC, all of whom looked as miserable as sin. After, I found out they only got in because they'd booked weeks in advance. Outside, touts were doing tickets for forty nicker, and they had plenty of takers. It was as hot as hell in the club itself, and the air was thick and blue with ciggie smoke, fashionable swearing, sweat and the slimy metallic sweetness of expensive perfume.

Dan the Man went on first and OK, he's no great shakes but he usually gets his laughs. He's the lovable-clown type. They ignored him like he was invisible. They didn't even lower their braying for a second. He came back into the mildew-stinking cubbyhole of a dressing room cheese-white and sweating. He said, *Christ*, and, *fuck me sideways*, about sixteen times and kept sneaking looks at Jamie, who just went on painting her lips like it was the most important thing in the world to get an even lipline. Next up was Cockette Cockteau, a black surrealist drag artiste, very popular during the drag explosion and a really sweet person, let me say, despite what the papers wrote. He did not get his dick out and scream *Suck it and see, whitey*, nor did he attempt 'an obscene act' with a member of the audience. Actually, he did ten minutes of his 'Marcel the Mime Comes Out' and ran offstage crying his eyes out. He sat next to Dan, sobbing and having swigs from the bottle of Bell's Dan was grimly downing. Everyone was now staring at Jamie as if she was being sent out to the firing squad. She just smiled. She looked calm and far away and she hadn't been to the loo more than once, when usually she went ten times – it was a bad sign. Dan and Cocky got up with expressions of dumb misery on their faces and left, just as Ricky Sharpe, the headline act, came in.

'Well, girlie,' he said, overdoing the cockney geezer as usual, 'you got 'em panting, ent yer, you got 'em nice and fuckin' moist . . . kiss an' tell is it tonight or shall we just leave 'em beggin' for more, eh, darlin'? Eh? Eh?'

8

I hated him then . . . Later, well, you just can't tell about people sometimes, can you? He must have seen me staring because he just giggled and rubbed up his ginger hair, fiddled with his tie and strutted off round the back way to the bar after the others. Jamie seemed not to have heard him; she seemed not to hear anything, even when the gofer-boy stuck his head round the door and said five minutes in a wobbly voice with his eyes on stalks to cop a glance at her.

The promoter was being compere (*quelle surprise*) and he was on already, rehashing his *Time Out* piece for the punters and the cameras.

Jamie got up, looked at herself tiredly in the flyblown mirror and smiled at my reflection.

'Greatest show on the road, eh, Lil? Take no prisoners, always go for the cheap laugh . . .'

We always said that, but tonight it was like a horrible ghost thing to say, it was like speaking ashes.

I heard the promoter; 'Ladies and gentlemen, members of the press, I am proud to present to you tonight a legendary comic talent, a woman whom I myself christened "Lenny Bruce In A Frock" – she's big, mean and firing on *all* cylinders, Britain's most cont-ra-versial artiste this or any other century . . . my name is Ronnie Rage and this is . . . Ja-mie GEE!!!!!!'

You've all seen the footage; if not, you can imagine how fucking shit it was. What did she talk about in that slow, dangerous way she had? I don't remember. Like I said, it was just me and Ricky standin' there, breathing in that horrible reek of fag-stale clubland air and a strange, goatish odour of mass anticipation; of the end of the bacchanal; of the nastiness of people. We stood side-stage, hand in hand like a pair of fucking schoolies.

They were silent for the first few minutes, the audience. They stared at her like they wanted to eat her up, suck the flesh off her face. She was talking about some ministerial corruption scandal or other, I think, when a wire-thin squeal went up from a woman in the middle somewhere.

'Well, did you or didn't you? Did you bloody know or didn't you?'

They all took it up then, screaming it over and over like a chant. A bottle flew and smashed on the lip of the stage, but Jamie didn't move. The reporters, at this point, seemed galvanized into action. They all stood up and started shouting and taking flash pictures; then some of the punters started grabbing at them and yelling how they'd paid forty quid to see this bitch so just fucking siddown. Jamie put her hand up and a sort of panting silence fell.

'People aren't telepathic, man,' she said in a low voice, as if she were talking to herself. 'How could I have known? I mean, I didn't; I didn't know, I thought, I just thought . . . he was with someone else, an affair or somethin' . . .' She didn't get any further.

'You bloody bitch!' A woman with a black bob and a posh accent threw her glass; it bounced off

10

Jamie's shoulder. 'Liar, liar, you fucking lying cunt . . .'

People think your posh types don't go on like that, but they do; oh yes, get 'em in a feeding frenzy and they're the worst of the lot.

Jamie was so brave, I've never seen such courage, but you could see, it was the end of everything. She walked off so casually, bolt upright, away from the howling melee in the club, until she got to the scabby dressing room and there she just literally fell on the dirty floor and cried, great wrenching sobs tearing and pulling at her breath and her whole big body shaking with it. I was practically useless, I was crying so much too – but Ricky shouted at us to stay put and went out slamming the door shut. I could hear him outside, screaming at the idiot promoter who was wandering around like a headless chicken, to get a security man up there fucking pronto. Man, Ricky just stood there while the reporters slavered at him, trying to get to Jamie. He even refused to go on until they got a guard – I'm not lying; it's true. Ricky Sharpe, The Man You Love To Hate, The Evillest Comedian and all that bollocks, he stood there like a little red rooster and defied them until the bouncer came. I was so sorry for all those times I'd rubbished him, I still am. Then he went on-stage himself, wound up as he was, to find a near riot going on with all the chairs overturned, glasses flying and women screaming. But I'll say this for him, he got them calm again, or as calm as they could be. Sheer force

11

of will, I suppose. I won't hear a word against him these days; I shan't forget.

We nearly didn't get out of that rotten hole, believe me. If you'd told me that was how people would behave I wouldn't have believed you. It's not that I'm naive – oh, maybe I am then – but it was so . . . shocking. Yes, it was shocking. They were like animals, those fucking reporters, just like . . . *things*, like beasts. They were all howling and jabbering, red and purple in the face, spit and drool flying, shouting horrible things . . . *Hey, Jamie, Jamie, how does it feel to shag a serial killer? Hey, Jamie, did he tie you up? Hey, Jamie, you knew, you knew, didn't you, did you join in? Did you? Hey, hey, over here, love, hey, slag, over here; what did he eat for his fucking breakfast?*

And in amongst all that red, splattery chaos, all that hysterical screaming, that poor, poor woman the reporter brought with him. Sara Evans's mother. I mean, how could they? That murdered girl's mother. We were trying to get to the car, shoving and running as best we could because the security bloke called Jamie a murdering cunt and left us to it; we were crying and suddenly, there she was. A face like a bone. She was like vengeance walking. Her eyes were terrifying, like great dark, shadowy pits and hate in them like I've never seen in a human being. She was incandescent – a human torch, burning with fury – and who could blame her, who could? Not us. Not then or now. That poor, savage, ruined woman. We both froze and she spoke dead low but it carried through that craziness like a cold flame.

'You . . . you *knew*, didn't you? My little girl, she was only a child, that butcher . . . you knew, how can you still be alive, how can you be alive, you disgusting . . . *bitch*. You should kill yourself, why don't you die? *Why don't you die?* How can you be alive when my baby is gone? You . . . you . . . you're a *monster*, that's what you are, a monster, a monster . . .' Her voice rose into a ragged screech and then she collapsed weeping and all hell was let loose again.

Jamie stood like a great statue carved out of slabs of stone. I grabbed her arm and tried to haul her towards the door while the ravening dogs frothed at the mouth with the pleasure of the vile thing they'd done. I saw someone half carry, half drag Mrs Evans away while a mess of photographers snapped and pointed and stabbed at her with their great insect cameras. She looked like she had no bones left, like an empty coat draped over the man's arm. Jamie was watching her too – her white, white face only flinching as the cameras flashed. She turned and bent a little to speak to me, as if that rabid pack weren't there.

'Lil, I didn't know, I didn't . . . God help me, Lily, he's killed me too.'

CHAPTER 2

I never liked him. That's not me saying it now, after the event, it's true. I never, ever liked him. I know people think I was jealous of her boyfriends, they say Jamie and I are gay, 'Gal Pals' the *Sun* called us. That's not it at all, we were never lovers – but these days it's like you can't just be friends, there always has to be sex in it. Sells papers, I suppose, but it's a crap way to go on.

We were friends, close to what having a sister must be like, I imagine, though people with sisters always say it's no fun. Still, it seems it would be, to me. I have no blood family, since I was abandoned as a baby (picture in the paper, held up to the camera by a nurse; *Who Is Mystery Babe's Mum? Baby 'Lily' Abandoned In Public Loo* – so you see, I'm used to being in the headlines). The nurses named me after the street where the toilet was – Lily Street. They kept 'Lily' at the Home I went to. Could have been worse, they could have called me Lily Street. No one ever claimed me or anything so I don't know who She was, my mother, if you could call her that.

I was adopted quite soon by the Carlsons. I'm

told babies go quite quickly, especially if white, or whitish, in my case. Ma, that is, my adopted mum, not Her who birthed me – Ma and I would have long discussions about what my background could have been, she was good like that. I was so lucky to get Ma and Pa, the old sweeties. We used to make up long stories about me being the child of wealthy aristocratic foreigners who had to leave me and flee due to political persecution; or, I was a common-or-garden old gypsy princess, accidentally lost and heir to the Romany secrets of fortune-telling, horse-doctoring and how to whittle a nice wooden clothes peg.

I reckon She was a half-caste – biracial, as they say now – and my father was white. Or the other way around, of course, how would I know? But I do know my tea-brown hair is ringletty Afro and my long, narrow green eyes look as if they've been stitched shut at the inside corners and my little rubbery nose is a tad flatter and broader than *white* white girls. My skin is a sort of rose-tan and freckled. If you think that makes me exotic and Creole-ish and pretty, think again. It makes me short and thickset, it makes me look, as Jamie said when we first met, like a White Dread Pixie on speed. I've got a gold tooth at the front, too, and a pierced lip. Do I sound defensive? Well, pardon *me*, wouldn't *you*?

But to get on; I never liked him. I disliked the vast majority of Jamie's boyfriends because they mostly ran to type. 'Bad Boys.' That is so pathetic, bad boys. It makes them sound harmless, naughty but nice. I read an article in some women's mag the other day about how women crave the illicit excitement of Bad Boy Sex. Bollocks. I could have spat, reading it. It was some sappy journo-ette salivating over how simply fabulous it was to have wicked encounters with butch, muscular, working-class young men who absolutely ripped one's knickers orf and just *had* one. Sex with a scaffolder: '*His rough, manly hands grasped my heaving breasts like suction cups, kneading, squeezing until my nipples ached and I was utterly aflame with lust for his brutal, hard body. "Give it to me, Kevin," I gasped, "give it to me now!!!!!"*' Golly. And these Mellors subs were so humbly grateful for the opportunity of rogering a real lady in Paloma Picasso lippie and La Perla pants they simply faded, strongly but silently, back into the great mass of the proletariat from whence they'd been plucked, without ever pushing their luck or getting *horridly* complicated. Then, of course, one smirkingly went back to one's normal life utterly glowing. Presumably the cheeks of one's arse glowing as well. Maybe one's arse smirked as well as it throbbed in one's silk chiffon drawers; oh, it was such crap, such crap. I know what that sort of thing really leads to, because I lived with Jamie, the Miserable Green Giant, for eleven years. In her case it led to Sean. And Sean, well, Sean was a nightmare from which we will never, ever fucking wake.

CHAPTER 3

I'd best fill you in about how Jamie and I met and all that, before I get on to what I thought about *him* . . . Sean, Sean Powers, say the fucking name, Lily, girl. God, it's so hard; I feel as if naming him will make him appear again. The 'Night Creeper', they called him. Jamie and I used to shake our heads over the stupid nicknames they gave these killers: the 'Yorkshire Ripper', the 'Hillside Strangler', the 'Green River Killer' and best of all, the 'Son Of Sam' We used to laugh. Why not the 'Nephew Of Arthur'? What would they call a woman serial murderer, the 'Auntie Of Brian'?

It all seemed so ridiculous, grown-up British coppers intoning nasally on the news about the 'Night Creeper'. We were so sure you'd be able to spot someone like that easily in real life. It was just the stupid straights and the media – so out of touch with everything ordinary. I mean, when you looked at the photos in the papers the killers all looked so demented, so weird, in a sort of falsely *normal* way – well, you'd just know, wouldn't you? All those poor sad next-door neighbours and Auntie

Madges who always said – Oh dear, he was such a nice, quiet chap, I never would have thought he was like *that*. If we thought a bloke was nerdy we used to say, Ooh, he's such a *nice, quiet chap*, in a meaningful way and make a comedy surprise face. It makes me cringe thinking about it now; I feel as if I could scrub myself raw and the guilt would never rub off me; my God, those women, those poor fucking dead bitches, their faces are in my mind like a tattoo.

Me an' Her Nibs used to laugh at just about everything, though, we had our own language, our own jokes and sayings – house speak, we called it. We never meant to shut other people out, not wanting to make anyone feel uncomfortable, but I suppose they sensed they were outsiders. Oh yes, we laughed at just about everything, when we weren't furious. I imagine we were pretty tiring to be with, a lot of the time. We didn't give a shit, though, we had each other.

But anyhow . . . I met Jamie Gee in 1987, at a benefit gig at the Windsor Hall in town. That it was a complete shambles goes without saying. Oh, sure, they *meant* well, they always do, that sort of earnest, holey-jumpered middle-class anarcho, fresh outta uni. They wanted me to be a gofer (you know – go fer this, go fer that) and to organize the bucket collection – unpaid, naturally, and once you say 'yes' in an unguarded moment, that's that. You end up having to do all their work as well as your own because they can never make a decision or get their arses in gear about anything, ever. They end up letting you do it all and then calling you a fascist control freak. Not very loudly, though, in my case, on account of me being nominally black, and utterly fucking unable to bear fools of any size, shape, race, creed, gender or sodding sexual orientation. At all. Ever. A-fucking-men. A tad intolerant? Yeah, oo-er, y'got me there, bro.

One of the most unwashed, untidiest and *foolish* of this shower, who called himself 'Liberty' (even though I knew his name was Nigel Bottomley because I'd been at Allthwaite High with him), sloped up to me at some point during the afternoon of overextended sound checks and general mayhem and stood twisting his bony hands together nervously.

'Wow, hey, Lily . . .'

'What do you *want*, Nigel?'

'Liberty, Lily, um, I'm called Liberty now – I feel it's like, a blow against, you know, against the oppressive patriarchy that forces sexist names on us when we're pre-persons and like, I feel . . .'

'Nigel, what the fuck is it?'

'God, you can be really hard, you know; I was just going to say we've, like, booked a womyn-comedian, sort of, just now; she's like, local, and Spike said you'd know what to do . . . but, I mean, I could probably miss the co-op meeting and, you know, deal with it if you feel it's a total hassle or anything . . .'

I refrained from mentioning we already had four

bands, a radical juggler and the Manningham Wimmin's Collective A Capella Chorus to get on. However, he must have seen the look on my face through the dope haze and he loitered off palely, muttering.

'Nige, wait!' I screamed after him over the sound of Sick Puppy tuning up. 'This comic, what's she called? What does she look like – *anything*?'

'Ah, yeah, gotcha – uh, she's called Jamie Gee and Spike says she's scary and big . . .'

Oh, how fucking wonderful, I thought, a big, scary comedian no one has ever heard of, from round here, who probably eats short, overtired and snappy gofers like other people gobble Pot Noodles. Then I forgot about this nightmare because another one was forming. The Committee, or at least the remaining inner core of three who had carried on after this morning's schism and the resultant loss of the communal van because it belonged to the rebel leader, had made a momentous decision. Led by the Wimmin's Chorus, we were all going to get on-stage at the end of the show and sing 'I Am Strong, I Am Womyn'.

Utter chaos reigned. The Committee and the Chorus were unshakeable. There was a distinctly male bias in the acts and this would help counteract it. The bands, including Sick Puppy, who were headlining as they had recently released their first single, were furious. The Chicken Skinners, who'd already had protests from Animal Lib about their name and were very edgy (or perhaps that might have been all the whizz they'd sucked up their unappealing noses all day), said they bolt refused to do it. Cries of 'sexist' rent the air. Lemon Pigs said they would, if they could just play as part of the accompaniment at the back of the stage. The Sickies gave in and said OK, but I didn't like the look in their eyes, it promised trouble. The Mad Scientists said yes, they'd be happy to do it, but only if their frontman could have a costume change and be in the middle, at the front, where the best lights were. No negotiation possible. More chaos. The Chicken Skinners started packing their gear in a jerky, furious way, and left.

There was a mass panic over this with anarchos wailing and keening and the Animal Libbers looking smug and vindicated over such a massive victory on behalf of the world's bunnies. I was so grateful that I had one less bunch of adolescent prats to butter up, I didn't realize that everyone was clambering on-stage to rehearse the bloody song. When I did, I ran as fast as my little legs would carry me to the Ladies. Bolting into an empty cubicle, I got up and crouched on the toilet seat, so even if they looked under the door, they wouldn't see anyone there. I know, childish, but I cannot *do* group things. The very idea makes me go hot and cold and full of resentment. It reminds me too much of school and college – oh, don't get me wrong, model student, me; lots of qualifications, no hassle. Never rocked the boat, never even cheeked the dense, patronizing halfwits

21

of teachers. Just did my time nice and quiet. But I hated it, every foul fucking queasy minute of it. Couldn't tell Mum and Dad because they would have been so upset, but the racism, the bullying – and that's just the staff. No, really, it was crap. And worst of all, were *Group Projects*. Having to try and survive those little exercises in 'Work Skills' were a horror. Ugh. Cringe. Trying to be nice to shitheads like dear Nigel; having to slow my brain down and make myself acceptable to them. Watching them just not *get* it, anything, ever. They didn't even manage the coursework, never mind recognize the hidden agendas inherent in the fucking *system*, Christ. And then it would be the Group Presentation, just like this bloody-be-dammed pissing singalong. No, hiding like a sulky brat was infinitely preferable to public humiliation.

I hugged my knees in their aged combat pants to my sweatshirted chest and waited. After a short while, I sensed something odd. I could hear someone breathing in the adjacent bog. We breathed together for a minute then curiosity overcame me and as silently as my monkey boots would let me, I crept off the bogseat and knelt on the floor, peering under the bottom of the cubicle side wall. *There were no feet!* It hit me straight away . . . someone else was escaping from the horror of the mass singalong. I got back on my perch.

'Excuse me,' I said quietly, 'but what d'you think you're up to?'

'What?' came the startled reply. 'Oh, shit! Look, whoever you are, please, please, please don't turn me in. I can't do shit like that fucking song thing, man. I mean, I'm sure it's great and everything but . . . I can't, I just can't . . . I . . . wait on, what are *you* doing – right – you're hiding too, are you?'

Shit, discovered.

That's how we met, crouched on the toilets in the Windsor Hall bogs, avoiding the ghastly embarrassment of the end-of-show singalong.

'Look,' I said, 'my name's Lily, I'm the gofer and probably the stage manager too, by the look of how things are going . . . I can't do that fucking shit either – don't worry, I won't turn you in. Who are you, anyhow?'

'Jamie Gee. I'm the, um, comedian; they only booked me at three o' clock this afternoon . . . I don't want to be rude, like, but it doesn't seem very . . . organized. I haven't got a fucking clue what they want me to do or anything . . . hey, are you the one they're all so scared of? Lily? Yeah, some bloke called Liberty said I was supposed to check in with you because he's going home for a bit of a kip. You don't know where I can get a coffee, do you? You fancy a coffee? Let's sneak off to a caff, they won't miss us for a bit and you could say we didn't know anything about the fucking singalong – then we won't have to do it, will we?'

'OK,' I replied with a distinctly frigid note in my voice, 'yeah, why not, fuck 'em.' Going home for a bit of a kip, eh? The sneaky little get. Well,

I'd done my duty. Fuck 'em double. I got down and opened the cubicle door. Until my dying day, I will never forget the sight that greeted me, never.

CHAPTER 4

It wasn't just that she was tall. I've seen taller women than her, often. It was the monumental quality she had, like a statue walking. She wasn't fat exactly, it was more like she had big bones covered in big muscles covered in a layer of padding. But it wasn't the size that got me, so much as the outfit in conjunction with the size.

She looked – well – medieval. Her outfit seemed to comprise of layer upon layer of raggy black clothing in thin fabrics – voluminous ankle-length, tight-waisted skirts, little skinny T-shirts one on top of the other, a tiny knackered cardie knotted under her bust – man, you name it. All home-made, you could see the stitching. And no wonder she seemed so tall, she was wearing a great big pair of boot-clogs – proper, Yorkshire clogs with a good inch and a half of wood and lace-up leather uppers. In black, natch. Huge silver rings covered her hands, and her hair – words fail me. It was long and *Shocking* Pink. Wound up high on her head with a mad arrangement of lacquered chopsticks and black muslin scarves – crimped strands escaped and fell around her face.

She smelt of sandalwood and of herself, if you see what I mean – warm and spicy. I gawped – she smiled.

'You're only little,' she said, 'aren't you? Are your eyes really that colour or is it lenses?'

I looked into her face as it loomed over me. She was heavily painted as the fashion was then, Gothic, I suppose you'd say. Her big, uncompromising nose was pierced with a thick little gold ring in the left nostril and her ears had six heavy silver rings on either side with all kinds of junk dangling from them. I looked into that face and into her eyes. They were grey, deeper than silver, lighter than thunder. Her gaze was like a child's, direct and without guile. I've never seen it matched, the intensity of that gaze. Maybe it's because she's so short-sighted, I don't know, but she looks at you, really looks, not like most people who just glance and look away. And it was without barricades against the world, that gaze, she had nothing between her and the terror that is humanity. Nothing to protect her from hurt, from love, or from destruction. I felt in an instant I wanted to take care of her . . . I know, I know, barmy, irrational; but the nakedness of those eyes was like a call to arms, and who would look after her if I didn't? I didn't know if she was married, single, gay, straight, celibate or shag-happy; I didn't know if she had lots of friends or none, if she had children, family or what. It didn't matter. I felt so deeply that she was, whatever her circumstances, alone. That she would always be alone no matter who she was with, and it cut me like a blade in the heart.

I felt like that too. Always outside, always out in the street looking in the warm and lighted windows of someone else's Christmas. Sure, I loved Ma and Pa, really, really loved them, but inside, somehow, I was alone too. But I had developed barriers, a shield that helped me to survive against those who love to hurt the likes of us. We're the ones who just can't *do* the sad dance of society as it is trudged through by the desperate, terrified straights of all classes. We're the scapegoat, the maverick, the wolf, the pariah; yeah, man, the freaky-fuckin'-deaky.

I know this might make Jamie sound weird and scary, and sure, some people found her scary, I won't deny it. But I wasn't scared. It wasn't bravado, she just drew me to her like blood, like the blood family I never knew and couldn't know. Here she was, my sister, my great helpless, savage, lonely, funny, loving sister and I would never leave her again because *she needed me.* She needed someone to look after her who wouldn't plunder that innocence or shut those eyes with weeping; who wouldn't try to douse that flame. No one could see how unbalanced she was. I don't mean that nastily, she just wasn't, isn't, couldn't be a balanced person. It made her vulnerable, that terrible strength and terrifying weakness, it made her what she is. I am proud of her and I always will be.

And yeah, it's bollocks about her being a liar. She *can't* lie, she's as transparent as glass. She's an Aries, if you do that astro stuff. If she tries, you can tell, because she goes all wooden and can't look at you, she's crap at it. So you just ask the question a second time and out will come the truth, she can't hide it. That's why I hate them saying she's a dirty liar. She is, and was, a lot of bad things – but a liar? No. She is my true sister.

But of course, I didn't mention any of this to her as she stood over me shaking with giggles and desperate to get some caffeine in her thick blood. I don't talk about feelings a lot, though as you may have noticed by now, I feel 'em good stylee. It's easier to write things down, I find. I've kept diaries for years. Jamie used to laugh at me when we were on the road, freezing in some hideous B & B, for sitting up and scrivening away by the yellow light of an unshaded twenty-watt bulb. But something told me to get it all down, to get it on paper or, later, on disk. She had her horoscope cast once; it said at the end, '*a great fatality hangs over your life*'. I felt that too, I felt as if it was all too good to last. But that's getting ahead of myself again.

We went into town, just a five-minute stroll in which passers-by dropped their jaws and bugged their eyes at her, or maybe us, because – man oh man – talk about the fucking odd couple . . . We nattered about how we'd never met before, which was just pure chance, just different circles, different clubs, different ways of life. Finding a caff, we sucked up some coffee and I asked her what she was going to do tonight. My eye was half on what time it was, since I have an overdeveloped sense of responsibility, so I didn't quite catch what she said first time, it sounded like, 'I've got no idea.'

I paused. I rewound. I pressed 'play'.

'What' I said evenly, 'what exactly do you mean, "I've got no idea"? You've gotta have a routine or something, jokes and shit. I mean, you're a comedian, what are you going to *do* up there?'

She sighed and reaching down hitched up her stockings, which, I noticed, were secured under her knees with red and black lace garters. She chewed inside her cheek and looked at me sideways. It all came out in a rush.

'Well, the thing is, you see, I've only done this once before and the first time was an accident. I was helping Graeham do the cabaret thing at the Cellar Bar, you know, just doing the door and stuff like that, and this bloke didn't turn up, so he said, Graeham said, that is, like well, get up there and tell 'em the story about the stripper you used to know who had an incontinent python. See, I'd told him it the night before and he thought it was funny. He said I ought to go on the stage because some of the so-called comics he booked couldn't raise their dicks, never mind a laugh. Hmm, so, when this bloke never turned up, I did it. It was great, I loved it, it was like jumping off the highest board at the swimming pool, only better because water doesn't shoot up your nose. And I told about some

29

other stuff that had happened to me or, you know, people I knew. Anyhow, they laughed and didn't bottle me off or anything, so I reckoned, why not? I've gotta do something with my life – I hate the fucking Social Security office, I hate signing on and I hate proper jobs, so maybe I could do this. Then that Spike bloke rang up Graeham this afternoon and said he'd been there that night and what was my number because he was getting piles of grief about there not being enough women on the bill tonight and he was desperate, and then he rung me up and I said OK. But, I don't tell jokes or anything, do you think it'll matter?'

I was gobsmacked. She looked so plaintive, I couldn't say anything except, yeah, it'll be all right, but my heart sank to my boots at the thought of her going out in front of a horde of pissed-up tosspots of the type I fucking *knew* would be there that night. Maybe they'll bugger off to the bar when she's on, I thought, she's only got fifteen minutes anyhow – what could happen in fifteen minutes?

CHAPTER 5

I'd like to say that when we staggered, weak with laughter, into the venue again, calm and happiness reigned. I'd *like* to say it but, yes, you guessed it, it would be a *lie*, mofo. I parked Jamie in the office with a book she produced out of her magic bag and tore down to the hall.

Horror greeted me. Everyone was screaming at each other and the Chicken Skinners had fucked off in a huff with not only their own gear, but a considerable quantity of everyone else's, too. The poor old Lemon Pigs had the most stuff missing and were practically in tears – or as near to it as super-cool heroes of indiepop ever could be. Musos – *Christ*.

When I finally sorted it, and showtime loomed, the hall filled up, alcohol was taken. We had a small glitch when I discovered the lighting man was tripping off his face. Still, the consequent substitution of his roadie proved a brilliant move, as said roadie had always fancied a go and turned out to be very talented as well as rather nice-looking ... We put the Lemon Pigs on without much trouble – they came, they played, they left the stage – yawn – only ten minutes over time. Not bad going for them.

The radical juggler, Sy, was indeed radical in that he couldn't actually juggle. Still, the punters seemed to think it was part of the act, his being incompetent and narky. Since most of the audience were still in the bar, the ones that were actually out front had a great time and laughed a good deal, especially when Sy nearly brained himself with a gaily striped club. Sy himself came off quite happy, saying that in his opinion, he wowed 'em – but that was only natural as a talent like his was bound to win 'em over, know what I mean? But I did feel his mother shouldn't have screamed, stamped and whistled like that everytime he managed a crossover.

Then the dreaded Scientists went on, to the roar of their four girlfriends and the conversation of the other six drunks in the hall. What can I say? Obviously I was so hip-less as to be beyond the pale, because I thought they were crap.

After doing three unrequested encores, the Scientists finished and we put the Wimmin on. We were now running massively late, but at least we had a good house and the punters were drifting out of the bar as it got too crowded, and the Wimmin's supporters and partners made a healthy audience. I took the opportunity to nip up and see Jamie.

I opened the door quietly, in case she was resting, and went in. She was stood staring out of the window at the city lights, smoking . . . I hadn't realized she was a smoker, and said so. She turned to face me and smiled.

'Yeah, but only when I'm nervous. I can take it or leave it, really, I'm not an addict like most . . . how's it going?'

'OK; the Wimmin are on, hear 'em? Yodelling their little fucking hearts out, bless 'em . . . you're on next, you know, fifteen minutes dead, I'm afraid, we're well over.'

'No, no, that's fine . . . fine; I can't think what to say to them anyway, my mind's a blank, totally.'

Now I know she always felt like that just before she went on, as if the terrible stage fright she suffered wiped her brain clean. It always came right when she went on; Dr Stage never failed her. But that first time, I was shocked. Was she a washout? One of those people who were 'ever so funny in the pub' but a dead loss on-stage. She was so sweaty under her slap and so palpably terrified I started feeling nervous, too. I stared at her gormlessly, then with a shake of my head, I said, 'Don't worry, honey, you'll be . . . wonderful . . .'

She looked at me, her eyes locking into mine. 'I don't know what to say to them,' she repeated numbly, and turned back to the window, the hand holding her cigarette trembling. I was aghast. She didn't have long to pull herself together and do it, but in this state? I doubted if she could.

Telling her I'd come back and fetch her, I ran downstairs two at a time. The Wimmin were joyfully murdering 'Respect', which happens to be one of my favourite songs. People were jigging about and clapping. I was a cat on a hot tin roof. When they came off, all fourteen of them, I ran up and fetched Jamie. She looked even worse. The stage was set for her. People were milling about in a vaguely anticipatory sort of way out front. I said, 'Go on, girl, you're on.'

She looked at me like a kiddie about to be smacked, and walked on.

And the magic happened. From the minute she set foot on that stage she was a changed person. I could see why she had said it was like diving from the high board. She looked as if she'd spent all her life up there, she looked suddenly calm and still. She kind of *sauntered* to the mic like she hadn't a care in the world. You wouldn't have thought she had a nerve in her body. She had a slight smile on her shocking-pink lips and she chatted with a few hecklers for a minute, then dovetailed straight into the stripper anecdote as if she'd done this all her life.

She was right, she didn't tell jokes. She talked to them, as if they were all friends, as if they were all in this together, partners somehow, not just audience and act. To be honest, it wasn't an act. It was just her, without any pretences or facades. She made that vulgar story into something comic and tragic, bittersweet and furious. She made you understand somehow, what it was like to get up in front of drunken, sniggering, wanking men and take your clothes off night after night. How the men weren't what they seemed, but were very often too frightened of what their friends would think to admit the whole thing embarrassed and shamed them. That some of them hated and dissed the strippers out of fear turned to loathing. How they wanted to fuck a stripper because they thought women like that were dirty cows who'd do any sleazy thing they wanted in the sack; not like their proper girlfriends who pretended to be virginal even though they wore 'exotic' lingerie and had been with half the pub before them. Those women were 'nice', the ones you wed. The strippers were slags, for fucking and forgetting after you'd boasted to your mates how she let yer stick it up her arse.

And she made you see the strippers. The ones who despised the men, truly despised them for being turned on by such a cynical, overtly commercial act. Money kept those women working at a job that froze my blood to contemplate. Or the others, who got a sad kick out of teasing men because they thought it gave them power, never wanting to see what the men really thought of them, never seeing how it was another form of abuse, of self-destruction, the pattern of their childhoods repeated like a scratchy, diseased refrain.

And then she had you laughing almost against your will at the incongruity of seedy glamour versus practical real life. Of the friend of hers from London who cycled to the peepshow with her still-damp-from-the-wash costume of lurid purple sequin G-string, bra, suspenders and fishnet stockings tied to her handlebars to dry. She had us in stitches over the bizarre costumes strippers were driven to think up in order to create a little novelty. Like, a Redskin maiden in home-made wash-leather chammy micro-mini, two bits of sheepskin fluff stuck to her nipples with eyelash glue and a black wool braided wig from the fancy-dress shop in town . . . And the poor old incontinent python, well past its prime and longing for a quiet night in digesting a rat, not being whipped about over the heads of the punters by some overenthusiastic artiste – who could blame it if it lost its self-control?

Did they love her? Fall down and worship her? No, not really. Oh, some did, you could see their faces in the crowd, they needed this, they craved the feeling of one-ness with someone they thought was strong. But plenty of others shut themselves up tight and fast against this unnatural bitch with her bad language and accurate eye. More than one man out there was looking well fucking moody after her fifteen minutes was up, and more than one woman looked outraged and self-righteous. But the rest? They applauded like good 'uns and off she came, beaming.

I patted her like a good horse who'd won her race. I was beaming too. I could hardly speak I was so fucking proud of her. I knew she had what it took, that she would improve and hone this ability into something extraordinary; I just knew. I also knew I wanted to be part of it, to get her on the path, and I knew I could do it. Because she wasn't just funny, she told the truth. It was like standing out in the rain when the summer thunderstorms come, electrical and fierce. She just needed someone who believed in her. She needed me. And the fact was, I needed her; she could speak out loud, fearlessly, what I, with my congested heart, could only feel. She would be my voice, I would be her shield. And that's how it was. Until that last, terrible moment when it all came down.

CHAPTER 6

I won't dwell on the backbiting, recriminations and disjointed noses that are the aftermath of every gig in the world. Suffice to say at around three a.m. Jamie and I fell into a curry house and stuffed our faces with Chicken Shashlik and Peshawari Naans until we could barely swallow another gulp of beautiful eggy-yellow Mango Lassi. As we stretched out groaning amid the clamour, I lit up a fag and offered her one. She refused.

'Honest, I only smoke when I'm nervous, really; I don't fancy them otherwise,' she said.

Reaching across I palmed a pinch of aniseed sweets from the saucerful on the table and chewed thoughtfully. Jamie stared off into the melee and bit her remaining lipstick off. It was odd, I didn't feel the need to fill the silence with chatter like I did with everyone else, so of course I said:

'Isn't it odd I don't feel the need to talk all the time with you?'

'Er, what, sorry?'

'I said, I don't feel obliged to do small talk with you, it's OK to just sit in silence, you know, just sit.'

'Sure, if that's what you want.'

'Well, no, I mean, it's like, we don't *have* to talk, but we could if we wanted to, or not, if we didn't . . .'

'Lil, do you have something on your mind?' She looked at me, squinting slightly. I considered telling her to put her glasses on, but I found myself saying:

'I realize we've only just met, and of course, like, I could be a first-water loony or a crazed stalker, but the thing is, could we live together, d'you think?'

I couldn't believe I'd said it. It sounded so totally mad. M.A.D. I felt myself go scarlet and sweaty and I swallowed, which sent my sweets down the wrong way so I convulsed in a coughing fit. At least it was a distraction.

When I recovered, Jamie poured me some water and said, 'Jesus, Lil, I thought you were a goner, are you all right now? Shame, though, I was really hoping to have a chance at practising the Heimlich manoeuvre – I've only ever tried it on my teddy.'

'How can you be so heartless? I could've died or something,' I spluttered.

'S'easy, years of practice, you haven't met my mother. So this moving-in thing, yeah, why not.' Her face closed in on itself slightly, her pale lips compressing like a winter rose. 'Yeah, now Andy's fucked off, you could have the attic room. We were wondering about who we'd get to move in. It's a slum, mind you, what if you can't hack it?' She smiled, her eyes unlocking. Her face split wider with a grin and her eyes went slitty with amusement. I smiled back. We started laughing.

I moved in the following Saturday. Mum made like I was off to Siberia and held funeral rites over the Last Supper (roast lamb, two veg, two sorts of taters, mint jelly, bread-and-butter pudding with *cream*, as it was a Special Occasion) and she cried like a leaky tap all the way to Ravensbury, where I was to take up my abode with demons. Well, that's what she thought, bless. Actually, she wasn't far off the mark. God, it was a fucking hideous slum, it really was. I cried out for Domestos, body and soul. My parents were truly horrified. I tried to make light of it, playing the 'young people going through a bohemian phase' coupled with 'nothing a good scrub-down won't cure' cards – but hey, napalm wouldn't have shifted the crud in that hole.

The house itself was really quite nice, if you ignored the pistachio-and-tangerine paintwork; a typical Bradford late-Victorian stone-built end terrace, with an open-ended yard round the back where someone had knocked the wall down to get a car in. Or in this area, where someone had knocked the wall down with a car. At least I could park the Mini off the street, which was comforting.

But whatever charm the house had once possessed in its heyday as a foreman's home was long gone. Once upon a time, end houses like this one had been a step up the social ladder, the rest of the 'through' terrace houses in the row being for workers. Now the hands of various landlords had rent (ha ha) any remaining charm from it during its long descent to the outer circle of hell.

This was what was euphemistically called a 'mixed' area, comprising equal parts students, poor Asian families and The Unemployed. If not lived in by a family, the houses were shared by groups of 'friends' of a type distinctly different from the Yankee sitcom version, believe you me. One person (known as 'Hitler' by the other tenants) would be designated senior tenant and assume the responsibility of collecting the meagre rent and delivering it to the landlord. In this case, by default, Jamie was senior tenant, her last boyfriend, Andy, having fucked off with the rent money and anything else of value he could scavenge from everyone's rooms. 166, Brunel Street was to be my new home. You should have heard my mam sobbing, it was like Niagara.

Trying to look cheery and devil-may-care, I hopped out of the car and waved to Ma and Pa who were sitting in the van looking horrified. I rang the bell. No answer. So, I knocked. No answer again, only the hollow boom of my increasingly clenched fist. I knocked harder. Pausing, I heard a strange shuffling noise. Then I heard a pathetic little cough. The door opened a crack on the safety chain and a sliver of pale face and a large light-brown eye appeared.

'Er, hi!' I said with false bonhomie. 'Is Jamie

41

in, I mean, she does live here, right – this is 166, isn't it?'

'Yes, darling, yes, yes and yes,' husked the face. 'You are Lily, attic, new tenant, welcome. Let me unchain the door, my love and let you in – oh, I am Mojo. The other tenant.'

The door was shoved open, raising a rill of mouldy carpet, and I met Mojo for the first time. I didn't dare look round at my parents lest I be turned into a pillar of salt by their expressions. Mojo held out a delicate hand, the almond-shaped nails painted deep crimson. I took it in my stumpy brown paw, and there it remained, like a long bundle of sticks wrapped in ivory silk. We didn't so much shake hands as hold them for a brief moment. Mojo's lustrous but dishevelled ebony hair hung in a deep wave over one heavy-lidded eye and fell to his shoulders. Yes, Mojo was a bloke. Well, sort of. He was a very convincing transvestite and only when this close could you discern the faint traces of manliness that clung to his long, skinny figure. He was wearing an antique satin kimono and pink velvet mules. I prayed my mum and dad just went on first impressions until I could break it to them gently. Better they thought I was living with a prostitute than a man in drag.

Huffing like a walrus through his greying moustache, Pa pulled bags and boxes out of the van while I dragged my rucksack and enormous barrel bag into the hall. Ma tremulously unloaded bags of food and 'freezer' loaves from the Bakery. I personally doubted the existence of a kitchen, never mind a freezer, but experiencing the hall was enough for them, to be honest. They were not impressed. I didn't bother asking Mojo to help us. It would have been inappropriate. Like asking the Pope for a condom. Mojo just *was*, in the Buddhist manner. Finally all my stuff was in and I kissed the Popsies (OK, OK, I know, what can I say?) ta-ta, received a huge, foil-wrapped fruitcake dripping with tears from Ma and waved gamely as they puttered off, looking like that couple out of *Where the Wind Blows* by Raymond Briggs. I was definitely Fungus the Bogeygirl, in that case.

I turned to Mojo, who was emerging from a grimy doorway.

'*Is* Jamie in?' I asked.

'No, darling, no. Just popped to the shops, shouldn't be long. Let's have a nice cup of tea and talk about me.'

We sank on to an enormous disintegrating sofa with a boing! of springs and a faint cloud of dust. Arranging himself in a Dietrichesque pose on the filthy ochre scatter cushions, he filled me in on his life and times. At one point I made tea in the appalling kitchenette (unhappily, it did exist), because whilst with Mojo the spirit was willing, the flesh couldn't be fucking bothered. We drank black tea, it was safer.

Mojo, legal name Mohammed Iqbal, was twenty-five, and the disowned son of Jahanzab Iqbal, the prominent local lawyer. I was shocked,

43

the Iqbals were pillars of respectable society. Mr Iqbal senior was a noise in Bradford; a self-made man – westernized, modern, big on the council and always in the *Telegraph & Argus* shaking hands with visiting dignitaries. His wife, the incredibly exquisite Shaheen, was occasionally glimpsed dressed in something unspeakably chic, her face rising like a perfect orchid from the negligent chiffon swathes of her dupatta. Girls all over Bradford shot off to the Bombay Stores when she appeared in public, longing to copy the latest cut of her punishingly expensive shalwar kameez.

Mr Iqbal was a short, stocky bull of a man, handsome, powerful and self-obsessed. That he acquired the gorgeous, aristocratic Shaheen seemed a dynastic alliance rather than a love match. Wrong. Mojo said they adored each other. They adored their darling boy until they came home from a pan-cultural civic function and found Mojo miming to the backing singers on a Nusrat Fatah Ali Khan tape at full volume dressed in his mother's second-best gold-lamé ensemble, dripping with her jewellery, painted like a houri and swaying in her ninety-quid bronze kid slingbacks. Wah! Horrorshow.

'It was terrible, darling, terrible. My mother screamed and ripped the kameez from my living flesh – you don't know how I mourned, I loved that costume, the embroidery! A fearful scene after that, you can imagine. Daddy went all Islamic and Mummy, well, the language! I *dare* not repeat what she said, I didn't realize she'd *lived* so much. They

44

threw me out, naturally, abomination that I was. Lots of chanting about waste of an expensive education, perversion, disgrace, heads never being held up again if anyone found out. Told everyone I'd gone to visit Granny back home. Lies. I did go to London, stayed with some Old School connections for a while, but I had to come back, you see, there's Someone . . .'

He paused, the glossy sweep of his lashes shading his amber eyes. Camp as buggery he was, certainly, but there was the iron self-will and self-interest of the public schoolboy there too, all right.

As I refilled our cups, gingerly fishing the wildlife out of mine, the door opened and in came Jamie, laden with Morrison's supermarket carrier bags. Her pointy nose was red with cold and her pink hair was scraped into a topknot spiked with one of her chopsticks; she was dressed in an astonishing voluminous black cloak, wrapped round and flung over one shoulder. She looked like the Grim Valkyrie. Only Disco.

'Hell-ohh! Oh, you've met – wasn't here, dragsville on legs. I bought food, lots of lovely food. OK, cheap food but lots and lots! Big scran tonight, kids; red spaghetti with orange cheese and *bottles* of Morry's best screwtop Albanian rouge. Fabby!'

'Don't say "fabby", darling, it's common. Such a big trollop. What *will* our new girl think?' Mojo purred.

'She won't care – you won't, will you? Sorry,

sorry, of course you might. Fuck, bollocks, shit. Overexcited again – wait, I'll calm down in a minute. Morrison's is too much for me, it really is. It gets worse and worse! The music! James Last does Punk Classics, I kid you not. The people, my God, the fucking *lights*! Honestly, I caught a glimpse of myself in the mirror over the veg display – I looked completely insane. Return of the Living Dead; Zombie Queen of Olde Bradforde Towne. I looked' – she paused solemnly – 'like a boiled pig.'

'No, darling, no, no, *poached*, perhaps . . .' Mojo's velvety lips curved gently. It was a smile, for him.

They looked at each other, well, in a way I can only describe as *tender*. Then they looked at me the same way. I did something I have never done before. I burst spontaneously into tears. I was home at last.

CHAPTER 7

Red spaghetti turned out to be Spag Neapolitan; and the violently orange cheese when grated on top made an interesting colour contrast. Jamie favoured the heavy-on-the-herbs-and-garlic, plenty-of-ground-black-pepper school of spag-making, which suited me fine. I wolfed down huge amounts, as did she. Mojo picked at a little bowl of the sauce and drank wine. We drank and talked all night – Mojo, who loved nicknames, christened me 'Tiger Lily'. I was secretly made up about it, it made me feel I belonged, was one of the gang, I suppose. Eventually, when the dawn rose with a chorus of coughing pigeons, I staggered off to bed with a hot-water bottle and slept all morning. Happy, happy, happy.

And that's how it was, mostly. We were a happy house, really, until Sean came. Nothing weird and occult went on, as the fucking papers would have you believe. No orgies, sorry. No biting the heads off live chickens and wild drug parties. We just lived there. We ate red spag and grey spag (with milk, bacon and cheese). Sometimes friends would come round and eat with us, not what you'd call a dinner party, more an eat-off-a-tray-in-front-of-the-telly kinda do. One of our regular mates was Gabe Smith, Jamie's best and oldest friend. I knew him by sight and reputation, and always liked the look of him – you know how it is, you want to talk to someone but you can't think up a good enough excuse. Now we had a friend in common. Synchronicity. He was a professional guitar technician for various fairly big bands and so away a lot, but when he was in town he often stayed with us. Sometimes we'd go to Lonnie and Ben's place, but on the whole, we were homebirds.

During the day, Jamie and Mojo pottered about at whatever it is the Unemployable do to pass the time – not housework, I can tell you. Jamie used to count it a personal moral victory if she didn't watch daytime TV. I know they both read a lot, which involved trips to the Big Library in town and the attendant drama of an outing. Jamie was beginning to try her hand at writing around this time; Mojo spent a lot of the day asleep. He could have slept for Britain, in my opinion. In the evenings if we didn't go out we'd watch telly or get a video from Ahmed's, read or make clothes for Jamie (lots of material, more than enough work for two). Sometimes the odour of hashish would seep down from Mojo's room and sometimes we'd knock on his door and he'd bring some of his favourite opiated black down to share. On the whole, though, we weren't big druggies; we all agreed that habitual drugsters were boring, sad fuckwits who substituted drug culture for real life because they couldn't hack it. We dabbled, we tried anything, but it never took hold. We knew it was just a bit of fun, nothing more. We felt somehow we were destined to do great things, be famous, get noticed. We didn't need drugs or anything except our own wits. Jamie and I thought we'd make it through showbiz; Mojo dreamt of being famous for just being Mojo. Well, we achieved those ambitions all right, man, just not how we thought.

As I was working freelance, most days I cranked up the Minski and puttered off to work for my various businesses; I am a *great* book-keeper, in considerable demand. I used to work bloody miracles. I liked it, I like numbers, making order out of chaos. I did Pa's books for years before I went to college, and then more and more of his chums in the Small Business Association cottoned on that I may look odd, but I'm shit-hot with figures. The work came in nicely, thank you. To a large extent I could pick and choose when I worked and if I got any shit off anyone, fuck 'em, I split pronto. I prided myself that my regulars couldn't do without me. Hah.

Not now, though, oh no. Might be catching, murder. Fuck 'em, they'll be sorry when they see the state of their accounts. Oh well, what can I expect? It's not their fault, really; it isn't – they're only human. They believe what they see on telly, or read in the papers. *Who'd have believed that nice Lily Carlson would have turned out to be a Homicidal Sado-Masochistic Lesbian Sex Toy? Well, she was adopted, it's Ken and Sylvia I feel sorry for, talk about a serpent in the nest, honestly, blood will out* . . . Yadda, yadda, yadda. I *won't* be bitter, I *won't*. He wins, Sean wins if I let this destroy me; he'd *love* to think of me getting bitter and twisted, with no friends and family. He loathed me as much as I loathed him. Loathe at first glance, so to speak. Rot in hell, you motherfucking son of a bitch. Rot and burn.

But enough with the Sean stuff – it makes my stomach cramp. Irritable Bowel Syndrome, the doctor says. Stress induced. Yeah. That and the nightmares, both waking and sleeping. You know, people don't understand about murder. How the murderer doesn't just kill the victim, they kill everything and everyone associated with the victim; it's like dropping a rock in a pond. The ripples just spread and spread outwards, swamping everything in their path.

Those families of Sean's victims – they've got no fucking *life* any more. They're bound up with murder forever. Not a day goes past for them that isn't a reminder of Sally, Mandy, Tina, Lucy, and Sara. Girlie names, girls' names, his victims' names. What if, oh, Mandy's brother gets married – where's Mandy? Standing by the fucking altar, a bloody, shredded ghost. How about if Lucy's sister gets her degree? Well, Lucy would have if

50

only she hadn't decided to walk home from the club . . . You see? No joy left in anything – no birth, marriage, anniversary, Christmas, holiday that isn't haunted by the pleading spectre of their dead girl.

Even friends, drifting away over the years, can never really be free of it. She was such a lovely girl, such a *bubbly, vivacious, pretty* girl; all the stupid, dehumanizing clichés just serve to call it back. Three of them were whores. One was a student and one was unemployed. But for the devouring fucking hounds of the media, they were just stereotypes to be packaged for the *News at Ten*, the *Sun* or the *Observer* – they're all as bad as one another nowadays. Oh, oh, those poor sodding *human beings*. No, it just never ends. He's still killing, still ripping, still mutilating.

I don't think He's dead, because I don't think He was ever alive. I think He was the savage, predatory brute in all of us, clotted into human form. What happened to Him at Lana Powers's hands was a shaping, a tempering. Lana made the base ore into a weapon; his own blood relative, his father's sister Lana, she *made* Him . . . and *she's* still alive, while those girls are just ghosts.

And we took Him into our house. We invited that horror across our threshold, and he came, laughing. I read somewhere that the devil cannot cross a threshold unasked. Oh, man – what did we do? What did we ever do to deserve all this? We printed party invitations, for fuck's sake.

CHAPTER 8

S orry, sorry, I didn't mean to go off on one. Sometimes I can't help it. Must try harder. Yeah, well; it was a happy house, we all got on a treat. We shared food and bill money equally, not like some houses where people write their names on their eggs and mark off the level of their cornflake packet every day. We didn't live high, partly because we couldn't and partly because we didn't really want to. It was that sort of time for 'alternative' types – yuppie rejection. We didn't want to be like Them, Thatcher's Whizz (and I mean that in the chemical sense as well) Kids. It seemed in bad taste, darling, as Mojo would say. We were the underground, the resistance, the last remaining warriors of Good. We were a bit special, to our minds at least. Yeah, why not? We were young and cool. The world was our lobster.

Well, after the first flush of excitement when I'd scrubbed the whole house with bleach, painted the tiny kitchenette, and thrown out seven binbags of rubbish, I put anything I couldn't chuck into the cellar and we all settled down to a routine of sorts.

Weekdays were as I said, pretty regular, nothing thrilling but cosy in a comforting kind of way. At the weekends, a flurry of activity would begin around three p.m. on Friday afternoon. Mojo would wash his hair and begin the long, ritual ascent to Glamour. Jamie (and me if I was there) would start getting baths and doing the hair-washing, leg-shaving, nail-painting, crimping, backcombing, clothes-sorting, face-constructing and general primping for a night out. Man, was I glad I'd got dreadlocks, at least I was spared the hassle of Jamie-style hair routines. What a palaver. Apart from the washing end of things and a light coating of lippie, maybe a freaky nail polish, I left nature to do her worst. I was a combats and crop top kinda gal then; still am really, it's just that fashion's caught up with me and now that look is *de rigueur*. Then I was a scumbag; now, *toute la rage*.

Mojo, who didn't usually frequent the same haunts as us – like, we were close friends but not in each other's pockets – Mojo played the field. Friday, hmm, cheong-sam and spike heels. Saturday, wash-faded jeans and a black silk shirt knotted at the waist, espadrilles. Sunday, I've got no idea – we never saw him until Monday morning. Jamie, well, she's had more looks than a naked bishop. It took hours to assemble her – she used to say, when she was finished, she looked like a portable shrine just tinkling with offerings. She would get quite trancey during this process, as if she were actually making herself; creating

53

herself. Everything had to be perfect and certainly she was an artist where make-up was concerned, either fantasy or the natural look.

She wasn't being false, but she did become Going-Out Jamie as opposed to Round-the-House-Jamie. I used to rib her about the fact that she was always performing, always on-stage in public; two people and herself in a phone-box was a gig to her. She couldn't help it, she just wasn't confident enough in herself to shut up. Two vodkas into the night and whoopsie-do! Heeeere's Jamie! She was a scream to go out with, honest, it sounds worse than it was. She was funny and full of fire and sort of carried you along. She shone and glittered; she loved being the centre of attraction, being Queen.

That was on good nights. On bad nights that flame turned to ash, blacker than coal and full of rage. It didn't happen often but it did happen, I won't lie about it. One drink too many, one bitchy comment too many, I don't know – wrong phase of the fucking moon, whatever. Then there would be violence – oh yeah, real fighting, proper punch-ups, the works. She'd fight anyone, and she was strong and fierce. She never hit anyone littler than herself or bullied anyone; I never saw her fight a woman voluntarily. She said no matter if the woman was a right snapping bitch, she'd come off worse in people's opinions because she was big. She hated the idea of being a bully. So she'd get into a fight with some straight lout, or some Crusty Thug (oh yes, they do exist, they're not all New Age Vegan

Bunnyhuggers) and there'd be all hell let loose, and then afterwards she'd be ashamed of losing her temper and cry like a child, nursing her black eye or busted knuckles.

I fought alongside her if there was no way out for us; I'm no saint. 'Bite-Yer-Legs Lil' she used to call me. That's how it is for the likes of us. You didn't let a mate down in public no matter how you screamed at them for being an idiot afterwards in private. Loyalty, pride, honour. That's what we had that separated us from the world's Bourgeois Scum. I know some folks find it inexplicable; they abhor violence, think fighting is the end of everything, but hey, it isn't. It's stupid, but it's not the *worst* thing you can do. Disloyalty, betrayal, cruelty – they're worse than any brawl. But that's just my opinion, and I know some will think the worst of Her Nibs because of this – well don't. You wouldn't if you'd known her in real life. You'd have loved her as much as we did, even if you think you wouldn't. She was *Jamie*, then, she wasn't like anyone else. She may have had a rep, but she had *respect* amongst the society we moved in, and for a woman, that's fucking good going.

CHAPTER 9

One night, after I'd been there a few weeks, I asked her when she had another gig lined up. We were off out to the Road House, a pub-disco on Manningham Lane, and she was just covering her eyelids with glitterdust.

'Hmmm, haven't,' she said, peering downwards into her mirror with her gob open like a goldfish.

'Why not? I thought you were up for it?' I queried.

'Am.'

'Well, why haven't you done anything about it, then?'

'What? Oh, Lil, I've buggered it up now! Pass me a fucking tissue, I hate this stuff – it's like moth-wing scrapings.'

'But gigs, Jamie, *gigs*. Don't you fancy it any more?'

She stopped dabbing and swiping and turned to look at me, her face awash with sparkles. 'I don't know. I did try for a couple round here, up at the uni and stuff, but it's so horrible having to phone someone up and tell them how fucking brilliant you are, it's naff, it made me cringe, to be honest. Maybe Graeham'll put me on again.'

'Maybe. But if he doesn't, what were you gonna do?'

'Dunno. I suppose I thought word might get round, or maybe I could send out some leaflets or something. Why?'

'Let me get gigs for you. I could do it, honestly. It's better if I do it anyhow, it looks better. I could say I was your manager or something, "Carlson Associates", something like that. I could do you letters an' contracts an' shit at Pa's on the machine – what d'you think?'

She looked at me narrowly for a few seconds while I got sweaty and felt stupid.

'Thank you,' she said, and kissed me on the forehead, leaving a big pink kissy-mark.

That's how we started. That's how Jamie Gee became Britain's answer to Lenny Bruce. That's how I got to be Machiavelli, only shorter. Naturally, I had problems in my attempt to be an *éminence grise*; the most major one being I didn't really know what the fuck I was doing. I mean, don't get me wrong, I was *willing*, God alone knows. It was an era in which we thought we could do bloody miracles if we only applied ourselves; oust the Conservatives, destroy racism; equality, liberty and fraternity – all that jazz. Turning Jamie into a household name was peanuts by comparison; at least it would be if I could get a handle on the *mechanics* of it . . .

I decided to go and see Graeham. I rang him and he said I could pop round the next evening and we'd have a chat, which I did. He lived in Heaton, which was kind of diagonally across town from us, and, leaving the two Mouseketeers to crimp their hair, I rattled off.

Graeham's partner Moira opened the door. She was, as the Bible has it, great with child. So great, in fact, I was somewhat fucking nervous; pregnant women get me that way, they're so focused on the event about to happen they frighten me. Moira regarded me with the insanely calm gaze of a woman about to have her pelvis stretched to breaking point and waved me in dreamily. I trailed in her wake like a tugboat following a liner.

'He's in there. Tea?'

'Oh, er, yes, thanks – are you sure – I mean I could do it – don't you need to rest – I don't want to . . .'

'It's OK. I'm pregnant, not crippled. Milk and sugar?'

'Um, sorry, er, no, just black, no sugar, strong. Thanks.'

'That's OK. I'll bring it in.'

She swayed off and I knocked on Graeham's door.

'Enter.' His voice was thick with cold, it sounded more like 'edder'.

'Hi, it's me, Lily, Jamie's friend.'

Graeham was sitting hunched into a knackered armchair bang up against a gas fire glowing

58

furnace-orange. The heat was astonishing. I perched on the chair opposite and took off my coat and two jumpers. I was still boiling.

'Sorry about the heat,' he said, coughing, 'but I just can't seem to get warm.'

'I can come back another time if you're not well, honestly, I don't mind.'

'No, no, it's fine.' He looked up as Moira entered bearing a tray with tea and digestive biscuits on it. She looked at him despairingly.

'It's all nerves. He's in more of a state about the baby than I am. Men, honestly, a bit of a cold and the world's at an end – cheer up, buggerlugs, it'll soon be over.'

I sincerely hoped it wouldn't be over before I left. Graeham sighed theatrically. He was a plump, curly-haired fella, going a bit thin on top, in his early thirties. I thought he was very old and wise. The Yoda of Alternative Comedy. He was the biggest promoter of alternative cabaret in the area, and his room was littered with toppling heaps of papers, posters and cassettes.

'She's got me where she wants me, the minx, I'll have to marry her now.' He watched Moira leave, his little round glasses fairly misting up with love.

I burbled into my tea.

'So, enough of my domestic turmoil; what can I do for you?'

'Well, it's Jamie. I want to manage her. I think, well, I don't really know what I think – she's got something, something special. I want to know what I should do, to help her – to get her gigs and the paperwork and, everything really.'

'Are you good friends?'

'Oh, yes, the best! I mean, not that we've known each other long, but really, we just got on straight –'

He held up a stubby hand clad in an unravelling fingerless knitted glove.

'Rule one. Never work with your friends. Nothing kills a friendship quicker than a life on the road and engaging in business together. As I see that advice is useless, take care to remember artistes' – he pronounced it 'har-teests', like a music hall compere – 'artistes are monsters of temperament, no matter how sane they appear. Criticize, criticize, but be careful how, when and where. Never do it in public. Your dear friend is going to require a lot of criticism, and I fear she is not well-equipped to deal with it.' He dunked a biscuit reflectively.

I was crestfallen. 'Don't you think she's any good, then?'

He looked at me carefully. 'Good? Yes, she's *good*. She's a Natural. That's where your problem lies.' I must have been gawping. He continued with a heavy, phlegm-laden sigh.

'You see, artistes, and in this case *comedians*, divide quite sharply into two varieties. The Natural, like Jamie, and the Worker, like, for example, oh, Tony Gecko. Now Tony, as you know, does

60

well for himself. A rising star. Don't make that face – you may not care for him, he's not a woman's comedian, but that's an advantage in this business – now, Tony is a Worker. He *works* at being funny. He memorizes his routine, his ad libs, his answers to hecklers, he learns it all by rote. It's the same show every night. Never varies. A real professional. Offstage, he's a boring little man with a huge ego, a coke habit and a monstrous ambition. He'd murder his grannie for a shot at the big time, his own series on the telly, that sort of thing. He will get it. His manager is ruthless, organized, well-connected and on a huge cut for his trouble. Can't stand the bloke myself but he's got what it takes. So has Tony. The only way Tony is "Alternative" is in the style of his promotion. Actually, he's just a club comic in a shiny suit and' – he squiggled in the air with his fingers to denote quote marks – 'a *crazy* haircut. Bog standard, really.'

Graeham heaved another sticky sigh and took a pull at his tea. So did I. I wanted desperately to write all this down but not wishing to appear tacky, I contented myself with concentrating on what he was saying very hard indeed.

'Now your Natural, well, quite another matter. Oh dear, yes. Your Natural is *naturally funny*. Born with it. Genetic, or whatever. They're a hoot in the pub and hilarious on stage. Born performers, larger than life and all that. They can do anything up there and people will fall about. Tommy Cooper,

Eric Morecambe, Betty Marsden, Joyce Grenfell. They make it appear easy, casual. I'm not saying they don't *work*; they work like devils but it never shows, never. They're in control, the stage is their home. Riddled with stage fright usually, too, poor sods. There's a lot of darkness there, in your Natural. The flipside, you might say, to that talent. And that is where your trouble lies. They're not reliable. Tend to burn out if not well looked after – but genius, no doubt about it. Too much so, in some cases, won't give the punters the easy option like the Tonys of this world. Of course, it's a matter of degree – some are more high-strung than others; some learn to control the darkness, some don't. They're special, though, very, very special. They do something like magic, like a kind of healing, they make us more human rather than less. You come away full of love and happiness, rather than feeling slightly stupid and grubby as you do after a night listening to some fella like Tony being cruel and clever at the expense of the weak. A Natural is like, well, like your friend.'

I choked on a digestive.

'Oh yes, she's got it all right. Pity she's a woman. Terrible disadvantage in the business. Never mind, never mind, things are changing, I suppose. Moira thinks so. I'm not so sure. There's lots of talk about feminism, equality, but the truth, bollocks. Jobs for the boys. Still, you'll just have to work a bit harder, nothing wrong with that. I see you don't approve of my attitude – I speak as I find. You'll find out for yourself soon enough. Your friend, though, she's got genuine talent. Knocks spots off that little fuckwit Tony, but he'll get on, she won't. Well, not as far as he will, let's say. That pisses me off. That's why I'm getting out. I used to enjoy all the wheeling and dealing, all the games. Not any more. Burnt out, I suppose. Soon as the baby's born we're off. Going to France, got a share in a bar on the coast. Quiet place, good for the child, good for Moira, good for me. No more of this.' He gestured at the chaotic room. 'No more bloody *comics*.'

He rubbed his gloved hand through his hair until it stuck up like Professor Whizzbang. 'Take care of Jamie, Lily. I've known her for quite a while, you know, on and off. She's a loose cannon, your friend. She'll either go off with a big bang and shoot the world down in flames or implode. Self-destructive. But you're a survivor, oh yes. You'll be good for her. Keep her sane – just keep her away from shits like Andy. She will go for that type. Addiction comes in many disguises, and Jamie's an addict, all right, stone junkie. Price they pay, Naturals, it's always something, drink, gambling, drugs, or . . . yes, well.'

He looked at me quizzically. I'd like to say I understood what he meant, but to be honest, I didn't. His talk of addiction lost me – I mean, we had an understanding about the drink and drugs thing, it was cool. So Jamie had bad luck with fellas – man, we'd *all* been there. I put it out of my mind and tried to concentrate as Graeham went through booking procedures and contracts and fished out lists of venues and copies of suitable contract forms, press releases, flyers, leaflets to send to promoters etc., that I could duplicate for Jamie when she got some publicity. It was brilliant – he couldn't have been more helpful. Finally, I thought I'd better go, it was getting late and I didn't want to be present at the home birth or anything.

Thanking him profusely and probably hysterically, I made my way to the front door, but Graeham stopped me and put his hand on my arm.

'Tell Jamie goodbye for me. I won't see you again. Talk to Jim at the uni – I'll ring him and put him straight, you'll get the gig. Do as I say and you'll be all right business-wise. But Lily, don't forget what I said about Jamie. She's easy to love – once upon a time I thought maybe – well, that's all history now. I've got Moira and the baby. I'm lucky. But be careful – I don't know – it's that darkness, it's strong in her, very strong. Good luck, you're a nice young woman, you'll do well – don't forget, take no prisoners.' He patted me and I went out into the cold night.

Driving home, I fretted over his last words to me. Sure, Jamie was a handful, temperamental in spades, but what did he mean by all that talk about addiction, darkness? Obviously he'd had a thing for her once, maybe it was just sour grapes. But he hadn't seemed that type of person. I made a mental note to keep an eye on Jamie's moods and get her sorted out.

It's amazing how thick you are when you're young, isn't it?

CHAPTER 10

I didn't tell Jamie much on my return, just that Graeham was going away and about the business advice – I made her swear on everything she held sacred never to throw away a receipt and to give them all to me. She was cool with it, nodding her plumey pink mane and not understanding a fucking word. I can never, ever comprehend how people get so dense about figures and tax stuff. It's *so* simple, as long as you're methodical and regular, it's . . . well, I suppose we can't all be good at everything, and Jamie is an idiot with money and numbers.

I waited two days then rung Jim at the uni. He was 'in a meeting'. I tried again and again until I struck lucky – between him rolling in around eleven a.m. and the pubs opening for lunch. I tried for the casual, experienced approach but I didn't get past the first sentence.

'Yeah, yeah, Grae buzzed me. Let's say, oh, the twenty-third? Is that good for you? It's a mixed cabaret night – your girl can go on second, after Sy – oh, you know him, great. Then it'll be Redskin Jack the ranting poet and headline, Billy Mental.

Not much money in it, sorry, funds are a tad low, let's say twenty-five pounds? Twenty minutes? OK, OK, how shall we bill her – J-a-m-i-e G-e-e, great, any blurb, any press yet? No matter, Grae says she's a winner, suits me. Must shoot – gotta meeting – 'bye.'

I felt somewhat deflated. I found my hands were shaking. Was it all going to be that easy? Shit, I never mentioned contracts, bugger.

It wasn't ever that easy again, but eventually, my hands didn't shake any more and I contracted the bastards before the fucking phone went down. The names they used to call me! Shocking. It really used to break my heart to hear some jumped-up London wanker call me a hard fucking bitch. Yeah, like really.

Jamie was astonished by my apparent ease at getting her work. Mojo graciously commented that he had known all along his Tiger Lily was a tiny little star. I twinkled obligingly and then made the tea while Jamie had hysterics about what she was going to wear, say and do on-stage, in that order. Although we had three weeks to wait, it was three weeks of ransacking the wardrobe and Jamie waking me up at two a.m. to 'listen to this funny bit'. She did it to Mojo as well, until he bribed her to stop by lending her his embroidered bolero.

The day of the gig dawned and an ashen-faced Jamie moved through the hours before we went to sound check like a zombie on Mogadon. Mojo said 'good afternoon, darling' to her and she burst into tears. I would have been impatient with her had I not soon realized she was genuinely terrified. This was what Graeham had meant by his comment about how unpleasant it was to witness real stage fright. Half of me wanted to pull the gig, if it made her feel this bad. But the other half knew that this was just the price she had to pay and somewhere in her heart, she knew it too. Oddly enough, it was Mojo who really couldn't handle it. He said it made him nervous just to look at her. It made me feel that way too, but I was determined not to let on. One of us had to remain human.

At the sound and lights check, which was minimal for this kind of gig, Jamie looked pale but fairly composed. She had understood without being told that her composure was valuable; it made her look in control. She was a good faker and even when Sy rushed up to her and gave her a *great big hug* she didn't bite him. He meant well, poor sap. The poet was a burly, thickset type, very fast with the aggressive abrasive rhyme and very funny, if played at half-speed. He was a nice, clever guy under his macho facade and he and Jamie soon had a bit of banter going. All of us were united in our loathing of Billy Mental.

Billy turned up late, as befitted a star from Manchester. He was accompanied by his manager, Slim, his girlfriend (trophy blonde) and his best mate, Doggo. Naturally, he didn't speak to Jamie, Sy and I. He did shake Redskin Jack by the hand in

68

a blokey, punches-to-the-upper-arm kind of way. They had worked together before and he must have known the poet was far, far funnier than he was. But Billy had it taped. He had a routine that dwelt long and hard (no pun intended) on penises and shitting. He collapsed 'em in the aisles with his 'just one Vindaloo' gag and they fell about everytime he belted out his catchphrase, 'I'm mental, me!' His concession to being alternative was his long meditation on whether Mrs Thatcher had a penis.

'Well, she's not a fuckin' woman, not a fuckin' woman, is she, be fair, well, I wouldn't shag 'er, would you? Would you? You would! You would! Fuck me, 'oo's the mental one 'ere, then?'

Sounds crap? Oh, no. Ironic, you see. The media loved it. He was playing a character. Very clever. Very *postmodern*. Of course it was a double-bluff, because in real life, he actually *was* a drunken, sexist bastard.

I suppose you think I'm just jealous. He did very well for himself, actually. Especially after he toned it down and went on the telly in the late-night Channel Four *Blue 4 U* series. I recall him being interviewed by the *Mail* in their piece about comics who'd worked with Jamie. He said he'd thought from the first time he met her, she was weird. That he'd tried to give her a few pointers, a bit of advice, but she'd damn near bitten his head off – a real radical feminist type. Pity, but it had all come as no surprise to him.

He never spoke to her. Oh, I'm fibbing. He once told her to get out of the fucking way, when she was standing side-stage. So jealous, no. Nothing so lighthearted.

Anyhow, he didn't really concern us, that night at least. Eventually, the show had to go on. Sy went on to thunderous disinterest (mum excluded) and since he had been forbidden to use the fire-clubs he'd wanted to try out due to regulations concerning burning the building down, he did some surrealist juggling using two dead cod and a cabbage. He ended up landing a cod in the pint of a huge bloke in the front row wearing a Bradford University rugby shirt. Something of a scene ensued and the cod did not escape in one piece. So, with the stage and auditorium littered with dead fish bits, Sy exited, stage left. Jamie was on.

I was, at this point, a bag of nerves and Mojo was drinking Black Russians one after the other. Through a straw. I had crowbarred Jamie out of the dressing room toilet and escorted her side-stage, where she stood like a condemned woman, waiting for the crew to sweep cod scraps off the stage, and the compere, a theatre studies student with hopes of being a comic one day himself, to announce her. She looked still and distant, her grey eyes fixed, her face closed and mask-like in the dim bluish light.

'Good luck,' I whispered.

'No, say "break a leg". Graeham said they say that in the circus; "good luck" means you'll tempt the devil into bringing you bad luck. Say "break a leg", Lily.'

'Break a leg, then. I'll be out front, we're here for you, it'll be great, really, it'll be . . .'

'He's announcing you now, get up there!' hissed one of the crew. I ran off round to the hall while she walked up the steps.

'Hey-hey-hey, folks, a real treat for you now – a home-grown Bradford lass with stars in her eyes, give a big hand for . . . JANIE GEE!' I could have slapped his pimply face – getting her name wrong, Christ, how would she take that?

There was a smattering of applause as she walked slowly to the mic and fiddled it up to the right height. She looked out at them and smiled slightly. It wasn't what they were used to and I felt my gut tighten, Mojo murmuring beside me, 'Come *on*, darling, *please* . . .'

Jamie looked out over the crowd, still smiling. They stared back for a moment in silence while they absorbed the astonishing facts that a) she was a woman and b) she didn't look frightened. Then a great hairy lout at the back shouted, 'Show us yer tits!' That got a big laugh, and cries of, 'Yeah, get 'em out!' resounded through the hall. They were mostly students, after all – the future leaders of our nation.

Next to me, Mojo groaned delicately.

'Why should I show you my tits?' Jamie enquired

71

affably. 'You wouldn't know what the fuck to do with them if I did. Look at you, really – a pint of shandy and you're making a fucking dick of yourself in public – no, get off home, kiddie, get yer mam to knit you a brain for Christmas. And stop pointing at him, poor sod – well, that's mates for you, honestly, talk about canaries – don't ever get arrested with that lot, matey, they'd have to torture them to get them to shut up.'

And for the next twenty minutes, she had them by the balls.

It's weird trying to write down what she said on-stage, the replies to hecklers, the routines. It was an ephemeral thing, made up of lights and cigarette smoke drifting blue across the space she inhabited. It was entirely of the moment; you could see her thinking on her feet, searching through the atmosphere for the thing that they wanted. The intimate, human banter and stories that made them feel as if they were part of something, as if she was a kind of big sister. Not handing them gags and saying, 'Look at me, aren't I the clever one?' Just being warm and real and not scared. Full of the life she'd led, the things she'd seen. The love and dying and healing she'd witnessed. Joshing them, being rude and funny to them, cheeking them and teasing them as if they were all her family.

I scanned their faces, those watching, smiling faces and felt a great surge of emotion that was hard to describe, it was like love, but it wasn't soft and sentimental. I loved them because they enabled her to do her thing; to walk the walk. They were what she needed to be free; they needed her because she was herself, and belonged to them wholly for her time on that dirty stage.

I'm not saying they all fell for her; by no means. I saw angry faces, I saw disinterested faces. I saw outrage and disgust, all of it. But on the whole, it worked. I was proud, too, of her and myself for having made this moment happen. It was a secret pride though, just for me. It was a now-try-an'-fuck-with-me-you-fuckas sort of pride. It set me free, too. It gave me something to work for. I was *needed*. My heart was full.

I looked at Mojo. He looked at me and we both went, 'Yes!' silently. Then it was over. They gave her the encore, but she stood there side-stage as if she didn't hear it. I was about to say – go on, go back on – but the Boy Compere bounded on and announced the interval.

He sauntered off and paused by us.

'That was great. Really. Very unusual. Do you write your own stuff? If you need any help, well, I'd be glad to get together with you – you know, polish your stuff up, that sort of thing. The Uni Comedy Club meets on Thursdays at the Shearbridge, come along . . .' He faltered as he looked into her shining eyes. Then he had the grace to blush and against his will, he muttered, 'Thanks, thank you. I . . . it was . . .'

'No, thank *you*, love. It was cool, yeah?' Jamie smiled at him and he smiled back, like the kid he was. I decided not to tear a strip off him for getting her name wrong. He was confused enough as it was.

Mojo swept up in a flutter of gunmetal silk satin and a waft of Poison. He held Jamie at arm's-length for a moment then embraced her gently, kissing her on both cheeks. He gazed at her gravely for a moment and then said, 'My darlings, a star *is* born!'

We cracked up. Then, leaving the two giggling idiots to their chucklefest, I went off to find Jim and get the cash. He was in his cubbyhole, morosely smoking a joint. The air was thick with dope fumes, indicating it wasn't his first. I coughed as my lungs filled with hashish.

'Yeah, OK, here's the ackers; sign here, bleed me dry, see if I care.' He sighed heavily.

'It's only twenty-five nicker, Jimmy, small change to a geezer like yourself, I woulda thought.'

'That's it. Be cheeky. You'll go far, you will. Do you know how much it costs me to put these gigs on? Do you know how much that gibbering fuckwit B. Mental Esquire and his fucking henchmen costs me? I have to put a bottle of Jack and God knows what all else in his dressing room and still find the money to pay you lot. It's heartbreaking.'

'You don't pay Sy.'

'Be fair. Would you?'

'My lips are sealed. He means well.'

'So does the fucking Pope, and look where

that goes. Oh, all right. She was good, as good as Graeham promised. 'Ere, come see me on Wednesday, come to the downstairs bar around two-ish. I said to Grae I'd help you out with a few contacts. I wasn't going to, but fuck it, she was good. Better than that dick-obsessed egomaniac, anyway.'

I kissed his unshaven cheek. 'Wotchit,' he said.

Slightly smashed, I weaved back towards the bar, looking for the Heavenly Twins. I found Mojo completely drunk, being earnestly chatted up by a big bloke in a rugger shirt that glittered with fishscales and smelt like a trawlerman's innersole. Mojo had a fixed, glazed smile hovering over his painted lips, and I knew by his unfocused eyes that he'd reached the 'no, I'm com-*pletely* sober' stage. The rugger-bugger glared at me and I felt like telling him exactly what sort of a lady he'd landed; but hey, I'm no party pooper, poor sap. Mojo was an expert, drunk or sober, at melting away leaving a puzzled and besotted straight boy wondering where the exotic, beautiful girl of his wet dreams had vanished to. Heartbreaker.

I cast about for Her Nibs, to no avail. I was considering breaking up Love's Young Dream and asking Mojo where she was, when I spotted her. She was leaning against a corner wall while a guy in a beaten-up leather jacket and two days' growth leant over her, propping himself up with his arm, which was extended over her shoulder to the wall behind. He had a sly, hawk's face, a heavy brow ridge and a beaky nose. She was gazing at him while he bent to whisper something to her. A look I'd not seen before crossed her face. I didn't like it. It was like *submission*. The bloke put his grimy hand on her waist in a gesture that should have been romantic, but somehow seemed curiously cruel. There was a weird feeling about the whole scene. It was like a power thing. I don't think it would be too strong to say it was like watching a sort of mental rape. It put cogs on me; the nape of my neck prickled.

I turned on my heel and went to the bar. I ordered a double Jameson and necked it straight off. I felt furious – for fuck's sake, what was she doing, messing with a waster like that? You could see he was a piece of shit, he may as well have had a sign saying 'bastard' in neon over his greasy head. We'd had such a good night, too – how could she let herself down like that? Let *me* down – just sod off without a word, with that *wanker*. Oh, I was getting more and more mixed up and cross. I felt the alcohol boil like acid in my blood, anger stoked up by whisky fuelling my adrenaline. I signalled the barman over.

'Another Jameson, mate, make it a double . . .'

A hand closed over mine on the bar. 'Cancel that, son, OK?' a deep, male voice boomed in my ear.

'What the fuck . . . my God, Gabe, what are you doin' here? I thought you were out all month . . .'

'Gigs got pulled – guitarist broke his wrist

76

fuckin' about piss-drunk. Silly bastard. Got the train up from London. Saw her. She were good, I thought.'

'But look, man, for fuck's sake, what's goin' on? Have you seen what she's up to, Christ. Look, I'm not her keeper, no – it's just, fuck, it's not right, I mean it's, oh – that *arsehole* . . .' I was inarticulate, as usual, but this time from anger. 'Gabe, what's with her, man? I've never seen her like this.'

Gabriel Smith is a big fella. He's a bit heavier now, but then he was slim, big muscles, long legs. What I call a paper-brown complexion, blunt features, brown eyes, black curly hair. A right gyppo to look at, really. His voice was rich and rounded and I always liked his hands; big, square palms with long spatulate fingers, always dry and warm. OK, I had developed a crush, it's not a crime. Not technically, anyway.

Tonight I was glad to see him, very glad. I needed his big, warm self, his good manliness, if you like. I needed protection and you could always rely on Gabe.

'I seen 'im. I know 'im. Name's Dodger, I know his family. Yeah, he's a waste of space.'

'Well then, we should *do* something, get rid of him – probably she's pissed, doesn't know what she's doin', please, it's horrible.'

'Nowt you can do, she's not pissed, I'll lay bets on it. It's how she is. Always 'as been. No, no "buts", I'm not bein' hard, it's a fact. Come on, get Mojo, we'll go home – go to yours.'

He put his arm round me. I leant against him, smelling the mixture of leather, fresh sweat and sweet blokiness that I liked so much. I felt suddenly exhausted and washed out. I wanted a nice cup of tea and maybe this time, more.

Mojo floated up. 'Darlings, oh, how lovely, the Angel Gabriel, my favourite. Tiger Lily, I feel rather drunk, to be frank, and there is an *extra-ordinary* man following me around like a puppy. Think he must be some sort of *sailor*. Seems to be covered in fish, very odd . . .'

We got a cab home. Taxis are very cheap in Bradford, not like other places. We fell into one, and apart from a short sharp exchange between Mojo and the cabbie in Urdu, which left the cabbie looking outraged and Mojo smug, it was an easy ride through the dark, wet streets.

But I was worried sick about Jamie. I hated leaving her, it seemed so wrong. And to be honest, it seemed so unlike Gabe and Mojo. What did they know I didn't? Back home I put the kettle on and some toast under the grill. After bringing it all through to the sit-ting room, I slumped on the sofa with Gabe. After a minute, Mojo came in. He had taken off all his make-up and was wearing a pair of black joggers and a long black cashmere jumper. His hair was in a ponytail and, suddenly, he didn't appear to be drunk at all. For a moment, his appearance threw me. Then I just thought – what an incredibly good-looking person he was, both as a man, and a woman. He and Gabe looked serious; I knew they wanted to talk.

I poured the tea and said, 'What gives, guys?'

CHAPTER 11

Gabriel's Story

'It's like this, Lily. I've known Jamie for years. My mam has a bit of land wi' some ponies on an' a bungalow out Ilkley way. My mam was a Traveller, you know that? Yeah, she married out, like, and there was a bit of trouble, like, her marryin' a gadje – a straight bloke, but it were love, straight up, so after some years an' stuff, it was OK. Well, after me dad died in the crash, like, me mam got this bit of land and the house. Nice place, we'll go visit sometime, she's great, me mam. Well, anyroad, never mind owt else, it's posh round there an' it meant me an' me brothers an' sisters got good schoolin', which was Mam's intention in movin' there. Now, I never went to school with Jamie or anything, because she were at that all-girls' school on the hill. But we all hung around together from about thirteen on. All the babby punks, the kids that didn't want to join the fuckin' tennis club. Jamie an' me, we liked the same music, the same books, the same everything. She were like another sister to me, only, more, like. My sisters are rock hard, real tough women, no fuckin' messin'. Like Mam, really. Great, an' I love 'em more 'n' me life – but hard, oh aye.'

He paused to drink some tea, his eyes seeming to fix on things far, far away. It gave me the shivers. Then he sighed, and went on. 'But Jamie weren't like that. Oh, she were a mouthy cow, allus goin' on about somethin', allus creating about somethin' or another. Scrappin' too. That's how I met her, pulling some kid off her who she were scrappin' wi. She were covered in mud with a bloody big graze on her cheek, bawlin' her eyes out and cursing like a trooper. "You can fuck off as well," she gives it me. "No," I says. "I won't." An' I give her my bandanna to wipe her face. She's still got it, she says, soft bugger. After that, we allus hung around together. She'd come up to our house and I learned her to ride the ponies and me mam would give her dinner along wi' us. We'd listen to records in the shed I done out for meself and swap books. We'd get stoned, or drink cider – Mam didn't know about that. Or at least, I'm fairly sure she didn't. I had mates, of course, but Jamie, she was mine, she belonged to me an' I loved her. Daft, p'raps – I dunno. Puppy love, mebbe. But I never fancied her, I never even snogged her an' I had my fair share of lasses after me from school, believe me. Me an' Jamie, we were family, like. Oh, folk made stuff up, they allus do – they still do, but no, it was never sex. She needed me, she really needed someone to take care of

81

her, an' I wanted to take care of her – she were
. . . lost.'

I sat up at this – it was exactly how I'd felt about Jamie. That she was lost. Now, perhaps, I'd find out why. The gas fire hissed and our cigarette smoke wreathed round the room, trying to escape. I did want to know what Gabe had to say – but somehow, I was apprehensive, too. What if . . . what if he told me something about Jamie that changed how I thought of her? I shook myself. That was just plain silly – how could he? She was my best mate, nothing could change that. His voice dragged me back to reality.

'Now, I only went the once to her house, although it weren't that far from me mam's. I went to pick her up. We were about seventeen. She lived on this sort of posh estate; bit o' garden back an' front – suburban. Crap houses – built cheap, sold dear. Her dad is some sort of executive, or so he reckons. Her mam's got a name for hersel' as a bit of a Lady Bountiful, charity work. You should hear what my mam says about her mam, fuck *me*. Still, her dad were in the same Lodge as my dad, so, well, nowt's said, like. Jamie takes after her mam, big, but her mam's just plain fat. Jamie's got more muscle, I saw to that. Her Mam wears all this fuckin' make-up, and pastel outfits, all got at the posh shops. Big on hats, too. Allus hats and big square handbags in public. Crap. Her dad's a little, weaselly sorta bloke, skinny, going a bit bald, soapy lookin'. Handshake like a wet sock fulla cold porridge. But big in the Lodge – big socially, like.

'Well, I turns up and I get told Jamie's not ready, which I thought was weird, but anyways, would I like a drink, some tea or Coke? Seemed OK, so I says I'll have a Coke. Her mam bustles about like it's a terrible big deal and I get a long, thin glass of flat Coke with ice, lemon and a fuckin' doily.

'Her dad, meanwhile, gives me the third degree, thinking 'imself a hard man, but never lookin' me in the eye, like. Where were we goin'? What time would we be back? Weren't we underage? *I hope you weren't thinking of drinking alcohol.* Where does your family live? Etc., etc. When I says about my family, he gives a jump, like, and says he knew my dad, sad loss, etc. I says, I know you knew him and mentions the Lodge. He gets all fuckin' matey then and goes, keep it under your hat, young man, your turn will come. I says, no, thanks, it's not my scene, like, at which he gets irate and goes off on one about the Youth of Today and leads into a kinda sub-fascist spiel about the Blacks and the Jews. I'd deck 'im, now, but then I were too young and anyhow, I were distracted.

'I could hear Jamie cryin', y'see. Upstairs. I could hear her cryin' an' her mam's voice dead low but carryin', like. I could hear scraps of it, like "dirty gypsy", "neighbours", "you little tart", "disgrace". That sort of stuff. It made me fuckin' mad as hell. I put the Coke – which I were glad not to 'ave touched – on a little table affair an' said, we gotta go if we don't want to be late. I weren't polite, like, just stared him in the eye an' said, Where's Jamie? He were gobsmacked. Everyone he knew kowtowed to him, I suppose, greasin' round him for favours an' that. But I knew what Jamie had told me an' I knew what went on in that house, an' somehow, I just couldn't be polite t' the sod.'

Mojo and I exchanged glances. We couldn't imagine Gabe being polite to anyone he didn't like, ever. I tried to unclench my hands and straighten my neck, which was cricked with tension as he continued in that calm, level voice.

'See, they were a fuckin' unit, him an' his missus. Tight, like they were made for each other. Why they had a kiddie at all's a fuckin' mystery, but they did. Just the one, just Jamie. Jemima Olivia Gerrard – Jamie. Named after some old auntie who they wanted to inherit offa. But her mam hates kids, really hates 'em. Other people's an' her own. Not interested, not bothered. Give Jamie to her nana to bring up – her dad's ma who lived in the "grannie flat" they built on the back. The other grandparents were long dead. Only Nana Gerry livin'. As far as Jamie's mam an' dad were concerned, Jamie were a bloody imposition on their lifestyle, y'see. It were like she were invisible to 'em. They just didn't take her into account. Never played wi' her, never went on outings, never went on holiday wi' her, never had a fuckin' picnic at the Rocks like every fucker else in Ilkley, never read her a fuckin' Pooh Bear story, nothin'. Nana did it all. Then when she were

84

nine, Nana died. Heart attack. Boom boom bang. Gone. It nearly killed Jamie, too. She musta had a breakdown, in my opinion. But her parents just ignored it an' – get this – went off to Cyprus with Nana Gerry's money an' left Jamie at home. With Uncle fuckin' Ted.'

He paused, and rubbed his face. Mojo leant forward a little, his hand outstretched as if he wanted to comfort Gabe – but Gabe didn't notice and Mojo sat back carefully, so as not to disturb Gabe as he coughed and spoke again.

'Fuck, I hate this, it fucks me up thinkin' of it. I'd kill the fucker if he hadn't killed hisself. Bastard. He were her mum's brother, Ted. Life an' soul of the fuckin' party. What a lovely, lovely chap. Oh aye. So fond of the kiddies, allus willing to babysit. Swimming coach, allus Santa at the Kiddies' Christmas Do. Oh yeah, Uncle Ted. Funny he never married. Just never met Miss Right, eh, Ted. You fuckin' bet. Christ. He'd been babysitting Jamie since she were a little 'un. Nana Gerry'd toddle off to her bridge evening or whatever an' Uncle Ted would be only too happy to oblige. Loved his Little Princess. So sad he never had any little ones of his own, blah, blah. Christ.'

He turned and looked at me directly. I jumped slightly, I don't know why. Then he said:

'I'm sorry, Lily, this int pleasant – I don't want t'be crude, like, but I think you 'ave to know the whole truth – otherwise you won't understand. You won't understand what my poor lass went through. See, when they were alone, he'd make her suck him off. Later, he'd fuck her. Oh yeah, the works. Front an' back. Everythin'. Tied her up, pissed on her, wanked off on her, rubbed his cum into her face, you name it. Poor little bitch. God Almighty, poor little lonely, helpless bitch. There weren't anythin' he didn't do. Showed her porno books wi' pics of women bein' tortured, said – this'll be you, if you say owt. Said – tell anyone and they'll die, I'll kill them, an' then you and then meself. No one will believe a dirty little cow like you anyhow – see? You're scum, filth. Even your mam an' dad can't bear you near 'em, but see, I love you, you're my dirty little secret love, ain't yer, Jemmy. My little secret.

'Fuck. Fuck. I . . . It were all ovver when I met her, had been since she'd were eleven. Too old for him. Said she were so dirty an' disgustin' he didn't love her any more – she'd started her periods, see. Said that were proof she were disgustin'. That it were God's punishment for her carryin' on wi' him, leadin' him on, like. Oh aye. He knew what he were about all right. She couldn't tell a soul. Nana Gerry'd just never believe anything like that could happen and anyhow, Jamie was petrified Uncle Ted would harm Nana, like he'd said. As to her mam an' dad, forget it. They thought the world of dear old Uncle Ted. She said the thing that got to her most were when her parents used to make her sit on Uncle Ted's knee and give him a great big kiss. If she looked unhappy or anythin' they said, "she was a rude, ungrateful little girl", an' that, "Uncle Ted simply loved her to bits". She thought they knew, you see, when she were little – she thought they knew but were so disgusted wi' her, they wouldn't mention it. Like goin' to the toilet, or stuff like that. An embarrassment.'

I could see the tears glistening in his eyes – yeah, the man everyone in town thought was so hard, so cool. He could cry – no, he could *mourn* – for that lost child. I glanced at Moj. He lay back in his chair, the cigarette dangling from his long fingers burning perilously low. His other hand was draped across his eyes. No, I didn't want to see these things, either. Gabe took a sip of his cold tea and continued.

'He topped hisself, Ted did. On her thirteenth birthday. Hung hisself in the garage. She thought it were her fault, that she were causin' all her family to die because she were so vile. I think someone else had found out what he were up to, an' threatened him. That were the vibe at the time but it were all hushed up. Ilkley, y'know. That sort of stuff don't happen in *Ilkley*.

'I met her about six months after that. She told me about Ted a couple of years later. Said it were no good us hanging around together because she were cursed – oh aye, that were her words; "I'm cursed, Gabe." I wouldn't let it be until she told me what were up – an' her shiverin' and shakin' an' crying like a beaten dog. I didn't know what angry were until then, I thought I'd burst wi' it. I think I weren't really a kid after hearin' that. Not again. I would 'ave been about sixteen. Oh, I'd allus thought summat serious were up wi' her on account of how wild she were – drinkin', drugs, shaggin' all an' sundry. She started drinkin' steady around fourteen an' the drugs soon followed an', of course, the lads. She were the original mixed-up kid. I can't remember how many times I bailed her out of trouble – oh, yeah, summat were definitely amiss there. I'd put it down to her parents bein' notorious wankers.

'She'd never told them owt about Ted, like – but when she were about eighteen, she read this fuckin' article in a women's mag – about child abuse. Well, she realized then it weren't just her. The article said to confront yer parents about it, get it out in the open, like. So she did, poor sod. They went ballistic. Fuck me. Screamin' an' shoutin'. Saying how dare she slander poor dead Uncle Ted who'd "adored her". That it were yet another attention-seekin' bid. That she were mad. She were a filthy liar, a whore, a tramp and allus had been. She were a livin' disgrace an' where had they gone wrong? She'd had the best schools money could buy, blah, blah, blah. The fuckin' works. They threw her out. Oh yeah, "Goodbye Was *All* She Wrote". Get out of our nice house, our nice fuckin' lives. Fuckers.'

The anger in his voice was palpable, thick and dark. His hands were clenched into fists; the knuckles showing white against his brown skin.

'She cut her wrists. I found her, on the moor up at Happy Valley, little sorta cove place that were our den when we were kids. Freezin' cold night.

Blood all ovver. The cold saved her, they reckon. Her blood ran slow an' thick 'cos of it. I don't know why I went up there – I had a date, like, but I blew it out, went up to our place an' there she were. White as white – she looked like a ghost. I ripped up my T-shirt and bound up her wrists then I picked her up, an' y'know what? Big as she is she didn't seem to weigh owt – weird. I ran down to t'pub an' got an ambulance. What a fuckin' scandal, man. They kept her in the hospital fer a bit, like, then her parents wanted her committed. But me mam says, no, bring her 'ere. So I did. Mam and me sisters took care of her. When they found out about Uncle fuckin' Ted – Christ, I were glad he'd done hissel because they'd have torn him apart. Her parents chuntered on fer a bit about puttin' her away but I told 'em – *no*. Straight out. Her old man tried to give me an' Mam grief about it, but really, it suited 'em just fine. They could play the martyrs to their buddies but to tell t'truth, they wanted rid, an' sharpish. So they just went, "She's made her bed, let her lie on it – she's not coming back to our house." I mean, that "*our* house" just said it all, right? So I said, "Great." Bastards.'

He paused to light another ciggie and I noticed his hands trembling slightly. I can't describe how I felt – how could Jamie's own flesh and blood treat her that way? It was – it was beyond my comprehension, really. Gabe took a deep drag on his cig and continued.

'Well, she were poorly for a longish while –

89

depressed, crying all the time. The docs wanted to force feed her all kinds of pills, but me mam said no way – she needs love. My mam, honest, what a case. I said to her, "Mam, this int one of yer injured foxes, or abandoned kittens, this lass is a right fuckin' mess." But me sisters chimed in sayin' they'd help, an' it were the only decent thing to do – 'sides, Jamie were one of the family. Mam just smiled, like. But she were right. It took a long time, an' there were plenty of setbacks an' worryin' times, but she come right eventually. Well, fairly right under t'circumstances. She were still a bit crazy, hanging around wi' the local bikers an' stuff but I got her to leave the drugs alone an' coaxed her into comin' to t'ai chi wi' me, an' walkin' on the moors – she still walks everywhere, don't she? We rode the ponies around an' went swimmin' at the Lido in summer – fun stuff. She got so she could sleep wi'out wakin' up screamin'. She tailed off the drinkin', too. At one point I thought we had a winner. But there's one thing she can't straighten out – blokes.

'She said to me once she knows she's doin' it – pickin' total bastards – but she can't help it. She said it's like a sorta drug, the whole thing, an' she can't kick it no matter how bad it ends up. I don't know what else to do for her – bar watchin' ovver her as best I can. At first, I used to try an' stop it – give the bloke a pastin', stuff like that. It were no good. She'd just crawl back to 'im sobbin'. I know enough not to try an' take the drug away from her

90

when she's on wi' it now. She'll just tear hersel' to pieces tryin' to get it back – you've never seen owt like it. Screamin', bangin' her head on the wall, cuttin' herself – horrible. Makes me fuckin' sorry I'm a bloke sometimes, the whole thing. They smell it on her, the bastards. Like predators, like fuckin' sharks. Like that twat Dodger. Man, I dunno. We just wait for her t'come home. It scares me shitless though. Can't tell you the times I've driven all ovver lookin' for her, but it does no good. Christ.

'Y'see, nothin' you do can fill up that ragin' black hole in her heart, nothin'. That's what I reckon. An' to my mind, that's why she can get up on that stage an' be funny like that. No, I know it sounds weird, right, but she were allus that way – makin' us all laugh, it were like a sorta protection for her, bein' the funny lass. It were like a bit of her that were of her own makin', nowt to do wi' her past. She needs it, she needs to be in control of summat. Mebbe if she gets on wi' this stage lark, she won't need blokes like that any more; who knows? At least it's a go, in't it?'

He turned to me again, his face pleading.

'Lily, you gotta understand. Don't hate her, it weren't her fault, it weren't. It ain't her fault now – she can't help it. If you really wanna be her mate you gotta watch ovver her, I can't be here all the time any more – she needs us – ain't that right, Mojo?'

91

CHAPTER 12

Mojo's Story

Gabe turned to Mojo and looked at him, you could see the pain in his brown eyes. Mojo reached out and patted his hand gently.

'Oh, Archangel Gabriel, what a good man you are. I know, I know, it's so horribly difficult. We're just flung out into the world to get along as best we can.'

Mojo offered his cigarettes round and we lit up. We smoked in silence for a minute then he sighed.

'I met her at Lucky's, you know. Terrible place. Crammed with types. She was twenty-one. I was . . . well, never mind. I'd just returned from London, was staying with a couple of friends who had a *cottage*, shall we say, in Bingley. Very chichi. They were quite the domestic pair, all quiches and Chianti. Oh, very sweet, but how they kept trying to pair me off – "Mo, dear, do meet Trevor, he's teaching English at the university, a terrific guy, really, just moved here from Penge, not at all *sceney*." All these raging closet cases simply draped in tweed and corduroy, and there's *moi*, in Versace. No. I kept meaning to move to my own place but the whole idea was so tiring. When Terry and Tim went off to the Greek Islands for a couple of months I just stayed to cottage-sit. Very convenient, I thought.

'But about a week in, I started having some difficulties. I'd come up here again to be with Someone, Someone special, you see, and things weren't going well. I was very blue, my dears, very. So I packed my handbag with necessities and my nose with coke and trolled out to trawl, so to speak. A disaster in the making, my God.

'I ended up at Lucky's very much the worse for wear. Fortunately Lonnie was there and I managed to fall on to a seat at her table; you know Lonnie, holding court as usual, madly Russian and dramatic. It was all "Darlinks", and "haf a leetle wodka", and "Illonka adores you, seet weeth me". Born and bred in Bradford, that one, but never let something as dull as the truth interfere in a good pose, I always think. Lonnie believes she's Anastasia, at the weekends. The rest of the week she's just Queen Catherine.

'Where was I? Oh yes. So I squeezed myself on to a disgusting little seat and drank some disgusting vodka. The place was like a zoo – full of horrible drunks and straights trying to be bohemian. I was in drag, naturally. Now, please remember, I consider myself a boy in drag, not a transvestite, that's quite another matter.

'After downing some of Lonnie's poisonous brew,

I staggered to the bar and tried to get a decent drink – rather silly, in there, but I wasn't thinking. As I stood there, in my leggings, heels and Gucci-esque tunic ensemble, a man hit me. He just hit me very hard on the side of my face. I went down like felled oak; quite unconscious for a few moments. I came round to find I was straddled as I lay on that filthy floor by a *tigress*, darlings; it was Jamie. She was standing astride my prone body, screaming at this simply *enormous* man. I struggled to get up and she stepped aside, without those blazing eyes ever leaving that brute's sodden gaze, and lifted me up. The Brute was wholly bemused. He was grunting about "queers" and "decent folk" but she just stood there with me fainting over one arm and tore him to pieces. I'm sure she would have fought with him for tuppence, but he was so utterly embarrassed by this harpy he shuffled off muttering. Then, naturally, we got thrown out.

'Her first words to me were, "Have you got your handbag?" She was shaking like a leaf and deathly pale; I imagine I was too, but I prefer to draw a veil over that. I was – well, I can only say, *moved*, by what she had done. I was not normally defended by perfect strangers, rather, the other way around. So of course, I said a very stupid thing. "I'm a man, you know," I said. Really, what was I thinking?

'"I know that," she said impatiently. "What does that matter – you're so beautiful, so beautiful.'

'It seemed to come from somewhere deep inside

her; it was too heartbreaking. It wasn't a compliment – I adore compliments. It was something else. It was like a child looking at a toy its parents can't afford; it was like some kind of unconscious reflex. I realized immediately she thought herself ugly beyond belief. I've seen that kind of damage before. I began to speak but then the pain just kicked in and I suddenly felt very frightened I'd been damaged more badly than usual. I suppose I *yelped.*

'We spent the rest of the evening at the hospital while nurses and doctors were rude to us. We were a pair, certainly. My face was quite purple – never my best colour – and Jamie, my God. It was her leather jeans and tight T-shirt phase; big boots, studded wristbands. Très butch. You could have written your name with your fingernail on her cheek, she had so much foundation on, as Colette says. But she was very funny, and well-read in a non-academic way. Eventually, even the nurses thawed slightly; the whole thing became quite a success, socially. I remember thinking how kind she was to a complete stranger; I imagine that's the influence of your family, Gabriel, my dear.

'Eventually, after the pills were dispensed and the lectures given, we were out in the car park and I found myself saying – "Do you have anywhere to stay, would you care to come to Bingley and stay at the cottage tonight?" To be frank, I simply didn't want to be alone – especially in *Bingley.* She only hesitated for a second, then just said, "Thank you." Lovely manners – your mother again, Angel?

'Well, we had quite a little pyjama party. It was as if we had known each other for years; extraordinary. I would never, ever have thought I would become so fond, so quickly of a person dressed as she was. She stayed for two weeks, and we decided to share a house together. That suited me, as she was quite prepared to do the tedious work involved and I don't really care where I live; public school does that to you. I can sleep happily anywhere and frequently have. We got a flat, first, in Manningham, but soon moved to Undercliffe and then here. We've tried various lodgers, so to speak, some lovely – I always adore *you* staying here, Gabriel, it makes me feel so safe – some just dreadful. And, I'm afraid to say, the dreadful ones have always been Jamie's Errors, as I call them. That awful Andy; such a foul creature. He stole my beautiful Cartier watch *and* my silver Tiffany bracelet. Someone was less than amused by that, believe me. Jamie was, as she always is – and I think you'll agree with me here, Angel – utterly mortified by the beast's behaviour. Then she always is – afterwards. Not for herself, but for the pain these Errors inflict on those who care for her.

'And I do care for her, deeply. Just not in the way you do, Gabriel. I'm not driven to *save* her, or anyone. You may think me cold and selfish, and perhaps I am. I am not in the business of redemption, like you, my dear. I very much dislike the pain she brings upon herself but it's her life,

96

only she can change it. I am not in a position to disapprove of anyone else's behaviour as my own is so convoluted. I will watch over her, certainly, and I will definitely encourage her to pursue her comedy aspirations, because on that, I agree with you. It will give her a purpose in her life, it will allow her to be creative and perhaps, just perhaps, it will, in time, free her from her past.

'I am not as emotionally intense as you, Angel, and Jamie is not my cause, she is my friend. I have a life outside these walls that concerns no one but myself. In a way, that's why I like to live with her. I simply couldn't bear sharing a little pied-à-terre with a bunch of screaming provincial faggots all jostling for the bathroom at once and reeking of poppers. This may be a slum, but that suits me, perversely. I don't have to care about it. I can be myself.

'And now, my darlings, that's quite enough soul-baring for this lady. I'm off to my little truckle bed. I love you madly, Archangel, quite beyond reason – and Lily, dear, dear Tiger Lily, try not to worry, please. Try to accept what you cannot change. She'll come home eventually, and then she'll need you. I don't fear for her physical safety as you do, Gabriel; I don't feel it's her destiny to be the victim of some maniac.'

Dear God. I'll never forget him saying that so glibly. 'The victim of some maniac.' Because, oh yeah, things like that don't happen to people like us, do they?

CHAPTER 13

I slept with Gabriel that night. No, we didn't shag, but believe me, it wasn't because I was playing coy. Oh, fuck. What happened was Mojo went to bed, then Gabe, who was sleeping in Jamie's bed as usual, and then after I cleaned my face and brushed my teeth, so did I.

But I couldn't sleep. The moon was a huge white globe hanging in the dark like a great spotlight. It shone in my skylight which had no blinds or anything. I tried counting sheep, deep breathing, shallow breathing, everything – nothing worked. I tried reading – no go. Wide awake. My mind was working overtime about the terrible things I'd heard and I felt totally mixed-up. I didn't know what to feel, what to do. On one hand, I felt desperately sorry for Jamie; on the other, well, I'm not proud of it but I thought, man, get it the fuck away from me. I know how bad that sounds, but it's the truth. Nowadays, we've all heard so many horror stories of child abuse we're kind of used to it in a grisly way. If a woman is acting crazy, people just assume she has some awful secret of abuse – guys too. But then, no. I knew there'd been a boy in my school who'd shagged his little sister, he'd boasted about it. We thought he was a wanker and I expect most people didn't really believe him. I didn't. I did now.

The thought of what had been done to little Jamie turned my guts. And her fucking parents! No wonder we never saw or heard from them, no wonder she just made jokes about them all the time. Defence mechanism. Now I understood what Graeham had meant by 'darkness'. I don't think he knew the story but I think he suspected something bad in her past. He wasn't stupid – but I fucking was. I mean, what dreadful stuff was going on out there in the big world while I skipped about wondering what colour lippie to wear and having my fucking dinner of an evening?

I wanted justice for Jamie and for all the other lost children. The walking dead kids; the pathetic little remnants of their elders' cannibal feast. My brain just whirled round and round with it. But at the same time I felt kind of resentful that I'd been given this savage knowledge. I felt ashamed of thinking that way but I couldn't help it. I was in a right state.

I got up and, putting on a giant T-shirt, crept down to the bog. I had a wee, then, as I was about to go back up to my attic, I thought, I don't want to be alone. I wanted to be cuddled. Oh, sod it, I wanted Gabe.

I'm not a bold, devil-may-care Modern Girl,

whatever I may look like. I can't abide the *Cosmopolitan* Girlie Predator types. I have my moments, sure, but generally I keep my hands to myself, if you like. Tonight was different; tonight I was trying to survive.

I opened the door of Jamie's room and stood for a second listening to Gabe's steady breathing. Then I went and sat on the edge of the bed and shook him awake.

'Wassermarrer? Uh, Lil, wa's up, girl?'

'Can I kip in with you? I feel awful, I can't sleep, please, Gabe . . .'

''Course you can, babby, hop in. Come on, snug up, right, off to sleepyland, kiddie.'

He went back to sleep immediately. We'd snugged up into spoons and I lay in his arms like a child. I could feel the strength of him and the warm swell of his big muscles; smell the sweet scent of his skin – the clean, comforting smell of a healthy bloke. I was glad he hated aftershaves and deodorants, I loved his own Gabe-smell so much. His breath was sweet, too, and his curly black hair smelt faintly of herb shampoo.

I knew I'd fallen in love with him.

What a fucking disaster.

You see, sometimes, the chemistry just isn't there. Oh it might be for *you*, but not for the Love Object. And nothing you can do will change that. I knew my beloved Gabriel thought I was a 'great kid'. I knew he was very pleased that his Jamie had a constant companion he could trust. I knew he would do anything for me if I asked, because I was in his extended family. But was he in love with me as I was with him? No. No point fooling myself – that way madness lies. I'd seen his girlfriends. He ran to skinny, neurotic blondes with big googly eyes and fuck-me mouths. They were bitches to a girl and he always thought they'd been hard done to, or the world didn't understand them. You see, in his own way, he was as fucked up in love as Jamie was. He just didn't see me as a potential lover. He never would, I knew that. Fuck all that shit about getting your man by appearing in something slinky, pouting and twanging your G-string at him. It never works. I would not humiliate myself that way, no, not for anything. Better Gabe thought I was a little sister than a sex-starved slapper.

Better to keep his good opinion and have a broken heart. So I lay in his arms and let the pain of it all bloom in me like a black flower. I just let go and at last felt the night shut my eyes. If I cried, it was in my sleep, and that doesn't count.

The next day, I woke as usual around seven, and leaving him sleeping, snuck off to get dressed for work. And yes, of course I kissed him as he slept. I'm not a fucking saint. I didn't want to leave in case Jamie got back, but I had some important bits and bobs to do for Carrington's, the jewellers. It wouldn't take more than the morning, and as Gabe and Mojo were in, I thought it'd be kosher.

I got through it all by twelve-thirty, after telling

old Mr C. that I was a bit wobbly due to incipient flu. After that lie, I actually began to feel shit and thought I really might have flu. I kept shaking and feeling out of kilter with everything; nothing seemed right and I was sweating and feverish. The idea it might be stress never occurred to me. I didn't get stress. Yuppie tossers got stress. People from London got stress. I was a stout-hearted Northern lass without a nervous bone in my tight-knit little body. Calm as a millpond, smooth as Galaxy. Oh yeah – I really believed that in those days. Ah, sweet bird of youth. Fuck. I decided to drive up to Ma's for a bit of scran on account of not having eaten anything substantial for hours and anyhow, I felt a strong need to see my ma. It was a beautiful day, and a beautiful day in Bradford is nearly as good as being by the seaside.

People laugh when I say I think Bradford is one of the most beautiful towns in the North, or indeed, England. What about York, they say, or Harrogate? Crap. No comparison. Bradford, you see, is built in a bowl. The city centre is the bottom of the bowl and all hills lead outwards. Upwards, in Bradford, is out of town. That means, as you weave your way down, say, the Leeds Road, the skies above you are vast, open and rolling with cinematic cloudscapes. It's just like cresting the rise and getting your first glimpse of the sea, only instead of water you can see the purple drift of the moors on the opposite hill.

As you drive along, the colours and textures of the fruit and veg laid out in front of the little shops

just knocks you out – mangos, figs, papaya, aubergines, carrots, sugar cane, plums, pomegranates,
potatoes, bunches of coriander, spinach and heaps
of apples, pears and cabbages. Everything you
could want from wherever you could think of. The
fabric shops take your eye out with great bolts of
sapphire, crimson, emerald, lamé, metallic tissue,
chiffon, silk and wacka-jacka polyester; a thousand
shades of pink make roses redundant and it's all
stitched, embroidered, laced and stuck with gold
and silver, paillettes, mini-mirrors and hologram
plastic. Just look at the Asian lasses in their sequins
and satins, glittering like goddesses as they wheel
the babby out in its pushchair for an airing and
some gossip. They get the best gear, really.

I love it, me. Of course, I'd like to say this idyllic
little gem is home to model citizens and cheery,
good-natured, honest Northern folk. But it isn't.
It's lived in by real people, which means for every
cheery etc., you get about four moronic fuckwits
of either sex, who have the brain of a trout and the
disposition of a rabid pit bull. We may be a smallish
city as cities go, but we have our fair share of gang-
sters, gobshites, whores, pimps, dealers, druggies,
con-men, chancers, fundamentalists, lunatics, vil-
lains, bully-boys, goons, viragos, hellions, wannabe
Outlaws, real Outlaws, blasphemers, fornicators,
paedophiles, robbers, vandals, Goths and plain old
wankers, both public and private.

Lists of good things and lists of bad things played
incessantly in my brain as I drove, like a sort of

chant. I kept trying to see which list was longer; but they just kept running like a chorus. I had a throbbing headache and the thick sunlight made it worse as it refracted through the scratched-to-fuck old windscreen. I was dying for a cuppa and two paracetamol.

I was so grateful when I pulled up at Ma's I parked like a right twat. I almost fell out of the Mini and up the step into the blissfully dark hallway.

'Ma, Ma, it's me! Ma, it's Lily, you in the kitchen?'

Of course she was. She gave me a floury-handed hug and I whinged about being headachey and fluey. That got me tea and pills plus the promise of a bacon-and-tomato butty, dripping with butter and ketchup on a nice white bread bun from the bakery, fresh this morning. I'm so glad Pa's a baker, I love carbohydrates and fat.

I watched her toddle around the tiny kitchen, frying and buttering things and offering me iced fancies for afters. I loved her so much I had to squeeze my face shut so I wouldn't babble on about it. She was wearing what she always wore; a blouse, a skirt, a cardi, an apron and a pair of fluffy slippers. All from BHS or Marks. Her one idiosyncrasy was her astonishingly long hair, which was tightly plaited and wound into a bun at the nape of her neck. She always wore it that way unless she was out walking with Pa in the Dales or wherever, when the outfit was old-fashioned ski-pants, Brasher boots and a jumper with the hair in one long braid, tucked into her waterproof. She never changed. Neither did Pa. It was so comforting.

I ate my butty in big mouthfuls and drank a pint of tea. As I started on a luminous-green iced fancy, Ma wiped her hands on a tea-towel and sat opposite me at the little table. There was a short silence full of meaning and then she said:

'What is it, lovie, what's the matter?'

Oh sod. She always sussed me. I 'fessed up. The whole thing. What I'd learned about Jamie, how mixed up about it I felt and how guilty, and how I was in love with Gabriel. It all came pouring out like a flood of darkness into that warm kitchen, with Ma just going, 'hmmm', 'I see' and, 'oh dear', at intervals. When I'd finished, I laid my hot head on my forearms and sighed. It was such a relief to let it go.

Then I was electrified with guilt. How could I have told my innocent, unworldly Ma about those dreadful things? I sat bolt upright and began to stutter apologies, explanations.

She didn't speak and eventually my burbling tailed off. We sat in silence for a moment, then Ma sighed.

'Oh dear, my poor little pet.' She looked sad and a bit lost; I felt a wave of sadness wash over me, too. She sighed, then continued gently.

'Well, dear, you know, no chap likes to be chased after, I don't have to tell you that. It makes a girl cheap. Oh, I know things are different now, but still, it's true enough. If he's as nice as you say, then just stay friends and he'll see your worth in time. I know it's painful, dear, but there's nothing I can tell you that will make it better. You're not a silly girl, thank heavens, I don't have to worry about carryings-on. But dear, I am sorry that you're hurt – your pa and I think the world of you, you know, we're so proud of you – this chap'll come round, just wait and see. If he doesn't, well, plenty more fish in the sea, it's him'll lose out, not you.'

I leant across and kissed her. She always said all the right mum things. Not like my friends' mums who wanted to be mates with their kids and who you had to call by their first names, as if they were ashamed of being mothers. I hate that crap. Mothers should be proud of being mothers, and fathers of being fathers, not trying to be kids forever – it's cheesy.

I was so busy ranting on in my head, I nearly missed what Ma was saying; but I came to pretty damn quick as her words floated in on my internal sermonizing.

'. . . your poor friend. But of course, I mean, round here for instance. Little Judy Esthwaite, you remember Judy, don't you, dear, you were quite pally at one time . . .' I did remember Jude; ponytail, spots, dozy as a fruitcake and pregnant at fifteen. What had Jude to do with Jamie's problem?

'Well, of course, it was her father's child, it'd been going on for years apparently, and the elder girl too – oh, what was her name?'

'Karen, it was Karen,' I said in a daze. Jude's father? Her red-faced, hearty, Friar Tuck-type Dad? Incest? *What the fuck?*

'Oh yes, Karen. Now there's a tragedy. The inquest said accidental death, but I think we all knew it was suicide. I looked after Betty Esthwaite as best I could while the court case went on – there were plenty round here fit to lynch her, but I said, we will never know what went on in that house – "let he who is without sin cast the first stone". And of course, afterwards, when Judy had the baby, it was a blessing, really, it didn't live – the little scrap. He got five years, Gordon Esthwaite, and it should have been life, in my opinion. I said to Pa at the time, thank heaven we never let our Lily stay over at that house, after all the other children he'd molested were discovered. He took photographs, apparently. A beast; I never trusted him. He struck me as too smiley by half, if you know what I mean. I remember Etta saying I was being silly – she let her May go there and look what happened. Awful. Those poor, poor mites. Betty never recovered from the trial; I don't know if it was true she knew what was going on, but the suspicions alone – dreadful. They live in Blackpool now, Betty and Judy. Did I tell you, dear?'

Did you tell me, Ma? Did you tell me? What? That two of my classmates were raped by a pervert and one of them his own daughter? That she sat in my bedroom playing Monopoly out to here with the child of incest and I just thought you were being

107

kind not to shun a girl who had a secret boyfriend and 'got in trouble'? And to be honest, I thought I was being pretty fucking decent having the class dweeb round, as well. Oh, and May Pollitt was 'weird' not because her mum was a dipso neurotic – but because she'd been systematically abused by a neighbour? That nice, jolly Mr Esthwaite went to nick and not to 'work away' as I thought? No, Ma, you never said a fucking dickey bird.

'No, Ma, you never said, I had no idea about any of this . . .'

'Well, I think your pa and I thought it was for the best, you were so young and it's not a subject for children. I suppose we wanted to protect you, keep you innocent.' She sighed again. 'But we all grow up eventually and here you are, with the same dilemma I had. Oh, it's a cruel world sometimes and no mistake. I felt like you do now, dear. I thought, why should I have to get involved with something as dreadful as this? But I had no choice. Your pa and I agreed – we weren't going to pass by on the other side and not try to help. We did our best, and I hope you'll do the same. It's not your friend's fault, you see. There are plenty of folks who'll blame her – you should have heard the things that were said about poor Judy and Karen and the others; cruel, evil things – but no, your friend was a little child, an innocent. She needs you to be her friend, especially now. Well, there you are.'

There you are indeed. My whole image of my

childhood as an idyllic, cosy storybook out the pigging window. Ma and Pa – not chubby, lovable potterers through life, but fiercely protective guardians of my innocence. The two girls I dismissed as losers along with everyone else at school, the victims of a hideous crime. What else was there in the world I was completely fucking ignorant of? Where did I ever get the idea I was a grown-up from? Christ. Fucking Christ. All I'd done all day was slop about in self-pity; just because I was too pathetic to help my friend, and just because, like a million other people on the planet, I was suffering from unrequited love. Oh pull-*ease*; I was ashamed of myself. But also, I felt something had happened to me. Maybe the cotton wool I'd been wrapped in so assiduously had parted a smidgen and the cold light of day had snuck in.

Things would never be the same again; and I was glad, in a funny way.

'I love you, Ma.' I mean, what else was there I could say? Some things just can't be spoken. Nothing I could say would make any odds except 'I love you'. And I did love her, but more than that, she had my respect for what she'd done; for facing up to what I'd been griping about. I held her red, soft hand across the table, and said I had to go. She nodded.

'Take care, lovie, and be a good girl.'

Bye-bye, Ma. It was time I started growing up.

CHAPTER 14

It was about four when I got back. I felt a bit guilty about staying out so long but I reasoned that Gabe would be there, or Moj. As it turned out, they weren't. Mojo was just nowhere to be found and Gabe had left one of his cryptic, semi-illegible notes sellotaped to the kitchen mirror.

'J. in. M. gone to Leeds says will be back late tonight. Me too after see about a van. Got key dont fret. Love and X's to both my girlz, G.'

Love and X's. Oh sod. I wish. My heart thudded painfully for a moment but I put the kettle on and gave myself a stern ticking-off. Then I went upstairs and put my head round Jamie's door.

She looked like shit. Her pink hair was a rat's nest of unbrushed-out backcombing and hairspray. She'd washed her make-up off at some point but there were clots of gummy black in the squeezed-shut corners of her eyes. Her pointy chin was red and abraded with beard rash and her neck was decorated with two big, blackish hickeys – I won't call them *love*bites. She was cheese-white and the room smelt of stale bed linen, farts, yesterday's perfume and unwashed woman. I noticed her hand, which was poking out from under the purple flowerprint quilt, was clenched in a tight fist. She was wearing all her jewellery.

I thought she was still kipping but as I withdrew, she said weakly, 'It's OK, Lil, I'm not sleeping.' Her usually tuneful voice was croaky and broken.

'Wanna cuppa char, babby?' I said gently. 'Kettle's on.'

'Yes, please. Thank you.'

I brought the tea – and some cake I'd picked up at Ma's – on her favourite cat-picture tray. After discreetly opening the window a bit, I sat on the edge of the bed while she pulled herself up and stuffed pillows behind her back. She wouldn't look at me.

Then she said in a small voice, 'I know Gabriel's told you – about everything. I s'pose that's it then. Don't worry, I understand. I know you've paid rent up till the end of the month but I'll get it back to you. I'll send it to your ma's or whatever.'

She was crying, the tears leaking from under her eyelids and running down her round cheeks. I poured her some tea and put a slice of fruitcake on a side plate.

'Drink this now, dear, before it goes cold.' With a slight shock, I heard my ma's voice issue out of my mouth. It was just what she would have said. I paused a second to collect myself, then I went on.

111

'Nothing's changed, love. You're my best mate.'

'But he told you – he told you what happened to me, an' my parents an' everything . . . oh, oh, Lily, how can you want to know a person like me? How can you? How can you? I'm dirty, I'm – not a nice person like you, I'm cursed . . .'

Gabe had said she thought herself cursed, but to hear it from her own mouth was heartbreaking. It was such a strange, old-fashioned idea. To be cursed; it was like something out of a Hammer Horror. But I knew what she meant; she felt that nothing she did would ever be good, or right. That she was *outside* of everything, worthless.

I took the mug away from her before she spilt tea all over everything and put it on the floor, then I took hold of her cold hand and held it.

'I love you, you silly piglet, you're not dirty, or cursed or anything like that. It wasn't your fault. I won't leave you until you want me to go away. Friends forever; best pals. The Dynamic Duo. Right?'

'Oh Lily . . .'

'Right?'

'Right . . . are you sure?'

'You betcha, babski, we're going to be famous. You're going to work your arse off. I'm going to be filthy rich. We got it made, we're unstoppable.'

Then she had a good cry and ate all the cake.

I found out the details about the dreadful Dodger later, over dinner. What she told me filled me

112

with a kind of cold fury made all the worse by the sense that she thought being treated like shit was all she was due. Naturally, Casanova behaved like a total fucking arsehole, I expected that. What I didn't expect were the little embellishments, like him getting up after sex to wash his hands at the bedroom sink so he could have a cigarette – 'Well, you don't expect me to touch me mouth wi' me hands after I've been messin' wi summat like you, do yer?' Oh yeah, that was just one of his charming lines. He threw her out around lunchtime after he got a phone call from his girlfriend to say she'd be visiting him that evening. He felt it necessary to inform Jamie that he needed to change the bed linen and air the room to get rid of the smell of 'that stinking fucking hippie crap you lot douse yourselves with'.

I won't dwell on the rest of the crap he doled out. Not that Jamie told me, or indeed, *ever* told me the 'gory details' of her sex habits. Unlike most women, she wasn't into dragging the secrets of the bedroom into the glaring lights of every Ladies in Bradford, usually at full volume. No, she was quite prudish like that; she hated dirty jokes as well. Funny coming from her, you might say, but there you are. Humans are contrary critters. To be honest, I didn't want a blow-by-blow account anyhow. I used to get embarrassed watching *Wildlife On One* with Ma and Pa when the mating bits came on. As for late night Channel Four – no ta. Maybe we were odd, but I don't think so, not really, not if people told the truth. People don't shag a quarter as much as the Media would have us believe. Hey ho.

I didn't have a lot of appetite for once, and neither did she. We put the best part of the food aside for the lads when they came in and sat with our tea watching *Blade Runner* on video. Sometimes we'd talk a bit about her past, or our future.

Only once did she say anything about why she did what she did with blokes like Dodger. The whole thing seemed to make her cringe with shame and humiliation. I asked her, very, very carefully, if she'd ever talked to anyone about it – a counsellor or some such person – someone trained to deal with these things.

She laughed bitterly. 'It's horrible, right? The whole shitty, stupid business. I know it's horrible. Everyone tells me it's horrible. But I don't know how to stop it; it's so much a part of me I wonder what I'd be without it. I feel like I'd be straight an' boring and grey if I stopped doing it. Stupid probably. I'd be a better person. Shit. I don't know . . .'

Her face changed – became defiant, rebellious. I thought – that's the face she showed the world when she was a kid. Yeah, a real little madam – if you didn't know the truth. She looked at the floor for a moment, then back at me, her grey eyes like stormclouds as she continued.

'I can rehash all the crap the docs flung at me but, man, they were on a major power trip too. A

114

real Good Guys Save The Bad Girl trip. Trying to make me fit their fuckin' image of what a girl *should* be. But, man, what the fuck, *what the fuck* did they know about how I felt? How could people like *that* understand what happened to me? Most of the spineless fuckers didn't even *believe* me. No, *wouldn't* believe me, is more like it. Some Freud thing – they said I was making it up. Christ Almighty, how could you make something like that up? I was just a delinquent to them, a bitch with a bad name – well, hang her if she don't do what she's told. So I think, you know, fuck 'em. Fuck all the straights – fuck straight society. It didn't lift a finger for me, an' when I fell, it stomped on me good style. Oh Christ, oh Christ – I don't know. Born bad, I suppose; "bolshie" my nana used to call me. Yeah. Born under a bad sign, or something.'

I just thought, yeah, she's right. When she needed society, society turned its back like she was scum. Well, we didn't need them, we had our own family – us against them. The Real Good Guys versus the Real Bad Guys. Righteous.

I didn't tell her about my feelings for Gabe. I thought, it's not the right time, I'll wait. I thought, if I don't say anything to anyone it will be easier to control – you know. I did wax lyrical about my Great Plan for world domination though. Got her smiling again with the castles in the air I built. She called me 'Fu Manchu' for years after that. I called her 'Lotus Blossom'. People thought we were barmy.

We were barmy. We were young and full of fire and bullshit in equal proportions; but you see, we had nothing to lose.

Oh Christ, yeah, nothing to lose – that's what we thought. We really did.

BOOK II

CHAPTER 15

I once had a teacher who asked us to think about Time. He said, if you were stood at a bus stop and you had to wait five minutes in the rain, that five minutes seemed like an hour. Now if you were at a great party, and it was five minutes before your dad came to pick you up, that five minutes seemed like five seconds. Yeah, we all went. Well, he says, what if it had really been longer during the bus stop wait and shorter at the party? But it's Time, we chorused, it just is. But who says it is, he goes, who's to say it isn't just how you see it; maybe Time is in your mind and time is something *we* invented to section up the daylight. He gave us that quote – 'Time is but a mode of thought'.

The rest of the class thought he was mental. It stuck with me though; I thought I knew what he was getting at. Bugged the hell out of me; still does.

The years went by like billyoh. So fast. I mean, not at the actual time; some years we were so frustrated by setbacks or finances that the months dragged like treacle. But when you come to look back . . . Yeah, the years just flashed by. I decided to work on the 'if-you-don't-ask-you-don't-get' principle regarding Jamie's (and mine, I thought of it as mine too) career.

I nagged everyone even remotely connected with showbiz for addresses of venues, journalists who might review her, radio programmes, anything. I got some mega-brightly coloured leaflets printed to send to every fucking venue in this country; I admit, I faked the reviews on them. Well, I had to, it was do or die. Just stuff like, *'Britain's fabulous new comedy talent . . .* Manchester Evening News' and, *'Quirky and innovative comedy styling . . . a talent to watch out for . . .* Bristol Gazette'. I mean, come on, everyone does it. No one ever *checks*, they don't give a shit at venues, it's just how cheap they can get you and will you bring in some punters. Bums on seats.

Initially, Jamie had a big advantage in being a woman. In those heady days of political correctness (or just being fair and polite, as I think of it . . .) every venue wanted a mixed bill. A Woman, A Man, A Black Man and if possible, A Gay. No one even tried for A Black Woman, there weren't any – and I don't think I need to explain why, do I . . . ? Oddly enough The Man usually got top billing but that always passed unremarked. The internal politics of the 'entertainment' business just do not bear close scrutiny; like, *at all.*

So in the beginning, if I got really desperate, I could always get her work on the 'You don't mean there are no *women* on the bill!' ticket. Naturally, at first I was fairly crap; but as I got more practised and the scales fell from my eyes regarding anything to do with 'glamour' or 'showbiz magic', I realized it wasn't that different from all the little businesses I worked for. Buy cheap, sell dear. Eventually, I got a rep as being ruthlessly efficient and hard as nails. Suited me. In that business it just means you don't exchange arse-licking or blowjobs for gigs and you don't let them off cheating you because you want them to like you. Fuck that. Promoters, agents, venue managers – man, they're all snakes, all out for their own wallet. Sure, I got dapped a couple of times, they were tough lessons – but I learnt from them. Polite but firm is my motto; and count your rings after you've shook hands with them.

And Jamie learnt too. She learnt not to lose her temper on stage with hecklers no matter how disruptive they were. She learnt to stop having a drink before going on and on one disastrous occasion, she learnt not to gum any whizz before going on. Christ Almighty, I thought she was going to have a heart attack that night. She was all over the shop on stage, yammering like an idiot. If I could of reached her, I would have smacked her face.

'But I was so fucking *tired*, Lil, so fuckin' tired . . . it's been eight shows in a row and no proper place to sleep. The stage manager gave it to me; he didn't mean any harm, honest . . .'

Oh yeah, sure he didn't. OK, probably he just didn't think twice about it. Everything's run on whizz – or coke in the upper echelons – I suppose the idea that someone *didn't* do it was totally fucking alien to him.

But Jamie had a point. It was a hard old slog in those early years. Driving for five hours, eating some crapola take-out, waiting for hours in a stinking, freezing filthy venue; on stage for twenty-five minutes, kip on someone's floor in a damp, smelly flat or squat if I couldn't make it home that night.

There were a few exceptions we could boast about to other acts who hadn't made it that far North. The rest of the time we were exhausted, dirty and hungry most nights. I was knackered all the time and I didn't have to suffer the hideous stage fright, then get over it and summon up superhuman mental energy to do the gig every night, like she did. I took heed and started booking three nights on, one off. Maybe it wasn't so financially sound but I wanted longevity for Jamie, not burn-out.

We worked about a gig a week steady, on average though. If I could string two or three together, fine. If not we'd just head off in the Mini and end up in Milton Keynes, or Oxford, or Carlisle – wherever. All the venues merged into one to me – but she remembered everything.

'What about the one where the fat bloke said there was a dressing room, only it was a cellar with a sofa in it and it was divided in two by chicken wire and behind that he kept two fucking Doberman guard dogs! Fuck me! D'you remember? Christ, as soon as we got down there the fucking dogs started hurling themselves at the wire baying like wolves and I had to sit there and put me eyeliner on straight! Drenched in flying dog-drool I was, d'you remember? It was Bournemouth, a pub venue called, oh . . . *Mindy's*, that's it, Mindy's – as in Mork, presumably. God, what a dive; it was me and Genghis Stanza, the comic poet bloke, you know, and – who was it? Yeah, it was Francine 'Scarlett' O'Hara. Remember her? They threw lighted fag ends at her, poor cow. Ruined her dress. She ran off-stage crying – you must remember, Lil, you were really nice to her, she fancied you – she *did!* Still, she didn't last long, did she? Not surprising though, funny, but too girlie-girlie. Not an old boot like me, eh? D'you remember . . . ?'

And on she'd go as we trundled up and down the M1 year after year. She got quite a lot of publicity very early on, mostly on account of what she looked like. You know – the 'Gothic Gagstress', the 'Queen of Goth' or, my favourite, the 'Morticia of Mirth'. It wasn't my favourite because of its intelligence, oh, quite the reverse. We used to wince when we drove up to a venue, or opened a local listings mag and there it was, some inane quip about her hair or her height. She got the front cover of *City Life* magazine in London, after a particularly freaky gig in a warehouse down by the river. It was supposed to be a 'happening' of some sort, but it just involved the usual comedians plus a stoned naked girl being wheeled around in a wheelbarrow full of jelly. Lime jelly, as I recall.

But the hack who covered it for *City Life* decided Jamie was hot. Or cool, whatever. He was the one who first called her 'a female Lenny Bruce', not that pea-balled cocksucker Ronnie fucking Rage.

I can't remember that journalist's name – what was it? If Jamie were here she'd tell you in a sec . . .

Well, anyhow, call him Fred. Fred and Jamie got on like a house on fire. Talked for hours. Then he arranged for her to have a photo-shoot with David Macavoy, *the* up-and-coming photographer. What a tosser, it took eight hours, they wouldn't let her do her own make-up but they couldn't do Goth and kept trying to glam her up with pearly lipgloss and shit like that. Davey-darling was a monumental fuckwit-cum-poseur and in the end, in *the* shot, sweetie, Jamie just looked bored stiff. But Fred loved it ('it's really bold, y'know, really *now*') and so did Fred's boss and so there she was – New Comedy Sensation – Jamie Gee. He was all right, Fred. I wonder what became of him.

I've still got a framed copy of that front page. She looks so young, so fucking young. All eyeliner and attitude, bless her. It did us the world of good though, gigs came rolling in. We got Glastonbury for the first time after that. They put her on in the big Cabaret Marquee; just ten minutes the first day, then after they saw how she went down, twenty minutes on the Saturday and Sunday plus a bit of compering. We did every year it was on after that. Regular. Her Nibs loved it – all the stalls selling bloody hand woven macramé ethnic friendship bracelets and recycled tie-dye sarongs. Body-painting. Henna tattoos. Circus skills. Crystal healing. All the fun of the fair. It did get a bit hyper after Dance came in, but we still went. Even in the fucking mud. Never mind, eh. I used to hire a tranny van from Rent-A-Rek, put a mattress in and we'd camp in that. Very snug. Wellies optional.

It was after that first Glasters that Jamie changed her look again. She just went out one morning and came back that teatime with chestnut-brown hair, still very long but instead of just grown-raggy ends, cut square across the bottom and with a really short, razor-cut edgy fringe. I nearly dropped me cuppa. Mojo actually gasped.

'Well,' she said a bit defensively, 'I got bored of pink. All them workmen singing "Pretty In *Pink*" – you know. I'm going to ditch the frocks, too. Bloke's black suit, I thought, from Oxfam – with my Docs and a scoop-neck kind of body effort underneath. Big jewellery. You know, different. Anyhow, the Goth thing, it's – what is it, Mojo?'

'Darling, I think you mean passé – but you look marvellous, *ma soeur*, marvellous. Now, I think a – yes – eyebrows, faint dusting of powder and a very beautiful red lipstick – matte lipstick – look for the *maquillage*, hmm?'

'Oh yes, that's great – but the lipstick, I mean, I take it you're thinking Chanel, here – what's that shade they do, "Cosmos", is it? Oh, lovely – but not cheap, that sort of lippie . . .'

I left them to it. I suppose I should have been cross with her, changing herself so radically but actually, I was secretly relieved. She was spot-on as usual. The Goth thing was a bit old hat and she hated being stuck in one thing too long. Oh well, new photos. Now, that student photographer . . . yeah, it was all about *keeping up* with Jamie, in those days.

Radio gigs started coming in; not Radio Four *comedy*, mind you, that sort of thing was for Oxford graduates only, thank you. No, guest spots on this or that magazine programme; a bit on *Woman's Hour* talking about a Woman's Life in Alternative Comedy. Jamie was good at that sort of thing. She could tone down her speech to suit the show, not frighten them. The times I heard one of them say – *Oh, we were all a tiny bit scared of you at first, but you're really jolly nice, aren't you?* – as if it was a compliment, the stupid bastards. No, Her Nibs was a real professional; we prided ourselves on being real professionals. We were amiable, but not grovelly. That was our line. Courteous, always shake hands. Never be late, pissed or temperamental.

We got a bit of telly, too. But my God, telly folk are idiots. Un*believable*. You know the type – they ask you a question but they never listen to what you say. They've got it all worked out beforehand, see, and if you don't fit into their concept they get nasty, as if it's your fault. 'We can't *use* you,' they say, and never get the irony. Jamie did a few magazine programmes, a few late-night comedy spots, but it didn't suit her style. It's all 'bright', 'fast' and 'whacky'. They want the Boy's Club, the Fizz! Award winners who were always in the right places, at the right parties, snorting the right cocaine and shagging the right producers. To be honest, I just don't think we understood the game; we thought it was all about doing a good show – making the punters laugh. Eventually, the offers faded.

But we thought, who cares about that sort of tosser? They'll come round to our way of thinking eventually, they'd have to. We had a wonderful grass-roots following for the live gigs. People loved her; we got loads of fan-mail – I got a PO Box as soon as we could afford it. Punters are fab, but you don't want 'em knowing where you live. You see, with an act like Jamie, the punters half believed she was someone they actually knew, their mate, if you like. So after a few showed up at the house wanting a chat and a cuppa, I drew the line and scraped up the PO Box money. I traded in the Mini – and I got a rather nice Peugeot – bright red, immaculate condition; OK, there was 125,000-odd miles on the clock but it was a steal at £1,500 plus the poor old Minski. I kept that car lovely, really. I do like a well-kept motor. Even Mojo sometimes deigned to travel in it – you could never get him in the Min.

We loved the life, though, we really did. Christ, it was a fucking scream, a lot of the time. Just her an' me belting up and down the country living like gypsies; like showfolk. All the hard work, the fatigue, the hunger – it didn't matter to us in the face of the immense buzz we got from the life itself.

Jamie blossomed, honestly. The terrible black depressions that had periodically haunted her like a kind of psychic migraine, reduced to just the occasional bout. We always did loads of stuff together, seeing friends all over the country, Christmas at my ma and pa's, then Gabe's mum's for Boxing Day. Holidays, we'd go after Glastonbury – pop down to Cornwall for a week in the hired tranny, cruise about – Polzeath, St Ives, Newquay. One year we went to Crete on a package. Simple stuff, not expensive. Jamie was keeping up her writing, too, and she started getting the odd article published in the local *What's On?* magazine, and once in *City Life*. She toyed with the idea of a novel, but in the end, I suppose it was too much work on top of gigging. When she retired, she'd say; when I'm old. I did my diary, got into computers more and more. I even set up a homepage for her, where we could put her gigs, biography and bits of her writing. She had a Zapmail account I set up for her – jamiegee@zapmail.com – and she got a lot of feedback that way. It made her happy to be in touch with folk; like penpals or fan-mail, but quicker.

Sure, she still had flings. 'Errors.' But she saw a couple of quite nice blokes, too. Not for long, maybe, but it was a start. Me, well, I carried my torch for you-know-who but I saw other fellas if one took my fancy. Nothing heavy, just friendly. I even turned down a marriage proposal from one guy, Ty Ellis. Nice guy – family from St Kitts – a session saxophone player. In short, a *musician*. Great in bed, very enthusiastic – but you can't marry a musician, can you? Disaster. It's the fuzzy end of the lollipop – everyone knows *that*. We're still mates though, fortunately. He probably wasn't 100 per cent serious about getting wed – I hope . . .

CHAPTER 16

At home, everything was cool. We'd even renovated the house a bit, well, *we* had; Mojo moved out until the paint was dry then moved back in and complained about the smell. His decorative effort was to drift around in black silk-satin pyjamas and a devore wrap reeking of Obsession, or Poison or some other deadly brew. He did pay for the paint, though. Or Someone did. Someone got quite domestic around this time and we got heaps of linen, towels and duvets given. All M & S. I once ventured to enquire whether Someone was Mr Marks or Mr Spencer, but I just got a Look in reply. Ah well, Someone moved in mysterious ways His wonders to perform. Gabe would come over when he was home and do manly building things with wood. Wearing just a white vest and combats. His black ringlets falling over his eyes, the intricate, curving indigo lines of his Celtic tattoos accentuating his muscles – oh, to trace those inky patterns with my fingertip and then . . . I used to be out on those days. There's a limit to what a girl can stand, after all.

We even started bugging the landlord to sell us

the house – he'd begun to waver at one point and we were all set to be a regular little family – two old maids, a drag princess and a neurotic cat.

Yeah, we had a cat – sure, we got broody like anyone else; we had hormones and got soppy over hip little baby items in Asda. Well, the cat got us, really. One day we were catless, the next we were with cat, so to speak. Moley, we called her; a little black silky smudge of a thing, all yowls and hugs. She just padded into the kitchen one day, sat down and asked quite politely for her breakfast, as if she'd always been there. She became Jamie's pet, to be honest. Mojo liked to show off his long hands stroking her, and Moley was all for it even if it only simulated love. But Jamie she really adored and she was Jamie's baby. I was allowed to feed her, for which I got the odd cuddle of a morning.

I often heard Jamie talking to her. It was strangely touching.

'Who's my girl? Princess, black shiny Queen of Love, my snake-head baby, my little ink-blot; does your mam love you, I think she does, flower-paws, satin-nose. Oh yes, I love you, midnight-fur, emerald-eyes, mouse-killer . . .'

On and on she would chant this litany of love to Moley, who just purred and dribbled on the quilt and tried to knead her mistress softer with her little black leather pads.

Oh yeah, everything was kosher. Sweet. Except, I was worried. Nothing personal, but a niggling little worry about our career. It was 1995, things were changing in the business; new young bloods were bounding down comedy paths that frankly, I just didn't find funny. I mean, of course there were exceptions – Eddie Izzard, absolutely hysterical. He didn't do telly, either, and it didn't seem to do him any harm. Mind you, he had a stone gimmick with the transvestite thing, perfect. But the others: Ricky Sharpe, Mona McLeish, Dermott Joyce. They were hard, clubby and cynical to the point of cruelty – and beyond. They got their laughs from a knowing, mercenary irony, from being elaborately anti-PC. The lowest common denominator – gutter laughs dressed in Paul Smith. They had dead coke eyes, those comics, and were in love with their own brilliance. The punters lapped it up. The Thatcher generation had grown up into hard-candy hipsters who pleased themselves and knew no better religion than 'Do What Thou Wilt And Let That Be The Whole Of The Law'. They wanted their comedy apolitical, amoral, elitist, and hot in the vanguard of the feminist backlash. So that's what they got.

It worried me. Sure, Izzard did Jamie's kind of anecdotal wittering, but he was a lone voice, and the rest of the pack chilled me to the bone . . . bookings were getting harder to find for Her Nibs. Oh, not much, just a tad. But the smell of winter was in the air and I wondered if Jamie realized. I didn't want her to change; I wanted the world to change.

1995. Jamie was twenty-nine; I was twenty-eight. We weren't *old* or anything, but we weren't kids, either. We'd had lives, if you know what I mean, we hadn't played it particularly safe but we hadn't wasted ourselves with drugs or booze. No babies, no abortions, no scary virus. We were lucky, but only because we'd been careful, in our way. But we were, well, not *bored* exactly, just not able to settle; round and round we turned, like Moley when she nested. Turning in our own little space; trying to get comfortable. Checking the mirror a bit too often. Checking our minds for the calcification of *age*.

We were both restless; change was coming, whether we wanted it or not. We'd been survivors too long not to smell it. Jamie especially. Some nights she was almost feverish on stage; pacing up and down, exploring topics more suited to a documentary than comedy. She questioned everything, dissected the corpse of postmodernism with a straight razor. The punters that loved her, her faithful FC, loved her even more as she anatomized their isolation, the alienation of their generation. Those that were frightened by this warrior woman who unpicked the seams of their safe lives, hated her. She was intelligent and well-read and she didn't try to hide it. She expected the punters to keep up with her, rather than playing it dumb to make them comfortable. She was tribal, wise, savage and her comedy was the type that gave more than it took; you remembered what she'd said days later. But she was searching for something, always searching – she just didn't seem to know what for.

So you can see why I was worried. I was one of the few people who knew what she was like in real life – knew her insecurity, lack of self-esteem. What if those things got a hold on her again, and everything we'd worked for went to the wall? Yeah, I was worried, all right.

So. *Do* something. And what was our answer to this bout of nearing-thirty-something angst? We decided to give a party. I know, great fucking solution, but the idea just took hold of us. Don't ask me why, we'd never done it before, but we just flipped for the whole deal. Even Mojo agreed – why not? Let's stop being so set in our ways, shake ourselves up – let's give a Hollywood Halloween party, yeah. It'd be fun, let's have some *fun*; decorate the house in kiddie-kitsch, let's do an Addams Family – the works. We'd photocopy invitations and we'd lock up all our valuables in my room – where all the computer gear was anyway – put Moley in there with her stuff, square it with the neighbours and wow! Party on down, dudes! Cool.

We could hardly wait, it was going to be a total hoot – ghosts, toffee apples, candles and pumpkin lanterns; big bowls of wine punch floating with cinnamon and cloves, retro sounds, ghouls and witches and . . . devils.

CHAPTER 17

That year, Halloween fell on a Tuesday, so we decided to do the Thang on the preceding Saturday, the twenty-eighth. We got Mojo – who was rather artistic when pressed – to do some invites, whipped down to Prontoprint and bob's yer auntie – instant party. Mojo wouldn't tell us who he was inviting. I tried to pump him for info as to whether we could expect a certain Someone, but he arched a calligraphic eyebrow and murmured, 'Hardly, darling,' before returning to Marcus Aurelius. In hardback. I wasn't crushed.

Lonnie and Ben said they'd meet us on the twenty-first, in O'Reilly's, the local cod-Irish begorrah-bar and we could have a drink and give them their invites.

'You don't need an invitation, Lonnie,' I said over the phone.

'Dollink, you rob me of my rights, eef zat idiott Marcus has an in-vee-tation, then why not I? Mojo has designed eet, I hear zis, Ben, she want one too, ees our *birrrrthrrright*!'

'You're quite mad, d'you know that?'

'Ho yais, but hey, a leetle madness ees a

135

good thing, not like you Eeeglish, wiz your steef upper leep.'

'Illonka, you were born in Bradford at the Infirmary. You're Yorkshire. Only your mum is Russian, please.'

'My *soul* ees Roosian, dollink – and anyway, being Yorkshire is *boring*. I'd rather be a *Roosian* dyke than a Yorkshire one any day.'

What can you say? Fasten your seatbelts, we were in for a bumpy ride.

It may sound odd, arranging to meet friends on a specific date, but in our business normal regular social life had long since gone out the window. That we were free on two weekends running gave me not a little twinge of apprehension, but I thought – oh, lighten up, for fuck's sake, girl.

I don't really know whether I should say this or not, because it sounds incredibly X-Filesey, but I felt really weird that day. I know people would say it's hindsight and all that, but I looked in my diary and it says in there: *NB 6 p.m. Feel as if there's going to be a thunderstorm. Feel queasy. Don't want to see* people. *Gotta go tho', everyone expects me. Feel* very odd. *Don't say anything, J. all excited. P'raps just PMT.* Oh yeah, blame it on menstruation.

Sometimes, your body tells you stuff your mind doesn't want to hear, that it can't *process*.

Naturally, I took two paracetamol and put my lippie on.

CHAPTER 18

The pub was heaving when we finally got there. It took about five minutes before we located Ben and Lonnie, who were sitting in a booth on the raised part of the floor space, as far away from the speakers blaring out imitation Irish music as they could. They looked pissed off and my heart sank. We sat down on the bench seat opposite them and I arranged my face into a sympathetic expression.

'Hi,' I said in a fake-cheery way.

'Oh yeah, hi,' replied Ben morosely, her broad face flushed over her black existential polo neck. 'Sorry. This place. The pits. Full of townies. My God.' Ben always spoke in short sentences, probably as some kind of reaction to being considered one of Britain's most promising young philosophers. I don't know by who – other philosophers, presumably, since Ben would never discuss philosophy other than when she was piss-drunk and then only to lacerate the philosophical community for intellectual sloppiness, xenophobia and rampant misogyny. Well, hey, I'll go with that – like, what the fuck do I know? I do numbers. I

137

liked Ben, she didn't feel the need to smile all the time, it was a relief.

Lonnie was in full voice, having started on Guinness and moved swiftly back on to vodka. 'My God, is a trink for peasants, for preygnant wee-min; eet is for food, thees black *soup*, not for dreenk. Aye hayte eet, I *revolt* against eet! Ben, Ben, dollink, more wodka, I beyg you . . .'

All of this was said in horrendously carrying tones while Lonnie threw the stiff strands of her long, bleached hair about like whips. Her dark, Slavic eyes smouldered under two pairs of false eyelashes and she lay back against the dark wood of the booth with a skinny hand placed tremulously on her knobbly heaving chest. Lonnie doesn't believe in food, she thinks it's indigestible muck. You'd think she'd get on a treat with Mojo, who is another camp non-eater, but it ain't so. They each consider the other wildly affected and tedious. Mojo just adores Ben, though, and they talk about dizzyingly highbrow concepts for hours while Lonnie casts baleful looks at them and mutters in what she says is Russian but I suspect is actually tosh. OK, so Lonnie is a pain in the arse, but she is also kind and very loving, in her way. She and Ben had been together since university and were just the most *married* couple I knew.

I sighed and told Ben to sit down, I'd get them in. I knew what everyone would be drinking so I struggled to the bar and tried to attract the attention of a surly colleen.

Fifteen minutes later when I sloshed my way back, Jamie and Lonnie were giggling together like idiots and Jamie was hissing, '*Don't look, don't look, no, there, there, by the jukebox, oh Lonn-eee,*' etc., etc. It was like the Youthie all over again.

Ben sighed and fiddled with the silver ring inscribed '*vous et nul autre*' she wore on her wedding finger.

'Over there. Blond fella. God. Tedious. Good-looking, I suppose. You know, if that's your thing. No, over there. Between the window and the fruit machine. There. White T-shirt. Jeans. Classic. Bet he's got Timberlands on. Dear God.'

I strained half-heartedly to see the object of Jamie's admiration. Then someone moved out of the way and I saw him, for the first time. I saw Sean Powers.

He was leaning against the huge one-armed bandit sipping a pint, looking over the rim of the glass at Jamie as she giggled with Lon . . . ah, sorry, this makes me fucking nauseous . . . no, gotta be done, gotta do it for Jamie's sake, and mine. Yeah, right. Yeah, the first thing I noticed was his eyes, they were that intensely pale, crystalline blue that looks as if it's lit from behind. It made him look blind, or like an animal. His whole face was a bit like an animal's muzzle, too; blunt nose – narrow, squared-off chin, wide jaw. His mouth was quite full for a man, and his hair was dirty blond, short back and sides, long on top, floppy fringe falling over those weird blind eyes.

I thought – he's a bit of a fucking straight boy to be interested in us. He looks like a poor girl's Brad Pitt. They played that up in the papers a lot, that faint resemblance to a celebrity, as if it was glamorous, important. '*The killer's film-star good looks* . . .' Yeah, maybe Brad will get to play him in the made-for-television movie, if he can do a *Brat-furd* accent.

I glanced at Jamie, thinking – not a hope, he's a screaming townie, he's just taking the piss. She was pink with excitement, fluttering like a bird in a net. Oh no, I thought, don't. But it was obvious she was game on and going for it. Lonnie was rolling her eyes and gesturing with her Sobranie – and all the time those crystal eyes were locked on to my Jamie's. Lonnie whispered something to her and she picked up her bag and announced she was off to the Ladies. To get there, she had to walk past him. His gaze never left her as she pushed through the crowd, elaborately ignoring him.

'Illonka, what are you up to?' said Ben, sternly.

'Nozzing, dollink, nozzing – I jost say, hey, inwite thees hunk to your partee, an' see if he comes – funny, no?'

I was furious. I tried not to tear a strip off Lonnie and her silly mischief-making – like, it was just a bit of harmless flirtation to her and she wouldn't have understood why I was that angry so I buttoned it. But Ben looked less than impressed. 'Christ, Lon. Look at him. Straight as a die. Trouble, that sort. You should know better. It's not *your* party. What d'you think he thinks of us? You know what, don't you – don't you?'

Lonnie sulked furiously and Ben apologized to me, which was crap so I just said, Hey, what the fuck – he won't turn up anyway. No harm done, forget it.

Afterwards, after the whole thing was over and the papers had waxed lyrical about our *'lesbian party friends, who introduced the smiling killer to showbiz swinger Jamie'*, Lonnie blamed herself for putting Jamie up to it that first time; she had a 'nervous collapse', or whatever the docs call it; Prozac, counselling, the works. She wouldn't see me, but Ben and I talked a bit. Not much, just circling round and round the unsayable. Poor Ben, she tried so hard to be rational; not to be touched by any of it. She and Lonnie split up over it; Lonnie thought Ben was being insensitive, apparently. I don't think so. She just couldn't weep and wail like Lon – doesn't mean it hurt her any the less. Christ.

But anyways, there we were in this fucking *atmosphere* and I spotted Jamie strolling back from the loo as if she was ice. Fooled no one, believe me. *Ever* so nonchalantly she stopped by Sean with a quizzical look on her foxy face. I realized they were the same height; they both had broad shoulders, long legs; I don't know why, but at the time that struck me as a bit odd because it made them look – like a pair. I saw her hand him one of our invites. I could imagine the cheesy conversation, though I

141

couldn't hear it over 'Black Velvet Band'. *Oh hey, we're having a little party, yeah, my mates and I wondered if you'd like to come . . . oh, great, well, here's an invite, make sure you bring it or you won't get in – ha ha ha.*'

She managed not to run back to us and carefully sat with her back to him, screwing her face up with excitement.

'Don't, don't look, don't look – what's he doin'? Ohh, what about *that*, gorgeous or what? Those eyes! That body! Fuckin' hell, I am in *heaven*; he says he'll come! D'you think he will? He says he thought we all looked so interesting! He says he likes arty types! He asked me if I was at the *Art School*! I didn't like to tell him how old I am – man, my heart's goin' like a fuckin' drum!'

For a good five minutes she didn't even notice the lack of enthusiasm her latest crush had generated round the table. When she did and it got explained to her, she just sat there looking like a kiddie whose teddy got took away.

'Well, look, I'll just go tell him it's not on, then – no, it's OK, what the fuck, I don't know him – you're my mates. Just say the word, honest, it's nothing, nothing.'

No one said the fucking word, naturally.

As we were all jerkily laying the blame on ourselves and saying how little the whole thing mattered, I glanced over to the gaming machine. He'd gone; his pint glass was stood on the machine's hood. I thought about saying, '*Oh, your fella's hopped it*,' or something like that, but somehow, I didn't. All I could think was thank fuck for that – with any luck he won't even turn up. I mean, a good-looking bloke like that won't be without a woman, he'll be off home to the wife or girlfriend and forget about his little moment of *artiness*.

The rest of the evening went with a whimper. Lonnie got arseholed and started mumbling about how if she wasn't wanted, etc., and Ben took her home. I knew I should have been nicer to Lon, but I was still unaccountably angry about what she'd done. No, what Jamie had done. We downed our drinks and wandered off for a curry.

Outside, in the damp, leaf-mouldy autumn night, Jamie bounced along humming a tuneless hum to herself, then suddenly she stopped and grabbing me, swung me round to face her. Her eyes were full of shining moonlight and her face illuminated by the streetlight above us.

'Oh, Lil, Lil! Did you see, wasn't he fabby! So good-lookin' and he liked me, he did, man, I could tell! I mean, he seemed really sincere, you know, about coming to the party! What a nice fella, he was dead, oh, quiet an' polite, really nice. I know it's stupid, bab, but lately I've been feelin' so low about, well, getting older, the way I look. These days, it's all skinny little chicks, y'know an' I'm twenty-nine, I mean, I was getting to think that was it, y'know, it was all over for me, romance an' that. But the way he looked at me! Fuck! A guy like that, he could have anyone, anyone at all an' he looked at me like I was special! He did, you couldn't see – oh, Lil, the old magic's still there, eh?'

I just thought, fuck, fuck, *fuck*. Another Monumental Error and all that goes with it. To tell the truth, I was a bit fucking tired of it. I thought, not again, I've got too much to worry about without the fucking emotional rollercoaster ride we were in for with that piece of work from the bar. Just when I thought I was winning with her, along comes Mr Timberlands with his wolf's eyes and rippling fucking pecs. And for the first time, I snapped at her about it.

'For fuck's sake, Jamie, he's another fucking waste of space; can't you see? Why can't you fucking see? You see everyone else so clear, why not yourself, Christ . . . Christ, Jamie, you're beautiful, you are, we all think so, it doesn't *matter* about your age, for fuck's sake you talk like you're a fucking grannie or somethin' just, just . . .' But my stupid words tangled up and I found myself facing her in the street, rigid with fury and my fists clenched.

She looked at me, horrified, with her pale face full of hurt. 'Lily, I'm sorry, man, uh, I didn't mean to upset you – God, I'm sorry, whatever it is, I'm sorry. Lily, don't, you're scarin' me. Is it because, well, because of Gabe? Because of me an' that fella an' you an' Gabe? He loves you, darlin', he really does an' he'll see one day, he will . . .'

I couldn't believe it. *She knew how I felt about Gabriel!* She'd never said a word before. I was stunned. 'How, what . . . what d'you mean?'

'Oh honey – I know how you feel about him. I never said anything to anyone and I won't, I swear. It's the way you are with him, girl, it's obvious – well, to me anyway, knowing you both so well. No one else has twigged. Don't worry about Mojo, he's got too much on his plate to fret about someone else. Lil, Lil, I love you, I love Gabe, it'd be the best present in the fuckin' world if you guys got it together, it really would! Don't be jealous, please, please, it'll come OK for you – an' that guy in the bar, fuck him! Forget him. Let's go eat. Come on, say you forgive me, please . . .'

I was totally gobsmacked; totally. Not only did she know about Gabe, but she thought I was jealous of her success with that guy. I could not fucking believe it. I muttered something unintelligible and followed her to the Rose of Kashmir like a sodding zombie. I ate my Masala without even tasting it while she chattered on, happy to have been 'forgiven'.

I was so caught up in my own shock I forgot about Mr Timberlands, Mr Straight-as-a-die. I was too busy sorting my head out to remember anything except how to get past this thing with Jamie. I knew I'd be OK in the morning, like – I suppose I had just been fooling myself I was the Great Inscrutable, but as long as Gabe didn't know, and Jamie swore he didn't – just like a bloke – it would be kosher. I'd manage, I could control it. I knew I could trust Jamie to keep shtoom, she wasn't the stirring type.

So I forgot about Sean. Just a brief entry in my diary: *21/10/95 . . . crap night, and another fucking Error on the horizon . . .* That's all.

I forgot all about Sean – oh, man, how he would have *hated* that.

CHAPTER 19

We only had one thing to do that week; on the Monday we had a local radio interview/chat show thing for Radio Kirkstall in Leeds. It was a national local, if you see what I mean, but that didn't make it any better. They'd approached Jamie directly because of her involvement with various AIDS events and she was just a gal who couldn't say 'no'. Personally I would have said go fuck yourself, matey-boy; local radio is absolutely notorious for stupidity, discourtesy and inanity in that order. I mean, six people and a whippet listen to Radio Kirkstall, but they behave like National Security was involved.

They trotted out the usual platitudes and idiocies, including, and I kid you not, introducing her as, *'Bradford's own local comedienne, the Gothic Queen of Alternative Comedy, notorious for her shocking-pink hair and shocking-blue jokes* . . . etc.' Pink-haired, blue jokes, fucking hell. I collared the researcher and complained. I asked her how they could introduce Jamie like that when they'd seen her, like, *in the flesh*, and where was the pink hair and Goth clothes? She squirmed and grovelled but she couldn't have cared less about how wrong and inaccurate they were and how bad it made Jamie sound; the apologies were just galvanic twitches. I sat outside in the corridor and cringed. The 'interview' was a joke by a primary school's standards.

'Now, Jamie, you get a lotta laughs all over the area, but there's one thing you're deadly serious about, isn't there? Yes, it's AIDS. Now, many of our listeners have written in about today's subject, AIDS, asking, well, does AIDS really exist any more? Has it gone away for good? Can we forget the dreaded condoms now?' – hearty chuckle – 'But seriously, Jamie, what do you, as a campaigner against AIDS really think? Are you just trying to put a damper on the nation's sex life? Isn't AIDS just a gay problem? Lines are open, folks, so don't forget to phone us with your views on AIDS . . .'

It lasted a little under ten minutes, with plugs. Jamie managed to remain fairly calm and didn't actually bite the presenter. I would've. She came out with a face like thunder, and we left with the researcher apologizing for not getting the presenter to mention the AIDS Awareness Benefit which was the whole reason for us being there in the first place.

Jamie was uncharacteristically quiet on the way home. We decided to go for a coffee in Bradford's one and only art café, the Espresso. While we waited for the waitress to stop pouting and twiddling her fringe long enough to serve us

(Espresso by name, Dead Snail by nature), Jamie stared out of the rain-beaded window.

'Don't worry about that shit at the radio, girl,' I said. 'You came out of it well, he was the one that looked a tosser. I got that researcher to swear she'd make him mention the benefit at the end of the show, it'll be OK.'

'It's not that. Well, it is, but it's not *just* that, it's everythin'. Lil, aren't you bothered about the way stuff's goin'? I mean, comedy and stuff. It's all money, money, money an' forget bein' creative, or achievin' anythin'. I mean, look at the bill on that Nottingham show – I felt like a fuckin' dinosaur. That little wanker Liam O'Hare came up to me after an' told me I was *so brave* doin' the stuff I do. So brave! He meant I was old-fashioned, past it; no one wants to hear what I want to talk about these days, they're all like her.' She jerked her thumb at our waitress, Clubland's very own Lolita. 'They're all clubs an' Es an' ooo, let's do some skag, it'll be an *experience*; and God, don't talk about politics, we don't *do* politics. We don't get *angry* about things because we're *all right*, only *losers* are angry because they're *losers*. Cop her, that little riot-grrrl – not. Fuck, she'd puke if you mentioned feminism. Puke.

'I know there are folk out there who want to hear me, man, I know it. Look at the FC, look how they bring their mates, and their mates go, Oh wow, you were great, you should be on telly, why aren't you famous? Well, I am

149

fuckin' famous – famous for being fuckin' *all wrong*.'

The child-waitress plonked down our dreadful trendy coffee in its oversized and chipped trendy coffee cups, then flounced off. Jamie sighed heavily and grimaced as she sipped the bitter fluid.

'It's like this fuckin' place,' she said, putting the lime-coloured cup down on the purple PVC tablecloth 'All fur coat an' no knickers. Dead arty-lookin', but the coffee stinks and it's so expensive. They make like it's *bohemian*, but d'you see the looks we get when we come here? The comedy scene's the same these days; makes like it's alternative but it's just shoring up the status quo; making all the Haves feel better about themselves and fuck the Have-nots. Christ, listen to me, how old hat can you get? This country, man, it breaks my heart, it really does.'

She was very depressed, and in my heart I couldn't blame her. I agreed with every word she said and I knew plenty of others did too, but fuck it, how could we reach them when we weren't telly material? Only the telly had power now – the Dead Eye, Native Americans call it, and it is, really. I'm an addict, man, I *know*. Drug of the Nation.

There must be a way round it, there must. We just had to keep the faith and work even harder; not listen to fuckwits like O'Hare, with his, 'God, I'm such a clever, fascinatin' Irishman' routine and his rat's face. Keep the faith – just try to get some publicity for Her Nibs, maybe a serious

150

piece about the *subject* of comedy in the Sunday *Observer*, something like that. Oh yeah, in those days I still thought journalists were basically decent types; well, on the broadsheets anyhow. Look at Fred, he'd been OK. Sure, local papers were the pits, but what can you expect? Jamie used to say if she won the Nobel Peace Prize, the *Telegraph &* *Argus* would have a headline on page two saying 'Local Girl Wins Prize' and a ten-year-old photo.

No, we just had to keep on keeping on. I told her that. It didn't make her less depressed, but she agreed with me. I mean – what else was there for us? When you looked at it, we had no choice. At least, Jamie didn't. I suppose I could have just done the book-keeping gig. I suppose. Nah, *we* had no choice.

Jamie was pretty down the rest of the week. She perked up a bit on Friday when Mojo came home in a taxi with a whole bolt of black muslin that I suspect Someone procured for him. We rushed out and bought some pumpkins from the corner shop and made lanterns. Mine looked like a biological experiment gone horribly wrong, but the others' looked very professional. I liked mine best though. I called it Brundle-lantern, poor thing.

CHAPTER 20

On the Big Day, we got up fairly early and moved stuff about. Moley complained long and loud and tried to trip up as many humans as possible, then made a muslin nest and thrashed about miaowling her lungs out. I took a picture of her, she looked too cute for words.

We moved everything of value into the attic and left just enough room for me to crawl into my bed. Mojo insisted on squashing his mattress and bedding up there too, as he didn't want people fornicating on it; fair do's. He said he'd just lock his make-up and other stuff in one of his two wardrobes. If people wanted to shag in his room, they'd have to do it on the bedsprings or on the floor. Jamie just tidied her room up a bit; threw a big old candlewick bedspread over the bed and tucked it in all round. Minimalist, that girl, at heart.

We went mad with the muslin, it was a total fire trap. Great swags and drapes everywhere and loads of bare-ish branches from the park, plus the lanterns and buckets of sand for ciggies. I put the food (just baguettes, bread buns and cake from

Pa's, plus cheese) on the kitchen table, which I'd pushed against the wall, and Jamie concocted a lethal punch. Quite nice, it was, actually, in small quantities. Halloween-print paper cups and plates, lots of pomegranates and apples for decor, a few judiciously placed candles, *et voila*! Let the Ball commence!

At least we had no neighbours to worry about. Next door was empty and up for sale and Mr Majid one up didn't seem to mind a bit when we told him – '*You young people, you enjoy your lifes,*' is all he said. What an old sweetie.

We were the corner house and only a rutted unmade alley separated us from the next row of houses on our side, which ran back three houses, not along the road. After them, on Brunel Street, was a bit of a knackered old sixties factory building and then the park. The three houses, Hardy Street, were due for demolition and had stood empty for a couple of years. At the far end of them was a small yard one of the blokes who'd lived there had used for storing scrap. It was still rustily chainlink fenced but the gates were sagging and the padlock and chain long gone. The front of our house looked over some wasteland, or at least it did from the second floor. From the front door you looked at a six-foot wall and some NF graffiti we had tried to remove and failed. Never mind, the view from Jamie's room was nice. If you liked Bleak Ex-Industrial.

So you can see how quiet we were, just the place for the World's Greatest Rave-up.

People started drifting in around eight – this wasn't really a piss-up-after-the-pub kinda do. Pete and Andy, two biker mates of Gabe's, came to 'look after things'. Gabe couldn't come because he was in Germany with Killzone; they were gigging in Munich that night.

But despite my missing him, I was still up for it. I even went so far as to put a kind of Alice band with light-up devil horns on by way of a costume. They were pretty cool after I sort of pulled my locks back over the band. Looked positively natural. Jamie looked lovely, really nice. She'd put a frock on for a change – an ankle-length, claret-coloured Empire-line number in velour. She'd got it during the week from Long Tall Sally, so it actually *was* long on her. A pair of metallic gold Chipie trainers finished the look. She'd had her hair done in red, copper, and dark-goldy highlights, just the top layer, and she'd left it loose for a change. It was nearly to her waist. She left off most of the jewellery, too, which I did think was odd. She just had her steel piercing rings in. She was playing hostess at the punch bowl (OK, punch bucket) so I let her get on with it.

Lonnie and Ben arrived with Lon in a white crepe shift embroidered with pearlescent beads; and just ropes of faux pearls. Huge earrings to match nearly touched her shoulders and she was smoking Cocktail Sobranie in a mother-of-pearl cigarette holder. Even Ben had dressed up in a heavy black silk shirt and black leather jeans. They looked so cool.

'Dollink, am I fogeeven, say I am, I beyg you, or my hearrt ees broke, troooly.' She rolled her eyes at me pleadingly. Ben rolled her eyes heavenwards.

'Don't be a silly cow, Lonz. God, you both look fab, I wish I'd made more effort.'

'You look *goor-joose*, dollink, I swear – thees leetle horrns are so cute, an' ze decor! Ay, mnyeh khochyeetsah peet! Skahryehyeh, Benska, my dollink!' And she rushed off to kiss Jamie.

'What was that last bit, was it actually *Russian*?' I asked Ben as Lon floated away.

'Don't know. Could be. She visited her mother. Always gets more Russian after that. Don't ask me what it means though. "Your poodle's arse is puce, comrade", p'raps? Can't tell with her. Quite mad. Do love her though. You've let her off, then?'

'Don't you get silly on me too. There's nothing to let her off of; forget it. Go get some of that stupendous punch Jamie made, that'll clear your sinuses.'

Just then, Mojo made his entrance, much to Lonnie's chagrin. He looked – what can I say? He'd borrowed a frock of Jamie's – an old one from her Gothic years, but one she'd never worn. It was from Camden Market, so she'd bought it without trying it on. The woman on the stall said it was pure satin Lycra and would stretch to fit, which it did – but on Jamie, it left nothing, but *nothing* to the imagination. She was too modest to wear it. It was black; a fishtailed tube, form-fitting even on Mojo. It had a V-neck front and a very, very plunging V-back. Long sleeves were cut into a point on the hand. Round the skirt from the knees down as it flared out to his stiletto-clad feet, were fluttering 'hankies' of chiffon and lace stitched with iridescent black sequins. It looked beyond knockout on Mojo, whose deeply waved gleaming hair put raven's wings to shame. His hands were covered in huge silver rings glittering with stones and he had a deep black lace choker at his throat. His full lips were blood-coloured. Words just can't do justice to him – he was the most beautiful Witch-Queen I'd ever, ever seen. People actually applauded. He shrugged gracefully and waved his dusky chiffon and lace handkerchief in acknowledgement.

God, was I jealous. But there you are – not a lot you can do about it. It did make me think I should put some lippie on though. At least I could do *that*. I ran upstairs to Jamie's room to nick some of her Chanel. Poor we might be, but we never skimped on the essentials.

As I was rummaging through her make-up box, I heard a car pull up and went to her window to see who it was. It was a taxi, and out of it got – yeah, you guessed it – Mr Fucking Timberlands. My heart sank. Oh bugger it. As I looked at him, I noticed he had a couple of carrier bags obviously containing bottles with him and I thought, oh, at least he's brought some booze. He just stood there, looking at the front of the house. It was odd. OK, maybe he's shy, I thought, but it wasn't like that; his posture was – strange. As if he was listening to what was going on – almost *smelling* the house. I drew back more behind the curtain just as those strange blue eyes swept over the window I was looking out of. Then he did a weird thing. He crossed over to our side of the road and I craned to see him come in, but he didn't. He went round the side of the house, into what had been Hardy Street.

I shot out of Jamie's room, nearly knocking over Marcus, who was going into the bathroom. I ran into Mojo's room which had two windows, one looking into Hardy Street and one out on to our backyard. Mr Timberlands was peering into the deserted, condemned houses across the alley. One after the other. Then he found the ex-scrapyard, and, pushing the gate open a little, went inside. I held my breath. What the fuck was he up to? Going for a piss before coming into the party? What? As I puzzled, Jenny and Magda came in to put their coats on the stripped bed with all the others. Marcus came in too, and his very earnest friend Saleem. I lost track of Mr Timberlands as they all exclaimed over how lovely the house looked and what fun, etc.

Still feeling a bit unsettled, I wandered downstairs. Things were in full swing with some cool sounds issuing from the old beatbox in the corner of the living room; I heard the doorbell ring and

Andy got up and answered it. I followed him. It was Mr Timberlands, all right. Standing there, invite in hand, smiling a little-boy-lost smile and asking if this was the right place. Like he'd just got here. Andy let him in. Over the threshold.

He walked in with a good pretence of being unsure of himself – that's not hindsight, I just didn't believe him, he was acting. I'd seen another side of him through that window. He ignored me like I wasn't there. Why, you may ask? Because he'd spotted Jamie, sitting on the muslin-draped sofa with Mojo and Ben. Lonnie was perched on the arm. He walked up to Jamie and I saw her face suffuse with light; with joy at his coming. She looked up at him, her eyes huge and bright.

I felt quite sick, to be honest. I thought, man, he's a smooth bastard. What a creep. I walked over to them, behind him. He put the carriers down and took out a bottle of Moët et Chandon, no word of a lie.

'This is for you, I . . . I thought you might like it; there's some beers an' that in the bags but, I thought you should have somethin' a bit special. For inviting me, like.' Jamie gazed at him like the Madonna googling at the Baby fucking Jesus. We all gawped.

'Look, I'm sorry,' he said, not taking his eyes off her face, 'but on the invitation it says "Jamie, Mojo and Lily", an' in the pub I was too . . . well, I never asked your name. Stupid of me, I'm really sorry.' He smiled that fake-boyish smile and I saw his teeth were very white and even – what I call American teeth. He pushed a lock of his blond hair out of his eyes, dead casually. Brown hair, actually, I noted. Light-brown with bleached highlights. I felt my neck tighten with tension. Mojo was looking at him with faintly narrowed eyes, like Moley looking at a sparrow. Ben's brow was furrowed and Lonnie was just plain giggling.

'It . . . it doesn't matter, I'm Jamie . . . um, this is Mojo, Ben, Lonnie – Lily, come over here – this is . . . ?'

'Sean, Sean Powers. Nice to meet you.' He put out his hand. She took it. He held it for just a beat too long then shook it and let go. He didn't bother with the rest of us. Oh no, you don't, my lad, I thought.

'Hi!' I said brightly, and stuck out my hand. 'I'm Lily – what was your name? Sean?'

He turned a little to look at me. Those crystal eyes locked into mine and I felt a wave of pure dislike run through me. Totally unreasonable. But I don't care, it's true, I loathed him. And it was obvious – to everyone except Jamie anyhow – he felt the same about me.

'Yeah, Sean, that's right. Pleased to meet you.' He hesitated for a split second, then shook my hand briefly. It was the one and only time I ever touched him willingly. He turned back immediately to Jamie and I surreptitiously wiped my hand on the leg of my jeans. Not that surreptitiously though, because I caught Mojo watching me. We looked at each other, with no expression – yeah, one of those 'no expression' looks that says *everything*.

I didn't hang around. What would've been the point? I felt like a right fucking gooseberry. I drifted to the kitchen and got a cold beer out of the fridge, then hung around with Pete and Andy for awhile, mostly talking about Gabe. God, how sad. Still, that's unrequited love for you; the stuff of poetry and bathos. I was cheered up though, by seeing how people were enjoying themselves. I was feeling quite smug and chuffed about what the beer told me was my brilliant idea about having a shindig, and I even kept my temper when I got into a long and tedious debate with Marcus and Saleem about the pros and cons of being a black child adopted by white parents. It was the usual rehash of cultural identity and search for roots. I remember saying that as a biracial woman my head was pretty well fucked-up anyway on the cultural thing, at which Saleem pounced. He was just beginning to get uncomplimentary about my parents, whom he'd never actually met, of course, when nature intervened and my bladder saved his face from a slap. I made my excuses and ran upstairs to the loo.

When I came out, Sean was standing in the passage.

'The toilet's in there,' I said somewhat ungraciously.

'Yeah, thanks.' He didn't make a move to go in or anything, he just stood there. I felt as if he

160

was waiting somehow; it was a bit odd, like his behaviour outside earlier. I decided to confront him about it. Or at least, the beer did.

'I saw you outside, before you came in, you were looking in those houses and then you went into the scrappie's yard; why? Why do that then make like you had just arrived?'

He looked down at me, and smiled slightly. It was as if he was *considering* me for the first time. I felt the hair prickle on the back of my neck and was in half a mind to call Andy and Pete and get him chucked out. But then I thought of Jamie, in her new dress and her naked face and I hesitated.

'You don't miss much, do you?' He was still smiling. I felt like a stupid kiddie who'd just said something embarrassing; it wasn't pleasant.

'No. I don't. So?'

'I wasn't doin' anything – just looking around. I haven't been round this area much – I thought I could maybe put my van in that yard next time I came. It'd be safer, like, what with me having all my stuff in it, you know.'

I felt my hackles rise. 'So you reckon you'll be round again, do you? Isn't that a bit fucking premature?'

'I don't think so. No, I don't think so at all, like. She's a special lady, your friend. I think we'll get on a treat. Don't worry, I'll take good care of her, you needn't fret. It's a very nice thing, bein' loyal to your friend, I like that in a woman. Can't stand them bitchy types meself.'

'Too fucking right, mate. She's very special and not just to me. She's got good mates, very good mates. I wouldn't forget that if I was you, I'd – I'd . . .' I was beginning to splutter, to get mixed up. He leant on the wall and turned his head to look at me. He was very calm.

'You know, you shouldn't swear so much, you really shouldn't. A nice little lass like you. Gives the wrong impression. People might think you was a *slag*, or somethin' and that wouldn't be right, now, would it? Eh?'

I was *really* annoyed. I knew, I just knew how he'd meant that, but I couldn't get my words right. I was just about to give him what-for, when Jamie came up the stairs. She was looking for him, it was obvious.

'An' here's our special lady' Sean said, holding his hand out to her. She took it and he pulled her to his side gently. 'I was just saying to your friend here – sorry, it's Milly, is it? Oh, *Lily*, yeah, Lily, right, my fault, I'm terrible with names, sorry – well, we were just sayin' what a special, beautiful lady you are, an' how many real good friends you've got. An' I just said, I hope one day, I can, you know, be one of them . . .'

Jamie just beamed. I gaped at him like a fool. I waited for her to demolish him for being so totally corny. But she just *giggled* and blushed like a fourteen-year-old on her first date. It was sickening. I felt my stomach churn and I knew if I didn't speak out now, say that I'd seen him outside

162

creeping around, that he'd insulted me, it would be too late, she'd be hooked good stylee.

I had my mouth open to speak when Lonnie, Magda and Jenny came running up the stairs laughing about something or other to do with Mojo and Andy, and grabbed Jamie, pulling her back downstairs and leaving me with Sean. It was over. I'd lost the battle. I knew that she'd never believe me now, I'd missed my chance. But I'd find a way, somehow I'd make her see what a bastard he really was before it was too late. I'd win the fucking war. I glared at him.

He looked back at me, still smiling that fucking horrible little smile.

'No hard feelings, eh, love? All's fair and all that. Let's try an' get along, for *her* sake, eh? We wouldn't want our special girl unhappy, now, would we?' The smile broadened and he – the fucker – he *winked* at me.

I was incandescent with rage. Honest to God, I don't think I really knew what hatred was until that moment. He had me like a cat playing with a mouse, and he didn't even bother to hide his enjoyment of it. I whirled round and flung into the bathroom, locking the door furiously, as if I thought he'd come after me.

I stood at the basin, my breath coming hard and ragged. Willing myself to calm down and stop being so stupid, I ran cold water over my wrists like Ma always told me to do if I was nervous or upset. I looked up, into the old bathroom

163

mirror. It was a nice thing, we'd picked it up at a flea market in Bristol, it had a gilt frame with a bunch of coloured flowers and ribbons moulded on the top. The glass was a bit tarnished and there were black age spots in the corners. It made your reflection look eighteenth-century, we thought. Now, it reflected my face back to me with the silly Halloween horns sticking out of my hair. I ripped them off my head and threw them in the bin. What had I been thinking of? I looked ridiculous, childish. I *felt* childish – and miserable. My hands were shaking, my lips were white and compressed. I wanted to cry, but my eyes just wouldn't make tears. Stupid! Fucking stupid! I was stupid – this party was stupid – everything was stupid, my life, myself, my thick, stubby body and my snaky locks; I hated it all. It was all wrong.

I sat on the toilet seat and rubbed my face, trying to breathe slowly and calmly. Why was I so upset by a wanker like that Sean? Who was he anyway? Just another user on the make, just another *motherfucker*. Jamie was my friend and my sister – just let him try his tricks and see what it gets him, yeah. Not this time, fucker, this was the last time I'd stand by and watch some bastard take my friend down to hell and abandon her. This time, there was too much to lose.

Very heroic. But even as I sat there chanting my little warcry, I was attacked by the kind of doubts and worries that always crept up on me when I was low. It was like that cartoon where there's an angel

164

on one shoulder and a devil on the other and both are whispering in your ear. The angel says all the defend-protect-be-selfless stuff, but the devil, oh, the devil knows how to get you. Why bother, it says. Why go through all this again for a person who just keeps on repeating the same mistakes? You'll have to put up with this bastard being round the house, coming to gigs and distracting her, eating his dinner with you. You'll have all the trouble of looking after Jamie when he's cruel to her and breaks her heart. And it's not like everything's going swimmingly with the work, either. Pack it in, take care of yourself for a change. You've done enough, no one will blame you. There are plenty of showbiz jobs you could get, never mind just doing the book-keeping – didn't Penny Kuchen's manager say only the other day she'd give you a job in their office any time you wanted? Why not go, move to London, abandon Jamie to her fate – it's her own fault.

Oh yeah, that devil knew its job. And I was tired. I wanted Gabriel. I wanted to sic him on that fella and watch Mr I'm-so-fucking-clever Sean deal with a man like Gabe. I briefly toyed with the notion of drinking myself insensible, but what was the point? I'd just feel like shit for two days and get nothing done.

I stood up and looked at myself in the mirror again. I straightened my shoulders and pulled my locks into order. *Get thee behind me, Satan*, I thought. I might be unwilling, I might be resentful,

I was definitely pissed off, but I knew my duty, and more than that, I knew who I loved. And that, Satan, was that. Shoo fly, you is yesterday, mofo.

When I left the bathroom, he was gone – I don't know why I thought he'd still be there. Anyhow, more people had arrived and I went downstairs to say hi and generally schmooze. Lonnie said, 'Oh sveetie, you taken your preety leetle 'orns off, shame!' But the dressing-up thing was a dead game now and I felt better just being myself; whatever *that* was . . .

I put my 'Disco Inferno' tape on the beatbox and things started getting lively – oh, not, you know, *trendy* lively, just loud and silly. I remember Marcus rolling himself up in some of the black muslin and 'being a cocoon', which involved worming round the living room making gurgling sounds and – yeah, well, you had to be there, I suppose. Things were cool, it was a good party and towards three a.m. people started drifting off. Ben practically had to carry Lonnie out she was so blasted, but she seemed happy enough. Ben volunteered to come round the next day and help clear up, which I thought was very nice.

Mojo appeared, freshly painted and with a black pashmina wrapped over his frock. He exuded an odour of sanctity – or possibly it was L'Heure Bleu. He ordered a cab. Apparently, Someone wanted to gaze on his loveliness and hey, housework was not his bag. What could I do? He swore he'd buy us a huge curry when he got home so I let him off with just a faint scowl and a big kiss.

In the end, it was just me, and Jamie. She lay on the sofa with her shoes off and we drank a pot of tea and ate leftover baguettes and cheese; I didn't want to talk about you-know-who, but she just *had* to tell.

'Such a nice fella – honestly, Lil, so nice. A real sweet guy. You know what he did when he left? *He kissed my hand!* Swear to God, truly. No grabbing, nothing, just really polite. Like, really old-fashioned, in a way. He says he'll come round tomorrow and we can go for a walk up Judy Woods, won't that be nice? Oh, I mean, I can't believe it, he's so good-looking and he's only twenty-four! I just don't know what he sees in an old bag like me – but he says he prefers a more mature woman, a real woman – he says young girls are borin'. I think he's the one, Lil, I really do. He likes all the same stuff I do – he loves reading, he says, but he doesn't get a lot of chance what with work, but he loves goin' to the pictures, an' walkin' an' all sorts of stuff. He was a proper professional athlete, you know, a sprinter, until he got an injury, but that's how he got this job because it's his old coach's company. He says he wouldn't work for anyone he didn't respect – he's got too much pride. It's why he's had so many jobs, just couldn't settle, couldn't take orders off idiots. Well, stands to reason, a guy like that. His dad owns Powers Motors, you know, the big place up by the roundabout; he's got two other garages too, like a chain almost, I didn't realize that. But they don't get on, apparently, sad really, you think anyone'd be proud to have a son like that . . .'

And on and on. What could I say? That he was a two-faced twat? I just couldn't be bothered, to be honest. I was knackered and she was so happy, just lying there in her pretty dress, her long white feet on a cushion like a medieval image on a tomb somewhere. I remember noticing her toenails were painted gold, and I thought, *She did that for him, she wanted everything to be perfect for him.*

I just nodded and ummed and eventually pleaded sleepiness. As I stood up and stretched, scratching my scalp and yawning, she sat up, suddenly serious, her eyes full of tears.

'Oh, Lil, you do like him, don't you? I'd hate it if you didn't like him. He likes you, he said – he said you were a real character; please, Lily, it'll be different this time, it will, I swear; he's not like the others, he's really not, I can tell. Oh, Lil, I want him so much, I do – I swear I'd, I'd sell my soul for a chance of him, I would, I really would. I just want us all to get on, be friends. Please, Lil, you're my family, my best mate, everything – but I . . . I want him, I . . .'

I was filled with the most enormous pity for her. I felt like a right shit for having even considered abandoning her. Poor little big girl, what a mess. Oh, why isn't life easy for the ones who need it to be? I was tired and shivery, but I knelt beside her and took her hand.

'It'll be OK, baby, it'll be fine. Just you wait an' see. You go beddy-bye-byes now an' tomorrow everything will work out just fine, I promise. Honest. I'm sure he's a real nice guy, and if he isn't, well, never mind, there's plenty more pebbles on the beach an' all that jazz.'

She put her hot cheek against my hand and smiled. I felt about a million years old. At least. Old and wise and shagged-out. I went upstairs and unlocked the attic door and crawled into bed with Moley.

Outside, the wind blustered and threw rattles of icy rain against my skylight. But I felt safe in my bed, with the cat and my snuggly quilts; safe in my own house, in my own safe life.

Out in the dark, the bogeyman smiled his little-boy-lost smile.

CHAPTER 21

Of course, he didn't come round on Sunday. Me an' Ben yawned through the housework – not too bad, really, considering, and put all the muslin in a binbag to take to the bagwash along with some other odds and sods like cushion covers. Luckily no one had chucked up, which is always the worst.

Jamie tried to help but every time the front door rattled or the phone went she nearly jumped out of her skin. In the end I told her to make the tea and toast – but she burnt it. Ben and I just sighed theatrically and rolled our eyes. Finally Jamie went upstairs and we flopped on the sofa.

'This love business,' said Ben morosely. 'Such a pain. Ultimate bad faith, really. How we lie to ourselves. This chap, don't know what to make of him. Not that he said anything . . . but I think Lonnie and I made him . . . *uncomfortable*. Mind you, nothing to his reaction when he discovered Mojo was a *man*. Nearly spilt his beer, choked. Sounds funny, but it wasn't, really. Don't like to make judgements, you know that, Lily, but . . .'

'But what? What? Oh, go on, who's here but

us? Don't be so bloody *philosophical*, what did you think?' I expected her to say something about him being a bit of rough, something about 'here we go again' – that sort of thing. What she said left me gawping.

'He's a homophobe. A racist. Dangerous, I think. Full of anger. A diseased mind. I would be careful if I were you. And Jamie. Be careful. You can always phone me, day or night. You know that. Don't know what I could do, but still. Just phone me if anything happens.'

'Ben, Christ – how'd you get all that? Did the bastard say anything to you? Did he upset you?'

'No, didn't have to say anything. Been queer all my life, you know that. Seen it before. Something in their manner, in their expression, how they speak to you. He tried to hide it, failed. He thought Mojo was anathema; could hardly look at him. Like Saleem and Ty. Racism, of the "you people" and "now, I'm not a racialist, but" variety. Not pleasant, not at all.'

'God – did you tell Jamie any of this?'

'No point. He hides it quite well. She's head over heels for him. But – don't get me wrong, no criticism intended – what does he see in her? Love Jamie to bits, wonderful, funny, clever woman. But – he's straight, younger than her, handsome, manipulative – what's the attraction there? Something wrong, I think. OK, going now, enough of this, just being an old fussbudget. Don't mind me; not usually so picky. Sorry.'

I saw her out with a heavy heart. Ben wasn't stupid by any means and if she thought something was wrong – well, in a way I was glad it wasn't just me being oversensitive. I wished Gabe would come home, but he was out in Europe until Christmas.

The afternoon dimmed into evening and Jamie got more and more depressed as the light faded and the cold night chilled the house. I bustled around and turned the gas fire up to Mach 4, put the telly on and tried to chat to her. No response. I knew what she was like in these moods and just shut up and we sat in silence watching an old movie.

When Mojo came home, we had a massive take-away, which I devoured like Ben Gunn on a cheese bender. Jamie just picked at a Chicken Tikka and stared off into the middle distance. Around eleven, she went to bed. I knew she'd be crying, but there wasn't anything I could do except fume.

Mojo delicately blotted his lips with a piece of kitchen roll and looked thoughtful. On the telly, John Wayne shot someone. I waited. He spoke.

'Darling, this . . . man. I'm concerned.'

'You're not the only one, matey. Ben was round saying all sorts of stuff, like he's a homophobe, a racist, all kinds of stuff. I've never known her be so down on someone – well, unless it was another philosopher. I think he's a shithead, but I can't say he actually said anything outta line, just, you know, implications, the way he said stuff. Really got on my tits.'

'Oh, our new friend is everything dear, dear clever Ben mentioned, and more, I fear.'

'But look, he said he'd come an' see her today, but he ain't showed – maybe he'll just vanish, you know, after seeing it's not his scene, that he's out of his depth . . .'

'He'll appear, believe me, my pet. That's what concerns me. Well, I shall ask that nice Andy person to put a lock on my door tomorrow. Such a charming boy, so willing. Yes, I think I'd rather keep my jewels this time. Never mind, darling, don't look so worried – it just makes lines. This *Sean* is just another one of Jamie's Errors, we both know that. Unpleasant, perhaps even more unpleasant than usual – but really, there's nothing we can do except wait it out. I take it you will be waiting it out? I thought so. Such a loyal little thing. Now, can I tempt you with some pistachio kulfi? It's in the fridge and I know what a *healthy* appetite you have . . .'

And he did appear. The next day after I got home from work and visiting Ma, who I thought was looking a bit tired, there was Jamie cooing ecstatically over a cellophane-wrapped bunch of flowers, tied with the usual florist's puke-green ribbon bow.

'Look – they're from *him* – aren't they fabby! There was a note – he couldn't make it yesterday because of trouble at home – poor sod, I know how that feels! God, no one's ever sent me flowers before – have we got a vase or anything? Where? No, I'll get it.'

That night, he phoned. I timed it – fifty minutes. We had two gigs that week, on the Thursday and Friday. The Thursday one was in St Albans, the Friday at the Pow! Club, Brighton. They were good payers and I was worried about how on the ball she'd be, what with her brain being turned to mush by *lurve*.

I needn't have been concerned – she was brilliant. Everyone raved about how incredible she was, what a great performer she was. I was really impressed with her, she just seemed to be glowing. Her crush on Sean seemed to have given her a real lift. Maybe we'd all been a bit hasty in our judgements – from what Jamie said, Sean was a man struggling to overcome his upbringing. Well, I thought, perhaps that's it. He's just a fish out of water with our lot, maybe he'll improve. I wanted to believe I'd been wrong, I suppose, because otherwise, he would be beyond redemption. Because otherwise it would put a heavy strain on our friendship.

We had a good time on those gigs though – real fun, like the old days. We went to the cult 'Perforations' piercing studio in Brighton on the Saturday and I got my lip pierced, and Jamie had her tragus done. I told her I wanted to get a tattoo and that Gabe had said he'd take me to Van Burgess, his tattooist. We had a laugh about how in the first note he'd left for me, I'd thought he'd said he was going to see about 'a van', not go and see Van, because of his terrible writing. We discussed my ideas for a tribal armband and wondered if it really hurt. We had crepes on the pier and ran about on the beach shrieking. During the long drive home, we talked and listened to Radio Four, or old tapes by Sisters Of Mercy, Killing Joke and New Model Army, and I made her sit through Tupac, Kate Bush, Cypress Hill and *Round the Horne*. She moaned a bit, but she secretly quite liked my stuff – anyhow, it gave us a chance to argue, which we always enjoyed. The miles flew past and everything was cool.

It was one of the last happy road trips we took together. Now, it sort of prickles like thorns in my heart to think of it; we were such a unit, so close.

The day after we got back, Sean came round. I had decided to give him my best shot, the benefit of the doubt an' all that. But it was just no good. No fucking good. Again, it wasn't what he said, it was just something about the way he said it, about the way every conversation revolved around himself and the way he'd been hard done to. I mean, Jesus Christ, his family weren't exactly fucking poor; he went to good schools, he had the best of everything. OK, his father may have been a bit rough an' ready – the original wheeler-dealer type, but the way Sean went on you'd think he was Hitler. I wish *my* daddy would've given me a flash motor when I was eighteen, but to hear Sean, his father was being a fucking cheapskate not giving him a brand-new one. And the athlete thing – oh, if only Sean had gotten the breaks, well, Olympics here we come. But everyone had it in for him, sure, and then (sob) he got his injury, a shot knee ligament – talk about the old war wound. We even got the bit about how much he wanted to join the Army and be a Marine, or a Special Ops bloke, or whatever the fuck they are – but dammit, they disqualified him because he got asthma when he was stressed. Gosh, my heart pumped custard over that one. I didn't believe a fucking word of it; it stank of spiel. You could tell he'd told the whole thing over and over; it was rehearsed. I was so glad Mojo was out, he wouldn't have stood it for a second and we'd have had a scene. But Jamie just lapped it up, serving his dinner for him, pouring his wine like a frigging geisha. I'm surprised she didn't anoint his fucking feet and wipe them with her hair. Urgh, puke.

It wasn't a great evening. I decided to turn in early and read the Yankee noir thriller I'd bought while we were away. I'd just finished washing and was in the kitchen making a last cuppa, dressed in my hideous old pink candlewick dressing gown, M & S boys' pyjamas and fluffy-rabbit-shaped slippers, when I felt someone behind me. I didn't *hear* anything, but I felt someone. I whipped round, dead nervy, and Sean was leaning against the doorframe.

'*What the fuck* – Christ, do you have to sneak up on people like that?'

'Did I frighten you – sorry. I s'pose I do move pretty quiet, me – it's a thing I picked up from a SAS bloke I know.' He pronounced it 'sass', as in 'Sass bloke'. He had a sort of knowing smirk on his face, as if that was supposed to impress me or something. When I didn't look suitably swoony, he put a serious look on and sighed.

'Look, Lily, I want to talk to you – I know we haven't, like, exactly hit it off, probably that's my fault. I – well, I'm a bit crap at social things, y'know, hey – always been a bit of a lone wolf. If I've offended you – well, I'm really sorry. I want to get on with you, I can see how much you mean to my special lady – an' I'd really like to be your friend, too. I'd like us all to get on, be mates. I feel a lot for Jamie. OK, I realize I've not known her long or anything but, you know, from the first time I saw her, I thought, wow, she's really something – I wanna get to know her better. An' now I have – well, *am* getting to know her, she's just great. Really. And, you know, hey, I've made some bad choices in my life – picked the wrong ladies, but I wanna put all that behind me, settle down a bit, have a life. Look, what say we bury the hatchet, be friends, eh? Eh? Come on, give me another go, I'll be a good boy, honest, I swear it!'

All this creepy baloney was accompanied by what he thought was a winning smile. I ignored the hand he held out and put my tea mug down before I hit him with it.

'Spare me the crap, Sean. I don't like you and

you don't like me. I can live with that. We'll have a truce, if that's what will make my friend happy. But you step over the line, you hurt her and I'll get you, one way or another. That's no idle threat, either, believe me. You're not the first bastard to take advantage of her good nature, but I swear to God, I hope you're the last. Like, I mean that, you know, so . . .' I started to lose it and decided discretion was the better part of whatever. 'So, if you'll, like, *excuse* me, I'm off to bed.' I picked up the mug and made to leave the kitchen in a huff.

It was as if a glass mask had dropped over his face, pressing down on his features. He was rigid with fury; his strange eyes full of blistering anger, like fire smouldering under ice. I flinched away involuntarily from that hideous, formless blast of silent rage. Then just as suddenly, he seemed to control himself and it was gone.

'OK,' he smiled tightly. 'OK, have it your own way. No, no, it's right enough – I admire your loyalty, like I said before. I understand loyalty, it's like in the Forces, buddies, mates. Comrades. It's a real strong bond. You an' Jamie've been through a lot together, I respect that. I'm just sorry you won't give me a chance. But, hey, time will tell. I know you'll come to appreciate what I feel about Jamie, how much I care about her – an' one day, yeah, we'll have a right laugh together about all this.' He nodded and gave me his rueful, misunderstood expression. It really bugged me how he *did* expressions, like he'd fucking learnt them or something, practised them in the mirror. It was yucky.

I brushed past him and went upstairs, seething. Oh God, let it be over soon, let it just be a short fling. Then we could get back to normal.

That night, for the first time since I moved in, I locked my bedroom door before I went to sleep.

CHAPTER 22

Well, it wasn't a fling. It went on and on. He'd be round most nights, though at first he'd go home to his parents' to sleep. I was curious about this, as most blokes Jamie saw used to stay over as a matter of course. Still, what with gigs increasing due to it coming up for Christmas, I didn't have time to pry. I found out something interesting though, after a while. They had a God Almighty row one evening, so bad I had to turn the volume of the telly up rather than sit through it second-hand. Thank God we had no neighbours. Moley was shivering on my lap and it was with some relief I heard Sean slam out the front door and chug off in his grotty van. Eventually Jamie came down and put the kettle on. She came in to the front room and sat on the edge of the armchair by the fire, white as a sheet, and it was pretty obvious she'd been crying her eyes out. I remote-muted the box and asked her if she was OK.

She sniffed and her lower lip wobbled somewhat. 'Well, I suppose you heard us rowing. I'm sorry, I don't mean to, like, disrupt the whole house. It's

Sean – oh, look, I know you don't think a lot of him – but he's got real problems, y'know. I mean, all right, he can be a bit – well, a bit annoying in public – all that macho SAS stuff, but it's just because he's so unsure of himself.'

I was about to say something snappy but the expression on her face stopped me. And again I wondered about why I disliked him so much. I mean, sure, Ben, Lonnie and Mojo and I thought he was a wanker, but like, Jenny, Magda and some of the other lasses we knew thought he was gorgeous and really nice. A real hunk. In fact, it was pretty obvious Jenny had a big crush on him and she kept making comments to Jamie about passing him along when she was done with him. None of them worried about his attitudes; I was confused. Was it just me an' Ben being overserious? I admit we could be pretty glum about stuff. I mean, I thought of him as an Error, but to be strictly honest, he'd done nothing wrong. He hadn't nicked anything, or hit Jamie, he was polite and . . . oh, I wished for the umpteenth time in my life I was articulate and cool. I heard Jamie continue.

'Look, I know you'll keep this between us, but he's – well, he's got a problem in bed – oh, it's awful for him, really awful. He just can't – well, he can't – he's *impotent*.' She was red-faced with embarrassment.

I leant forward and put my hand on her knee. Her legs were trembling. 'Sweetie, you don't have to tell me anything you don't want to . . .'

'No, no – it's a relief to talk about it, actually. I mean, it's never happened to me before – well, not me, but you know what I mean. I thought it was just older men, but he just can't – he wants to, but nothing happens. It drives him crazy, he keeps sayin' he's not a man, and that I must be laughing at him. But it's not true, Lily, I'd never do somethin' like that – I tell him over and over that it doesn't matter but he gets so fuckin' angry. Then this evening, we – you know, tried again, but it was worse than ever. I tried everything but – nothing. He just got furious, and said terrible things – he doesn't mean them but it's killing him. Now I don't know where he's gone. I'm frightened he's gone to Lisa's.'

'Who's Lisa?'

'Oh, she's his ex-girlfriend. She's really got a hold on him – he says she's really hard, you know, all gold jewellery and stilettoes; she threw him out and kept loads of his stuff, and money. That's why he's so skint now. But you know, it's the way he talks about her, like he hates her, but he can't forget her. I feel like a substitute sometimes, not up to Lisa's standard, not good enough. Then he says he loves me an' she just wants him back to prove she can do it; God, she sounds like a real cow. Oh, I don't know, I want to help him, but I don't know how.'

The kettle was boiling its toes off, so I brewed up. We discussed what we knew about impotence until we decided that in the end, patience and love were the best you could do. Eventually, she went to bed. Shortly afterwards, Mojo came in and I told him what Jamie had told me. Yeah, I know, blabbermouth, but it bothered me and I wanted to talk to him about it.

'So you see, not only can he not get it up, but then he takes it out on Jamie and taunts her with this Lisa woman, who sounds like a real piece of work.'

'Hmm – closet case, I wonder? He is *so* macho, it does make one suspicious, certainly. I admit, I don't like this at all. I rather wish the dear Archangel would come home, I feel at least he could talk sense into Jamie and perhaps even – shall we say – *encourage* our friend to find pastures new. But then, that has been tried before to no avail. Oh dear, dear, dear; I shall never understand this love business, so messy. And even little Moley doesn't like our houseguest, does she, my sweet, no, not at all – and I must say, to be vulgar, he gives me the fucking creeps.'

I hadn't thought about it before, but Mojo was right. Moley didn't like Sean. I'm not a great one for that stuff about animals having sixth sense, and Moley was a notorious tart who sucked up to any bloke going, even Jamie's previous Errors. But now Mojo mentioned it, I had noticed her being very nervous of Sean, and he certainly just bolt ignored her. Also, for Mojo to descend into the vernacular was an indication he was genuinely disturbed. I just repeated my plea to the Almighty to let it be over soon. Sure, I felt a kind of second-hand sympathy for Sean if he really was impotent – after all, it must be crippling, especially if you were young and good-looking, with everyone assuming you were a super-stud. But I still distrusted him, and this business with the ex-girlfriend just reeked of manipulation and game-playing. Oh bugger, *bugger*.

Christmas just seemed to rush at us that year. We had some good shows in November and December – Jamie was certainly firing on all cylinders. A telly researcher had phoned saying someone had told her Jamie was the female Billy Connolly and that they were thinking of *using* her for a new pop-music game show, so that cheered us up a lot career-wise. She also had a couple of good reviews in local papers – Aberystwyth and Oxford, if I recall correctly, which was useful. But her mind was with Sean when she wasn't on-stage and it made things a bit dull, due to her talking about him all the time.

I managed to get all my presents bought – I got Her Nibs a pager, which I thought was a cute idea – but then Jamie hinted Sean was getting us presents and I thought, fuck. So I bought him a book token – it was one of the things about him that irritated me, his big porkies. One of the biggest was that he loved reading. Such a whacking ham-out. You only had to talk to him for five minutes to see that apart from his collection of fucking Special Forces

184

manuals ('six ways to kill a man silently', 'mantraps and their uses', 'my dick's bigger than your dick', etc.), he was virtually illiterate. We all read like bastards, so he thought he'd scored a hit by giving it big licks on the book front. Sa-ad, really. Mojo and I made a pact not to bait him about it, because when we did, he used to get totally pissed off, and take it out on Jamie in one of their increasingly regular bust-ups.

Well, sure enough, Sean came round on the twenty-first and gave me and Jamie our presents; nothing for Mojo. He gave Jamie a pair of obviously second-hand big gold creole earrings, the sort of thing she'd never wear normally, and insisted she take out a pair of her piercing rings and put them in. She did, and they looked crap, but he was dead chuffed – probably just because he could make her do what he wanted. We all got silk thermal underwear as well. Jamie got long johns and a long-sleeved T-shirt in black, and I got a beige T-shirt. I'm not going to dwell on what I thought about it. We got a long rigmarole about how they were pure silk, the latest, latest thing in the sports world and how the RAF used them and how his boss Mike imported them from China directly and Raptor Sports were the major seller of this gear in Yorkshire and . . . I thought, *He's nicked them from work, cheap bastard.* I put mine away in my drawer and never even took it out of the cellophane. You'd think Jamie'd been given the crown jewels, not bloomers and a pair of trashy earrings.

It bothered me he didn't get anything for Mojo, but Jamie said Sean'd thought with Mojo being Asian, he didn't do Christmas. That was a bit weird – I mean, Bradford's so mixed-up, everyone does everything, Christmas, Diwali, Chanukah, Easter, probably Beltane, too, if you know where to look. Sean must have known lots of westernized Asian folks did the Xmas trip, too. Or at least, he could have got Moj a card; but he treated Mojo like he treated Moley – they were invisible to him; he blanked them as much as he could.

Well, any road up, as usual Jamie and I went to Ma and Pa's for Christmas Day – Someone whisked Mojo off to the South of France, or some other exotic location, like They did every year. We always got our prezzies duty-free, which was nice, if late. Mojo said that being a nominal Muslim, he had a great excuse to flee the dreaded English Yuletide Fayre; sometimes I wished Someone liked short biracial women as well, especially after Turkey Kebabs *Flambé*.

That's just me being horrible; actually I loved mince pies and Christmas Cake – every mince pie a wish, as Ma always said. Yeah, I was a bit worried about Ma, she seemed increasingly tired and I wondered about just how well she was. Still, there was no point asking her, I tried several times and she just put it down to her age. I asked Pa, too, but he just said she'd taken longer than usual to get over the bout of flu she'd had at the beginning of December.

Jamie was a bit downcast, as Sean had told her he was off on a skiing trip to Glencoe with a bunch of mates for the holiday – since I'd never ever seen him with the 'mates' he was always going on about, I was suspicious. Off to his mum and dad's, or the Bitch-Goddess Lisa's, more like.

But there was no point in going on about Sean, I was just glad to be rid of him for a bit, and we had a nice, family Xmas.

On Boxing Day, we went to Gabe's Mam's. I hadn't seen Gabe for months, and I was really pissed off when I got there to find he'd brought home his latest flame, a German girl called Silke. She was a real Gabe-girl, too. Anorexic, neurotic, eyes like sooty black holes – a real clubland babe. We called her the Schtick-Insecte. Fortunately, we didn't see much of her, because if she wasn't in the bathroom, she was asleep. Suited me. It took me about two seconds to tire of her skinny charms. I got mighty sick of seeing her badly done belly-button piercing peeping gummily out of the top of her hipsters and hearing her whining baby-doll voice going, *'I can't eat zis, I can't eat zat, where iss der shower, Gay-bree-elle?'* Not that I was jealous or anything – I'm far too mature for that. I am, honestly. Oh, suit yourself, then. The fact is, I've known lots of Germans (hey, I snogged an exchange boy called Gunther once when I was fourteen) and I don't have the usual English prejudices about them – it wouldn't have mattered where in the world Fräulein Silke came from, that type is uni-fucking-versal. Neuro-chicks, we call 'em. It just makes me eat more. Well, yeah, go on then, everything makes me eat more.

Mrs Smith always insisted she wasn't going to put on a spread, and every year there was more food than you could possibly imagine. Even the ponies, dogs, cats, ferrets, canary, rabbits and the goat – who was called Concepta – got special dinners. It was mayhem.

Eventually, after a monumental pig-out, we retired beaten to the front room with coffee and various bottles of brandy, Jameson's and Mrs Smith's favourite, Bailey's. It was red-hot from the log fire and carpeted with animal hairs. The owners of said hairs lay around like living rugs and panted, purred or squeaked. So did we. Silke sulked off to Gabe's room and ran up his mobile phone bill. Mrs Smith turned to Jamie with a glass of alcoholic custard-slop in her big, work-reddened hand.

'So, my girl, I hear you have a new fella – is he nice? What's his name?'

'Sean Powers, Mam, his dad has the garages, you know, Powers Motors.'

'Ah, I know Paddy Powers – or now, should I say *Patrick* Powers – he's gone up in the world these days. Sean will be the eldest, now – aren't there two girls, oh, Katherine and . . . Theresa, that's it. Gabriel, you know the Powers girls, don't you? Caitlin, pour Lily a coffee there, she must be parched . . .'

'Yeah . . .' Gabe shook his head, looking

troubled. God, he was so handsome, it made me reach for the chocolate. 'Well, I knew Terri – Theresa – more than Kathy. Both of 'em stuck-up little madams though, an' no mistake. That whole family's a right old mess, if yer ask me. Summat not right there – don't you remember that stuff about Paddy's sister Lana and her friend – what was that, Mam? It's a while since . . .'

I saw Jamie's ears prick up at a mention of anything to do with her beloved – but I was in a gossip-frenzy now, as were we all. Gabe's second sister Rosary flapped her hands about to get our attention and said in a fake newsreader's voice:

'Lana Powers's friend, Simone Something-or-other, was found *horribly* dead in a *compromising* situation in a hotel room in Leeds with Miz Powers herself *dragged* to the po-leece station . . .' All the sisters, Caitlin, Rosary and Grace hooted in unison and rolled their dark eyes. They're terrible girls, really.

'Oh Rosy, enough of your nonsense – no, it was a scandal, to be sure. Now, wasn't the friend, Simone, all dolled up in some crazy costume, and got herself strangled or something . . .'

Gabe looked serious. 'Well, it were all hushed up, y'know. Mam, in't Old Man Powers in the same Lodge Dadda were in? Yeah, I thought so – same one as your father, Jamie. Anyhow, this bit o' bother were all taken care of. Seems that Lana an' her friend were in the habit of havin' little *adventures* of a *particular* kind – no, I can't tell, ladies present an' all that – OK, OK, it were heavy bondage and rough stuff with hired fellas . . . oh yeah, honest – no word of a lie. Well, they holes up in this hotel in Leeds for a bit of a *private party*, like, an' it seems summat went a bit haywire – an' whoops-a-daisy, Lana's buddy's a goner. There were an inquest, an' a "accidental death" verdict. I'll give you cash money the coroner does the funny handshake an' all. Mind, she's a right 'un, that Lana Powers. I got it all offa Tommy Garrat – yeah, Cait, the lanky one – he worked cleaning cars at Old Man Powers's first garage. All the lads call Lana "The Black Widow". She's allus in these tight black leather skirts – tons of make-up, Joan Collins style – an' her hair dyed jet-black an' all done up in a mass o' curls. Tommy says she's allus slinking around ogling the young lads an' offerin' them a bit of how's-yer-father. You know what I mean. Mutton dressed as lamb, sorta thing. Only goes for really young blokes, an' all. Old Man Powers thinks the world of her though, won't hear owt against her – funny, in't it?'

'Well, now, son, she's his only sister, it's natural enough. But the mother, now – Rosalie – she's a strange one. Very pious, mind you – oh yes – pillar of the Society of Mary, always singing in the choir, an' such. Keeps the Fathers well supplied with cake and Jameson's. She was on that trip to Lourdes I took last year – very quiet, never said a word. Just tellin' her beads and starin' out the coach window. Little blondey mouse of a thing, and Paddy such a

190

big fella . . . don't you be so vulgar, Gracie, I don't know where you get it from, I'm sure . . .'

There was a bout of cushion-throwing and hysteria then, until the sisters said they were off to the pub, and would we like to come. No one mentioned the Schtick-Insecte, who was still in Gabe's room – probably picking her belly-button scabs – so we said, no, we'd just stay here and digest.

Mrs Smith declined all offers of help to clear away, saying since Gabriel had bought her the dishwasher she was a lady of leisure and it wouldn't take her a minute to fix up the kitchen. Gabe, Jamie and I lolled about in the heat like pythons after eating a – well, better not say *goat*.

It didn't take long for Jamie to ask Gabriel what had been on her mind for the last half an hour. She plonked down on her knees at his feet and looked up at him earnestly. I sighed and allowed my attention to wander somewhat.

'Gabe, honey, how come you know the Powerses? I mean, d'you know Sean?'

'They're an Irish family, same as us – Bradford-Irish. Though sayin' that, they kinda look down on us on account of Mam havin' been a Traveller. It's a bit of the "oh, Tinkers" crap, you know. Anyways, I like knowin' stuff – I like havin' the gen on folk; it's a kinda hobby, like – dead nosy, me. No, the Powers lot are well fucked-up, everyone knows that, girl. 'S a case of money not buyin' you happiness, like – 'cos they're not fuckin' poor, that I *can* tell yer. Now, I knew Terri Powers on account of her goin' out wi Franco from Ultimate Angel – I were doin' some work for 'em at the time. Terri, she quite fancied hersel' as a rock chick. Still, she picked a wrong 'un there – rock an' roll's a pussy factory for the likes of Frankie-boy. All came down at the Town And Country Club in London. Angel were giggin' an' Terri was stuffed to the gills wi' coke an' Jack, teeterin' about on six-inch heels – she were only a young 'un, too, but she made like she were very *so-fis-ti-cated*. Well, the band comes off and next thing we know, all hell's broke loose in the dressin' room – seems like she caught Franco gettin' a blow-job offa some slag an' she went ballistic. Stormed off back to the hotel, an' won't let Franco in his room. Early next mornin' your man Sean appears in a flash motor an' off they go. Daddy sent him to fetch sis. You ask him about it, pet. It were a nine-days' wonder. Did Franco's rep as a Casanova the world o' good. Didn't do a lot for her though, I imagine.'

'What about Sean, though, did you ever hang around with him?'

'Nah. Not my scene – he were a bit of a sporty type, runnin' and such, from what I hear. I do know Old Man Powers traits him like a fuckin' gofer, though. Traits him like a hired hand, not like a son, by all accounts. I don't see him inheritin' the Powers Empire – more like Kathy'll do that, I should think. She's a hard piece. Mind, he's a good-lookin' fella, that Sean – he's got those weird eyes, int he? Same as Lana, an' Terri. Not the others, though. Funny thing, genetics.'

Gabe smiled, and patted Jamie's head indulgently, like she was a kiddie. 'You just go easy, darlin', just go easy on the lad, eh? Poor sod, he won't know which way's fuckin' up at your house – Powers's place is all Waterford and Chinese rugs, Mammy says. Not a nest of fuckin' hippie squalor like yours.'

We beat him up. He liked that. So did I – but hey, that's *private*.

CHAPTER 23

In the New Year, I had a bit of trouble. Ma got sick and I was worried outta my mind. She got another bout of flu after she an' Pa had done their usual New Year's winter hiking trip up Helvellyn or thereabouts an' she just couldn't shake it off. Then it turned to pneumonia. I can't tell you what I felt like – like, oh, totally fuckin' helpless. She got taken to the Infirmary and just lay there looking like a rag doll with her long plait hanging down on the outside of that hideous hospital bedspread.

Pa an' I practically lived in that hospital room, despite considerable opposition. I suppose it just made us feel like we were doin' something useful. God, it was awful. That place – Christ, I'm sure the patients go out sicker than they come in. The nurses were sweet though, just totally overworked and knackered.

But my ma, God – I just prayed an' prayed for her not to die or anything. To hear her poor lungs heaving and gurgling like that was dreadful, just awful. Pa went grey and looked like he'd go with her if she went; he was wrecked.

Jamie and Gabe were a tower of strength, they couldn't have been nicer or more helpful in practical ways. Even Mojo – who my parents had long ago accepted with open arms – brought useless but nice things, like copies of *Vogue*, bottles of lavender water and a huge bouquet of roses from Someone. Poor Mojo, hospitals just weren't his thing at all; but he did his best by his lights, bless.

Mrs Smith went over to Ma's and cleaned the house and did the washing more than once – what a saint. All our friends sent cards – Ben and Lonnie sent a fruit basket as well. It's times like that you really do find out just who cares.

One night, we were really scared. It was freezing cold and the ward outside Ma's little side room seemed full of the dying. Jamie had been and gone that afternoon, but I stayed by Ma's bedside as the evening wore on. Pa was sleeping, it must have been about midnight. I was wretched with fear and worry. Suddenly, I felt a cold hand on my shoulder, God, did I jump. Looking round I saw Jamie unwrapping a big black woollen scarf from round her head, it was sparkling with frost.

'How – how did you get in?' I said.

'I told 'em I was your sister – they don't know no different, I said we were both adopted. Anyhow, their security's crap. Lily, you *are* my sister. I love you. I love Ma an' Pa, too. I just want to be with you, quiet, like. You don't mind?'

I hugged her. We held hands by the bed as Ma struggled to breathe, the fever boiling in her blood.

195

'What about . . . Sean? Won't he mind you being out so late?'

She bowed her head and I saw the pain in her eyes. 'You're so good to me, girl,' she said. 'I don't know where he is; I think – I think he's with someone else, with Lisa. He's been so strange recently, so wired. Look, it doesn't matter, *this* matters.'

I nodded, too worn out to even comment. We just sat there, holding hands in that little side room. It was a long night, and the dawn came slowly, grey and soft like the brush of wings.

My ma got better after that night, slowly, but she got better. The rest of us were absolutely knackered – but never mind, at least Ma was on the mend – I felt like a boulder had been lifted from my heart.

I began to be able to leave Pa and Ma alone a bit and get out into town. The whole city seemed very agitated and there was a definite atmosphere; I found out why when I picked up the local paper. Banner headlines screamed, '*Brutal Murder: No Leads In Sara Evans Case*'. I nipped in to home and while I was sorting out my laundry, I asked Jamie what it was all about. It wasn't reassuring news.

'Crap, isn't it? Poor little cow. Cut to bits apparently, really awful. Now they're saying there've been two others similar, but get this, right – *they* were prostitutes, this is a *respectable* girl. Makes my blood boil, honestly. Well, you know what everyone's thinking, don't you?'

'It's the Ripper all over again.'

'Too right. Three women murdered an' the police doin' the "no comment" bit all over the telly and the papers. Town's swarming with reporters – well, not that I've seen any. Mind you, sayin' that, I wouldn't be able to tell one from a human being, unless they had a ticket with "Press" written on it stuck in their hatband.'

'Two others though – like, when?'

'I dunno. Somethin' like one last year an' one maybe a year before that or thereabouts. Seems no one connected them. Naz at the shop says his mate's a copper an' he says the plods are holdin' back loads of horrible details because of people that come in an' pretend they did the deed – for attention. Like, really – I thought that only happened in films, but apparently not. Go down the nick in droves, they do, givin' it – "It's a fair cop, guv'nor, it was me that offed the blonde" – an they have to keep somethin' secret to check out the loons. Still, Naz's mate says whoever did it damn near cut their fuckin' heads off and made a right mess – says hardened coppers were pukin' like kids. God, I wouldn't have that job for anythin'. Yuk.'

That night, Sara Evans's mother was on the news. I remember thinking – why is she doing this? It seemed so awful, her with that desiccated, ravaged face, weeping and showing a photo of Sara. I kept seeing not the girl's young, rather serious face, but a bloody, hacked-up ruin of flesh. It made me shiver. We all agreed that if anything happened to us like that, the rest of us would never go on telly. It was obscene, the stupid questions they kept asking Mrs Evans. *'How do you feel about your daughter's killer?'* For fuck's sake, what was she supposed to say? *'Oh yes, some nutter's carved up my only daughter but I don't mind a bit, really.'*

And all the stuff about how normal the girl was – she'd been waiting at a bus stop (up on Manningham Lane, near the Adult Education Centre) after her Poetry Appreciation evening class. Oh, *she* wasn't given to wearing 'provocative' clothing, or being flighty, no, none of that. She was a good student trying to improve herself and get a job – and then bam! Some old wino bloke found what was left of her in the shrubbery of a boarded-up old house off the Lane where he'd gone to drink his meths in peace, or whatever. *'Brutal slaying'*, they called it. *'This savage attack on an innocent young girl'*. Like the other two were just scum, nothing, not worth bothering with. So bloody sanctimonious, it took your breath away.

Everyone was talking about it. I mean, Bradford did have a history, what with the Black Panther and the Ripper – but we weren't *'Murder City'* like they said in the *Sun*. People were getting very cross about being labelled the whores an' psychos capital of Britain – I mean, what about Manchester? They did this really scary 'vox pop' thing in the local rag – you know the kind of thing. Mini-photos of people nabbed by the Arndale Mall, with their answers to the question *'What can be done about Bradford's bad reputation?'* It was all young white and Asian blokes with casual haircuts and counter-clerk ties giving it, '*I think they should run the prostitutes out of town*', and, '*They bring it on themselves these women and then decent people suffer*'. Plus a sprinkling of young Mums and Grannies saying they were terrified to leave the house at night. The paper ran the usual warning to women too, the one about not dressing in skimpy costumes and not going out late. I liked the skimpy outfits bit – like, did they know what the temperature was outside? Even the Ladies of the Night were in moon-boots and ski-suits, or so rumour had it. People invented the usual sick jokes as well, but I'm not going to repeat those.

Eventually, the whole thing died down a bit as other things took over the news – more gossip about the tedious Royal Family's goings-on. Good luck to 'em, we said – the inbred fuckwits.

Gabe had taken Jamie to the couple of gigs I'd missed because of Ma's illness, which was nice, but shortly he was off out to America with Salamanca. He reckoned if he could stand them, he'd be away for months again and my heart sank. Fortunately, Der Schtick-Insecte had chittered off home to Köln so we decided to give Gabe a big going-away spaghetti. Jamie was still pretty depressed over Sean not coming round or even getting in touch – I really hoped he'd decided to fuck off and thought, how bloody typical! That sort always just bugger off without a word. We kinda decided it was all over, really. I knew she was hurting, but she was pretty good about it, even going so far as to cracking a few lame jokes about him.

The night of Gabe's dinner, Sean paged her. *I love you, Sean*, was the first one. I thought she'd burst with joy. My heart sank, natch. *My special lady* came next, followed by *See you tonight* and *Please forgive me, darling*. What the pager people must have thought about all this slop I can't think, still I suppose they're used to it. I wished I'd got her a jumper for Christmas.

He turned up with a bunch of gas-station guilty flowers and a big white teddy. I let him in and before he went through, he paused and said in a stage whisper:

'Soz about this, Lily, you must be real mad at me, an' look, I don't blame you. But it was family troubles. That's all over now, I promise, on my honour! I just want to make it up with Jamie and be happy – so, how about a truce, eh? Eh?'

I grunted. I couldn't say anything because I was pretty damn sure that he knew Jamie could hear what he said. It was everything for effect, with him. Mind you, I had to suppress a smirk when he got into the front room and copped a glance at Mojo and Gabe there. I think in his mind he'd pictured just Jamie, or at the outside, me and Jamie. Not the whole tribe.

He put his rueful look on and gave Jamie the flowers and the toy. She was trying to make like she was angry but it was a pitiful attempt. Mojo picked up the flowers, murmuring, 'Shall I put these in water?' That was a shock, as manual labour usually didn't enter his brain, and I realized he wanted to get away from Sean. Wow, I thought, they *really* don't like each other. Mojo dumped the wilting chrysanths in a jug and, draping his new long black coat over his shoulders, said he'd forgotten he had an appointment elsewhere and would we excuse him?

It was an outright lie. Gabe got up and hugged him goodbye, while Jamie said in a puzzled voice something about having cooked for four.

'Darling, now dear Sean is here, you *have* four and really, I must dash. Love you, Archangel, be safe in the Land Of The Free, kiss kiss . . .'

I went out to the door with him, and stopped him before he opened it.

'Where are you goin'? You weren't goin' anywhere tonight an' you know it.'

'Darling girl,' he said; 'I simply can't stand a cosy night in with our Charmer. It's . . . he's – oh, never mind.' Uncharacteristically, he was stuck for words. It was an odd, unsettling little moment and I wished I'd tried to talk to him more as he swirled out into the night, heading for Mega Kars Taxis.

I drifted back in feeling a bit at a loss. In the front room, Sean had ensconced himself in the armchair by the fire and was holding forth to Gabe – who looked decidedly disinterested – about the Sara Evans case. He had opinions about everything, that bloke. The killer, as far as our Sean was concerned, was a dead cunnin' fella.

201

'Stands to reason. Like, he'll be one of them ex-Sass blokes, a trained killin' machine, like – out of the Service an' on the loose. The government knows all about them guys, knows they're out there, like, but won't let on in case it causes a panic. Your ordinary plod don't stand a chance with a guy like that. Used to covert operations, a man like that. Moves unseen, camo expert.'

'Yeah, but why would a fella like that go after some little lass?' said Gabe equably. He took a swig from his beer bottle. 'I mean, bit of a, watchamacallit, a soft fuckin' target, some little studently lass on her way home.'

Sean was silent, his jaw working with tension. 'Well, you know, he'd have his reasons, like; I mean, you know, there'd be more to it than meets the eye with a fella like that. Could be anythin'. Probably, like, probably we'll never know, see, 'cos they won't catch him an' so, how would civilians ever find out. All classified information, government secrets an' that.'

'Nah, bollocks, it's just some sad fuckin' loony who wants to shag his own mam, I reckon.' Gabe smiled lazily and I realized he was baiting Sean, who was white with fury.

'You . . . you can't say that, I mean, huh, that's crap. This fella's an expert, like I said, clever, not some nutter – no, he's like them blokes outta them Vietnam films, like that *Platoon* an' *Full Metal Jacket* – real experts, you know, like, deadly force – Christ, he's not, not what you said . . .'

202

'Mebbe, mebbe not – but come on, he'd not be right in the head – a bloke who cuts up little lasses? Be fair . . .'

Sean grinned mirthlessly, dry lips skinned back over his perfect teeth. 'OK, OK – but see, some – I say *some*, mind you, like, not all lasses, obviously, present company an' all – but you know, some lasses, well, they're no better than they ought to be, if y' get what I mean. You've seen 'em on the Lane an' round town, skirts up to their arses, practically naked – mekkin' shows of themselves – it's not decent for a lass to go on like that, is it? It's not right.'

'It's their business how they want to get dressed up – what 'arm do they do? Granted, these days, the outfits are a bit – but that's no reason to *murder* 'em, is it?' Gabe had lost his amiable air and was looking a bit narked – me, I was downright livid. Even Jamie had the grace to look embarrassed. Who the fuck did Sean think he was? The Archbishop of fuckin' Canterbury? Guardian of the nation's morals? Wanker.

Sean leant forward, his face strained, his elbows on his knees. 'It's not murder, it's – I mean, they're like a disease, those prostitutes an' lasses who're no better 'n whores an' such – they're infecting decent people's lives. I've read all about it – there's nowt worse than a woman that's gone wrong. It's a crime against nature. That bloke – well, I've heard – people have said, like, he's doin' the world a favour almost, keepin' the streets clean – doin' society's dirty work, like them Charles Bronson films – an anti-hero sorta thing.'

We all said, 'Bollocks!' in unison. Then Gabe put his beer down and sat back, really eyeballing Sean, who looked away.

'Yeah – like, who says that?' Gabe's voice was low, but carrying.

'Blokes in the pub – all sorts – come on, Gabe, all blokes – all proper blokes – feel that way about whores – they mek yer skin crawl – they're better off dead. I mean to say . . .'

'I think you should shut yer mouth, mate, that's what I think – an' stop reading so much bully-boy crap. Don't fuckin' tar me wi' *that* brush – I int one of yer fuckin' pub gobshites, just leave me outta all that – you'd do better to think about what muck's comin' outta yer mouth an' all, round 'ere. These lasses are my family, mate, an' don't forget it . . .'

Sean blanched and a weird little flicker twitched under his eye – one of those ticcy things you get when you're really stressed. He looked like he was going to burst and two red patches appeared on the sharp points of his cheekbones. Ey up, I thought, now we're for it.

But we weren't. He just subsided into the chair, spreading his hands in front of him. 'Right, right – no offence meant, boss, no offence – I wouldn't want to upset these lovely ladies wi' my – *ideas* or whatever – I'm sure you're right, eh? It's just pub-talk – you know how lads are . . . sorry if I, y'know, upset anyone . . .' He smiled that joyless smile again and Gabe picked up his beer and took a swig, dismissing him. I just thought – how long will I have to put up with this *pig*? Oh, get *rid* of him, girl . . .

Jamie stood up quickly, and started bustling about pointlessly. 'Oh, what does it matter, leave it alone, you guys – let's not argue; honestly, it gives me the shivers, the whole thing. Those poor girls, it's them *I* feel sorry for – God, it must've been awful for them. Doesn't bear thinkin' about. Right – dinnertime, I reckon. Lily, give us a hand with the stuff, will you?'

By the time we brought the dinner things in, Gabe and Sean were discussing football – if not amiably, at least not at each other's throats. Gabe even winked at me when, after we'd had some coffee, Jamie and Sean 'went upstairs for a chat about stuff'.

'What d'you think?' I said, wishing heartily I was upstairs for a 'chat' with Gabe.

'He's just a gobby tosser – I hear stuff like that every time I go out in town – dickless fuckwits. It's all hot air – y'can tell – no balls, that 'un, just like the rest. Bit tiring wi' the SAS business, all that "covert ops" crap – but I know a few lads like that. Wannabe-soldiers. He probably can't get it up, poor fucker.'

I blushed scarlet. Talk about hitting the nail on the head. 'Well, strictly between you an' me, they have had a bit of a problem, like.'

'Don't surprise me. Still, that's their business,

I reckon. He's a bit whatd'ymacallit – *immature*, like. Not the worst guy she's been involved wi' – Christ, d'you remember that Dodger fella? I don't give it long though, they int got much in common an' he's not her usual rough-an'-ready type. Look at it this way, Lil, mebbe it's a good sign – mebbe she's settlin' down a bit, tryin' to find a softer sorta bloke.'

'But Ben says . . .'

'I know what Ben says. An' Mojo. I don't doubt your man's fulla crap when it comes to gays an' black people, as well as all this bollocks about pros; but like I say, it won't last long, an' his bad attitudes will be the thing that drive 'em apart. Jamie won't put up with him dissing her friends or saying racist stuff. You know she won't.'

'I know, but he never actually – well, he always wriggles outta stuff an' – it's just the way he *is*, it's, oh, it's . . .'

'Come on, girl, you can't like the whole world, an' everyone knows you think no one would be good enough for our lass. He's just a pretty-boy, a wanker. Forget him.'

That night, when he left, he kissed me goodbye. Oh, not anything resembling a snog, but a kiss on the cheek. He had his arm around me an' I thought I was goin' to faint, or throw up. It was the first time he'd ever kissed me, even as a friend. God, that sounds so childish – but it made me have hope, you know. That maybe, one day, me an' him *could* . . . yeah, well.

CHAPTER 24

The next morning Jamie looked like Moley with a yoghurt carton; from her blissful expression I surmised union had been achieved. When I made interrogative eyebrow movements she nodded happily.

Slowly but inexorably, Sean moved in. First off it was the litter of his wash-stuff in the tiny bathroom – a tangle of manly, disinfectant-smelling shower gel, shaving gear, deodorant in giant-sized spray cans, corrosive aftershave – which thankfully, he seldom wore. The little plastic pods of his daily disposable contact lenses collected like flotsam around the wastebin and his grubby sports socks lay in greyish heaps in the corners.

Then one night after I got in from visiting Ma, I heard a God Almighty banging and clattering coming from the cellar. I pushed open the door and shouted down the stairs.

'Hello? Hello? Who's down there – what's goin' on?'

Sean came to the stair foot and grinned up at me winningly. 'Oh, now then, Lily – I was just gettin' this place into shape – I thought I'd put my weights gear down here – dead handy, eh?'

'Sean, that stuff belongs to Mr Suleiman – you can't go chucking it out – anyways who said you could . . .' I stopped. I knew who'd said he could.

'Oh, don't worry, I'll just shift his stuff into a corner – plenty of room down here. It'll be like a proper gym, you can use it if you want – Jamie says she's gonna have a go!'

I retreated to the living room and turned the telly on loud to drown out the thumping and banging. Typical – a gym. He was so vain about his body and his fitness. It was turning warmer now and at any hint of mild weather, he'd lounge around in just a pair of marl-grey trackie-bottoms rolled at the waist. I don't deny he had a stupendous body; I'd like to, but I can't. It was all smooth, hairless pecs, bulging biceps and a six-pack. He had hideous feet though, which cheered me up, and his fingernails were bitten to death. Ugly.

Increasingly, as Sean crept into our house, Mojo and I crept out. I'd invested in a mobile phone, something I'd resisted – partly because of the money aspect and partly because of looking like a dealer. But Ma's health situation persuaded me to. We weren't that skint, really, and I felt happier knowing the Popsies could get in touch easily wherever I was. I gave Gabe my number, too. You know, for when he phoned from Boston. Well, he might need it, who could tell . . .

Mojo's – I can't say relationship, I don't know

what it was – let's say his mutual antipathy with Sean got worse and worse. I know people will say, why didn't you just move out? But we were used to these invasions and usually they lasted a couple of months at the very outside. We just thought we would sit it out and one day – abracadabra! – Sean would vanish in a puff of smoke.

But Sean stayed and stayed. Sometimes he would sod off for a week at a time – the eternal, never explained 'family troubles' or outings to sports events with his invisible mates. If he and Her Nibs had a row, he buggered off implying that there was someone else who he could stay with. That of course, was the Ogress of Elmsford, Miss Lisa Taylor. Personally, I didn't believe in Lisa. If she was as hard and cruel as he said when he wanted sympathy, why did she take him in without question whenever he turned up in the middle of the night with his Adidas bag stuffed with dirty laundry? Nah, I reckoned he just went home to his mam, the long-suffering Rosalie, Mater Dolorosa, the Madonna of Sorrows.

On non-gig days, I'd either go to Ma and Pa's or, more often, to Ben and Lonnie's to avoid sitting watching telly all night with the lovebirds. Jamie had virtually stopped reading because when she read, it made Sean uncomfortable and jealous. She'd stopped writing for the same reasons. They just stayed in watching the box, or went to the pictures to take in the latest testosterone epic from Bruce, Arnie or Jean-Claude. I can honestly say I do not know what she saw in him. I mean, aside from his looks, he veered between self-obsessed and dead boring. But she said he *needed* her – that inside, he was just a big kid trying to fight his way through a confusing world. O yeah, an' I'm Kate fuckin' Moss.

But Jamie wasn't the only one who was bowled over by his dubious charm and good looks. Oh no. In case I've given the impression *everyone* we knew hated him, I'll have to say that just wasn't the case. At all. Gabe and our male friends (Mojo aside) thought, oh hey – he's a bit of a tosser but what can you expect from a pretty-boy? They talked about bloke-stuff quite happily and never understood my antipathy to him.

Our women friends divided quite sharply down the middle: Lonnie and Ben on one side and all the straight lasses on the other. Worst of all was Jenny, whose crush on Sean developed alarmingly, and culminated in a very unpleasant incident.

Now, normally, like, you couldn't get Sean out of 'his' armchair by the fire for cash-money unless it was to do something for himself. But one night we'd all decided to go to O'Reilly's for a change – even Her Nibs. At first, Sean refused to go, but after Jamie got all dolled up, he suddenly changed his mind and came along after making us late waiting for him to get ready.

We rushed into the pub to the tinny wail of a mutilated version of 'Star of the County Down' and joined Ben, Lonz, Magda and Jenny, plus her boyfriend Guy, who we all called Bloke (Guy = guy = bloke . . . oh, we thought it was funny). Bloke was a real cutie – one of those nice, stocky, deadpan sorts who looks like he ought to wear a trilby and trenchcoat. He worked on the rigs. We all really liked him and always looked forward to his shore leaves. Jenny was Bradford's answer to Grace Kelly, in a lot of ways. Very pretty, very groomed, very WASP – a club-babe WASP in a floaty layered slip dress, mini-cardie and high-back bob. We thought they made a sweet couple, rather like those old Hollywood comedies featuring a wisecracking hero and a beautiful gal.

First off, there was nothing amiss. Bloke had the same kind of reaction to Sean that Gabe had – you could see him dismiss Sean as a lightweight, summat and nothing. But not Jenny. I hadn't realized how gone she was on Wonderboy. Within minutes she was flirting outrageously, the whole tinkling-giggle, fluttering-mascara, knowing-pout routine. And Sean just lapped it up. He flexed his biceps, he boasted about his 'connections', trundled out his covert operations crap and gave a whole new dimension to eye contact.

The atmosphere started to get sub-arctic, to say the least. At first, everyone talked vivaciously about complete bollocks, hoping Sean and Jenny would just pack it in – they didn't. Then sporadic fits of silence dropped into the brittle chat until the conversation shut down totally and we watched glumly as the two of them had a great time together.

Bloke just downed pint after pint grimly, like a man on a mission – to oblivion. Jamie was obviously on the point of tears and Ben looked at me meaningfully until I said, too loudly, that I just *had* to go to the Ladies. I got up and, nearly knocking my drink over, exited stage left. I was joined in double-quick time by Ben and we stared unhappily into the clouded mirror over the sink.

'What the bloody hell is all that? Some outing. Poor Bloke. Jenny's gone loopy. Look, I'm taking Illonka home before she says something. Want to come?' Ben sighed heavily and, probably, existentially.

'I can't, can I? Christ, Ben, I can't leave Jamie and just bugger off – and Bloke as well, it's not right.'

'I know. I mean, I know you're right but I just can't stick it. That bloody man. Nothing but trouble. Got to go – really sorry. Makes me sick. Call me tomorrow – come for dinner.'

I knew who the bloody man was all right and when we got back to the booth, Jenny and he were practically drooling over each other. I was disgusted, how could they go on like that? Ben and Lonnie went and Bloke got up unsteadily. Uh-oh, I thought – here we go, here we go, here we go.

'Jen, *Jen*, I'm – I'm going home now. You coming?' There was no reply and he leant over and tapped her bare shoulder – gently.

She flinched up like a fly-bitten horse, eyes flashing.

'Thank you – I *did* hear you. You're pissed, Guy, just go home. I'll be along later. Go on, before you make an idiot of yourself.' The Ice Maiden spoke. It was very cruel. Bloke hesitated for a second but her attention had returned to Sean, who was leaning back against the booth wall with his arms folded behind his head and a smirk on his face. I willed Bloke to whack him with all my might. But he didn't. He looked beaten, as if there'd been some contest between him and Sean I hadn't twigged, and poor Bloke had lost. He looked weak, confused, somehow. He just mumbled something and stumbled off. I ran after him.

'Don't go, Bloke – we haven't seen you for ages. Look, let's go for a real old Bradford curry – come on, whaddya say? Oh, Bloke, forget them, forget them, it's not worth it, honest – look, it'll all come right in the morning, it will, I know it . . .'

He just looked at me as if I was mad. Then he slung his jacket on and went out of the bar. I trailed back to the table miserably. When I got there, Jamie was on her feet with her coat on.

'I'm off too,' she said loudly. Magda stared at the table as if it were a treasure map and Jenny ignored her. Sean smiled.

'See you later, then. Think I'd better escort Miss Jenny here home since her fella's deserted her. Town's not safe for a pretty lady with this murder business goin' on. Go on, off y'go.'

She turned and walked out – real quick, but not

213

quick enough to hide the fact she was crying. I rounded on Sean and Jenny.

'What the fuck do you think you're playin' at?' I demanded.

Jenny looked at me as if we were strangers, not two women who'd known each other for years.

'Piss off, Lily. It's none of your business. Run after Jamie like usual – why don't you? God knows she needs a minder.'

'Jen, leave it out.' Magda rubbed her forehead and looked embarrassed.

'Shut up, Maggie – in fact, why don't both of you just *shut up*. I don't see why everyone has to get at me just because I'm enjoying myself. It's just jealousy – plain old jealousy. Go on, Lily, run after your *girlfriend*, leave the grown-ups alone, for once.'

I realized how drunk she was – the vodka had been flowing pretty freely, but that was no excuse. I felt anger welling in me like a black tide.

'What the fuck d'you mean by that?'

'Oh, really – I think you know. I think you know full well – *Lily*.'

'No, I don't – d'you wanna fill me in?'

Sean took Jenny's arm and whispered something in her ear. She burst out laughing. Magda got up and went to the Ladies, her face stiff with humiliation. I noticed vaguely that people were staring at our booth, at us; I could see the gawping white faces of the student clientele looking like sickly blisters in the coiling blue ciggie-smoke. I could hear the atrocious strains of mass-produced jig music squeaking and stuttering through the sound system and it seemed to irritate my nerves and scratch in my head. I snapped at Jenny, who was casually lighting up.

'Oh, very good – you have a good laugh, ha-fuckin'-ha, why not. But come on, *Miss Jenny*' – I threw a look at Sean who just leant back and shrugged – 'why don't you say what's on your mind – what there is of it.'

'Christ, you think you're so bloody clever, don't you? I am *so* sick of the way you go on, like you were something special – just because that bitch gets up in public and makes a show of herself. God, you and that big, fat *cow* – come on, Lily, everyone knows you're queer for that slag, it's pitiful – playing housey-housey with her and that, that *pervert*. Pathetic. I don't know how a decent *man* like Sean sticks it, I really don't.' She grinned viciously and I felt my stomach heave. I'd liked Jenny – OK, she wasn't my number-one best buddy or anything, but I'd liked her, admired her looks and her style. It was horrifying the way she'd just shrugged off our friendship for a crack at Sean. That's straights for you, I thought. You just can't trust 'em. I felt suddenly intensely miserable and my retort to her abuse was lame, to say the least. Once upon a time I'd have smacked her pretty, spoilt face – but I just felt too tired – too beaten by Sean's games.

'Shut your dirty mouth, just shut it – you're not

fuckin' fit to lace her shoes, you . . . you . . .' I was tripping over my words and I could feel my face burning.

'Now, now, ladies – enough's enough. No need for name-callin'. Jenny, why don't you fetch Magda an' I'll see you to a taxi, eh? Off you trot. We don't want to get chucked out of here, now do we – that's it, go powder your nose.' Sean patted her bottom as she left, unsteadily, to find Maggie.

I was pulling on my coat as fast as I could, desperate to get away from this fucked-up scene and find Jamie. I felt dirty and somehow, used.

'And you, you fucker – I won't fucking forget this – we were friends until you came along, bastard,' I hissed into his smiling face, into those unnatural eyes.

'I've said it before, an' I'll say it again – you shouldn't swear so much, Lily. Take a leaf outta Jenny's book – always the lady. I s'pect Jamie's waitin' outside – tell her not to make a mountain out of a molehill, now – it was just a bit of harmless fun, a bit of flirtin' never hurt anyone. Everyone had a bit too much to drink, I expect – it'll all be different in the morning.'

I nearly laughed. Sean never drank alcohol. He'd known exactly what he'd been doing and he'd enjoyed himself immensely. We never spoke to Jenny again. I saw Maggie a couple of times, and Bloke, but it wasn't the same – somehow or another, they blamed Jamie for bringing Sean into

216

our circle. Not that they'd say so straight out, but you could tell. When I told Ben the next night, she just shivered and said something about looking into the abyss, which I didn't understand – it was something philosophical, I imagine.

But it was depressing – really depressing. I thought Jamie'd be bound to split up with him now. Yeah, like – how wrong can you be? It was becoming a dreadful routine – he'd do something crap, she'd forgive him because he was so 'mixed-up' and he 'didn't mean it'. If it was a big row and he thought he was losing, he'd say how much he needed her and (yuck) *cry*. This was presented as evidence of his sensitivity. I blamed his contact lenses, personally.

Time rolled on and we acquired neighbours. We'd really hoped the nice young black couple who came a couple of times to look at next door would move in. But no, we got the White Trash Family. They looked like they'd been sponsored by Netto. The day they moved in, the husband came round and knocked loudly on our front door. I answered it – thank God it wasn't Mojo.

'Oh, hi!' I said cheerfully, trying to ignore the red face, a-dog-bit-my-hair-off barbering, Liverpool FC shirt and stripe-leg nylon joggers. Don't judge a book by its cover, is my motto. Even if it appears to be *Rednecks Are People, Too!* by Fuckwit and Braindead.

'Now look. I just moved in 'ere, like, an' I wanna

be clear straight off, I don't hold wi' weirdos. Any fuckin' carryin' on, noise or whatever, an' I'll 'ave the cops on yer pronto. I 'ave a wife an' babby to consider, so that's that, right?' His lumpy face was flushed with the effort of this speech and he looked the dead spit of the crappy British Bulldog tattoo on his meaty forearm.

'Sure, mate, sure. No probs. Er, welcome to the neighbourhood.'

'Don't get fuckin' clever wi' me. I know my rights – I'll 'ave the coppers on yer, fust sign of trouble. Don't you fergit it, neither.'

'Right, I've got it. Well, ta-ra, then.' I shut the door and leant against it, giggling. I suppose I should have felt threatened, but the sight of him marking his territory like a ginger chimp just made me hoot. Goings-on. Weirdos. Oh my God – wait till he really got to know us, he'd have apoplexy.

I told the others about this encounter and Jamie and Mojo just sighed but Sean was all for goin' round there and 'sorting him out'. Yawn.

A few days later I was in the backyard doing something or other and I saw the new Her-Next-Door in their yard with a large, turnip-headed baby engulfed in pastel acrylic knit clasped in her skinny arms. Christ, it was an ugly kid.

'Hiya!' I said, and waved.

She looked around furtively and then hurried over to the wall that divided us.

''Ello,' she said breathlessly. ''Ere, I'm dead glad I seen yer – look, I know 'ow as our Gary give you a 'ard time, like. Now, see, 'e don't mean owt by it, love. 'Is bark's wuss than 'is bite, like. It's jus' that 'e's very protective of me an' Charlene here, on account of 'im not 'avin' a fambly of 'is own, like.' She dropped her voice conspiratorially. 'Children's 'Ome, y'see – 'e jus' wants the best for us. Don't mind 'im, lovie, 'e'll settle down. Oh, I'm Reena, by the way, an' this is my little darlin', Charlene – pleased ter meetcha.' She smiled beatifically and jiggled the baby who drooled attractively.

'What a lovely babby,' I lied. She beamed with pleasure. 'I'm Lily, an' the others are Jamie, the tall lass, an' Mojo, the . . .' I was stuck for words.

'Ooh, I seen 'er, int she *bee-yootifull* – that Asian lass. Jus' like a film star! I says to Gary, you can tell she's a real lady, such a way about 'er! I int a racialist, me. No – I think how as we're all 'uman bein's, int we? An' your friend, well, lovely clothes – she a model or summat?'

I was lost for words, honest. I nodded – well, what would you have done? We smiled at each other, genuinely pleased to have met, then she cocked an ear towards the house and scurried off. I went in to tell our 'model' to ring *Vogue*, his time had come.

CHAPTER 25

Things just went on and on more or less the same; it was weird, the dreadful *normality* of the situation. Once or twice Mojo and I discussed moving out, getting somewhere together perhaps, but our hearts weren't in it, to be honest. We kept on thinking that after the next row, Sean would just piss off and not come back. I mean, he was always going off and not letting on where he was – it drove Jamie frantic. She began to get funny about going to gigs if he'd done one of his runners; in case he came back and she wasn't there, I suppose. I'd like to make myself out to be really caring and nice and say I tried to talk to her about things, but hey, it'd be a lie. I just wanted it all to be over and our lives to return to normal.

But she talked to me sometimes. He had her totally under his thumb – it was as if he was some kind of predator and she was his prey. He fed all her insecurities about her looks, her age, her intelligence – and then said, but to *him*, she was beautiful, timeless, lovable. To him, mind you, not to anyone else. He'd imply (I gathered this from the way she put things – I'm not a mind reader) no one else would tolerate her and that he was the only person who really cared about her welfare – who wasn't trying to get anything from her. He, of course, being young, handsome and in demand, could have any woman he chose – and he chose *her*, more, *needed* her. She was immensely flattered by this and it pressed all her loyalty buttons. She wouldn't hear a word against him.

The weeks turned into months and soon it was Glastonbury time again. Sean was not impressed by the idea of her going off to some 'bloody hippie festival' and leaving him behind. Not that he actually wanted to go or anything, he just wanted to stop her going, to exercise his will. He never bothered coming to her shows – he'd been to one and frankly, I think it embarrassed him – he notoriously had no sense of humour. Glastonbury to him – like a lot of other 'normal' people – meant a three-day orgy of drugs, nudity, shagging and 'goings-on'. He didn't want his woman outta control for five minutes, never mind three or four whole *days*. He went on and on and on about her not going, not *leaving* him, like she was off for a year or something. He tried every trick in the book – sulking, silences, crying (I heard him from the corridor outside her room, crying and whining like a child – what a wanker) and vanishing for days on end. But for once, Jamie was obdurate. This was her treat, her little escape from reality, if you like. She met other performers there, friends she'd made in the business, she enjoyed it. I could hear her trying to reason with him, saying it would only be a little while, and he went off with his mates for longer jaunts than this would be. The more she resisted him, the more he was determined she wasn't going. I, on the other hand, was determined she was going – that *we* were going. She had a good rep at the festival and it brought us a lot of other gigs – it was important, special.

Then one evening, it all exploded. It was about eight o'clock and they had gone up to Jamie's room to talk about 'things'. It developed into a belting, no-holds-barred screamer of a row. The language was dreadful. I was on tenterhooks waiting for Gary-next-door to knock furiously on the front door or the plods to appear. Then I heard Jamie's door crash shut and I came into the hallway in time to see Sean thumping down the stairs with a face like thunder.

Little Moley was on the third step from the bottom. When she heard the thud of Sean's boots she panicked and froze. In the same split second I ran to pick her up, he kicked her squarely in the ribs really hard and sent her flying into the front door. She bounced off the wood like a rag doll and skittered off, screaming in pain.

Without thinking, I flung myself at him in a blind rage at his cruelty. The next thing I knew, he had me up against the wall by my throat and his furious, burning white face was thrust into mine, its features contorted into a gargoyle of rage. I could smell the damp muskiness of his breath; see his perfect white

222

teeth bared in a grimace as he pushed his muzzle towards me. Like an animal, like a beast. He reeked of sweat and cheap deodorant.

And then something bizarre and, to me, intensely shaming happened. I realized that he was not only charged with a terrible violence – the violence I'd seen before that night in the kitchen, but also with intense sexual excitement. I don't know how I knew, only his hand was touching me, holding my neck, but I knew. It was like a chemical fume rising from him, it caught in my throat. And, oh my God, *I felt my body respond.*

It was as if my mind and my body were, for an instant, wholly separate. My mind was revolted by him, but not my body – my nipples hardened, my arms and legs got quivery and hot. I wanted to throw up, and at the same time, to kiss his swollen, perfect mouth.

He knew it.

'Oh no, girlie, no – it's not for *you*, not for the likes of *you*,' he breathed into my face.

Then he flung me aside. As I slid to the floor, he crashed out of the door and I heard him racket off in his crappy old blue van.

I could hear Jamie crying but I couldn't move. I felt filthy, defiled. How could I have felt like that about a man I despised? All right, I admit he was handsome, really handsome, and had a fantastic body – but for Christ's sake, I hated him. I was revolted with myself and totally confused. Did this mean that I secretly fancied him or something?

What was *that* saying? Something about love and hate being two sides of the same coin? It couldn't be true, I was a rational, thinking person, not some sort of nympho driven by animal instincts.

But that's what it had been like. Animal. He'd looked like an animal almost, with those pale crystal wolf's eyes and his blunt, brute's face. It had been the smell of him, that powerful fleshy, hot smell and the strange musky-sweet odour of his breath. I'd responded like a creature, like some sort of fucking *bitch*.

As this ran through my mind in a torrent, I heard someone banging furiously on the door. Picking myself up wearily, I opened it, knowing it would be Gary-next-door.

'Right. That's the last fuckin' time. I fuckin' warned you lot. Any fuckin' more an' it's the coppers. I won't 'ave my –'

He stopped dead. I suppose he must have seen my face.

'Christ, you OK? 'As that bastard 'urt you? You look fuckin' awful – 'ere shall I fetch Reena? Look I didn't mean ter upset yer, like, I were just pissed off – look, let me get Reen . . .'

'No, no – it's OK. Sorry, Gary, I'm really sorry. Oh Christ, man, I fuckin' hate it too, I'm sorry, I . . .'

'Nay, never mind, love, fergit it, like . . . fuck, though, if that fucker's done owt to yer, look, we can get the coppers on 'im – you got rights, y'know, same as anyone. An' the other lasses, an' all. He's no good that 'un, no fuckin' good, I tell yer.'

I laughed hysterically. 'Yeah, yeah, I'm with you on that one. Look, I'm really sorry, I'll try an' . . . well, I don't know but I'll try summat to sort it all out.'

He looked all pink and confused; but not half as confused as I was.

After I shut the door, I thought, Fuck! Where's Moley? I ran into the kitchen but all I found were some little wet paw-prints like damp flowers on her newspaper. I went upstairs and roused Jamie to help me search, ignoring her apologies for Sean and her tears. Hurting people was one thing, hurting animals was quite another. This time he really had gone too far. I searched the house and the surrounds with a feverish intensity which I knew was all the more focused because I didn't want to think about what had happened between Sean and me. Even going into the abandoned scrapyard and poking about in the weeds and bits of metal calling for Moles gave me the heebie-jeebies; last time I'd paid any mind to the place had been the night of the party, when Sean had been nosying around in there. I half expected to find Moley dead amongst the trash littering the ground – the whole place seemed to reek of Sean somehow, of the way he kind of invaded places and infected them with his nastiness. I felt dirty, filthy with that indefinable muckiness – what had happened between Sean an' me – oh, I didn't even want there to be a 'between' Sean and me. I wanted him to vanish, die, fuck off. I wanted not to have even *dreamed* that horrible, beast-like attraction could have existed in my ordered life.

When Jamie tapped me on the shoulder I nearly had heart failure – I just wanted to get out of the ratty, choked yard and breathe fresher air. I couldn't get rid of the creepy feeling Sean was watching us all the time we were in that place, like he'd watched the house the night he first came. I knew it was impossible, but that's how he made me feel – he sort of got into your mind, like a stain, or a shadow.

We searched all evening and into the night. Even Mojo helped when he got home, flapping through the dusk in his black coat like a camp bat.

We never found her, and she never came home. I still miss the little scrap. I know it's pitiful in view of all the other things that happened, but Sean's brutally kicking that little animal with no more thought than if she'd been a football; the sheer, thoughtless cruelty of it, always makes me shiver.

Sean stayed away until after we got back from Glastonbury – no Cornish holiday for us that year, well, even if Her Nibs had wanted to, my heart wasn't in it. I couldn't tell her what had happened, and it lay heavy in me making a barrier between us. I decided to go with Ma and Pa to the Lakes for a week, it was their annual blow-out, bless 'em. All yo-ho up mountains and cream teas. I was buffing up my hiking boots when Jamie's pager bleeped. If I'd had the fucking boots on my heart would have been in 'em.

I left for Ambleside on the Sunday night; he turned up again on the Monday.

I rang Mojo on his mobile a couple of times, but he only said the atmosphere was terrible and Sean was even more difficult and tedious than usual – very jumpy and irritable, doing things like changing channels on the telly with the remote when the others were watching a programme, and hanging around unwashed and unshaven eating them out of house and home. Mojo was seriously looking for somewhere else to live now, and I felt very, very sad at the prospect of losing him. I felt that if he moved out, I'd never see him again. I don't know why, but I suppose it was because we were so different, really. He'd go off with Someone and have a glam, fabby lifestyle or something. I'd be stuck in Bradford with a disintegrating friendship and an unrequited love. Boo-hoo. Oh, *bollocks* to it.

I also felt secretly that perhaps Sean's behaviour was caused by what had happened that evening. What had happened between us. It had been so strange – I thought it had tipped his balance, what there was of it. I seriously considered just packing my stuff and leaving before I had to deal with him again. In the end, I thought, I'll go back to sort my stuff out, and if Sean tries anything – *says* anything even, I'm off.

★   ★   ★

When I got back I saw Mojo had been right. Sean was a right mess. Still, he showed no interest in bringing up what had happened and after a while I thought – he's just forgotten, it means nothing to him, just like poor Moley meant nothing to him. I felt a mixture of relief and, irrationally, anger at being so utterly without meaning to someone – like a ghost or a servant.

He just slormed around like a proper slob. Jamie indicated their 'problem' was back with a vengeance and put all his behaviour down to that. When I taxed her with the Moley thing, she insisted Moles would be back any time and that Sean was mortified about what he'd done. Yeah, right.

We did a couple of bread-and-butter gigs and looked forward to the autumn season. The newspapers were full of another attack by the new Ripper – he'd gone for a prostitute but she'd got away – cut to bits, poor cow. Naz, our police leak, said a loving couple, or another whore and her punter, had disturbed the bastard just as he was about to kill the girl. He said his mate reckoned she'd be able to give a description and everything. We felt relieved, like every woman in town – sorry for the lass, but relieved that the plods would catch the fella now.

How wrong we were.

CHAPTER 26

We went off to the South Coast to do a couple of gigs, and Jamie perked up a bit as the sea air worked its magic. We even had a serious talk in our room after the Pompey gig, and I really felt we'd made some kind of headway. She actually admitted that his treatment of Moley had changed something in her attitude towards Sean, that she felt she ought to seriously consider whether they had a future together.

But she talked like an addict; it was all 'I would if I could', and 'I can handle it, just give me time'. I was more hopeful, though, much more. It was the first time she'd ever even *thought* of jacking him in. It was a kind of progress. I mean, she'd never jacked any of the others in, ever – they'd always dumped her.

I was so excited I phoned Moj from the bathroom – but I just got the *This Vodaphone may be turned off* business. I tried a few more times and got the same baloney. Yeah, like, I bet he was off drinking champagne and smoking opium in a swanky hotel somewhere, the posh git. Lucky git, in view of our 'quaint' B & B.

On the way home, we stopped at Leicester Forest for a cuppa and a bun. Jamie went to get the Sunday papers and came rushing excitedly into the café.

'Wow! Look at *this*!' She was waving a newspaper around and pointing at the headline.

It said: *Night Creeper Exclusive – Victim Tells Her Horrifying Story.*

'It's that lass the new Ripper got – except they're calling him the "Night Creeper" 'cos he *creeps* up on 'em – urgh! She's sold her story, I bet she got a packet an' I bet the coppers are *livid*! 'Ere, look, middle-page spread, oo-er!'

'Don't be so morbid – 'ere, give it us, then.'

There was a full-colour pic of the girl, Tina Ferris, sitting up in a hospital bed, her head and face swathed in bandages and plasters, clutching a big fluffy teddy. She was obviously very young and her huge dark eyes, ringed with bruises, looked vulnerable and scared.

The text was the usual appalling crap these fuckers churn out; I don't know how they live with themselves, I really don't. Jamie read it out to me in the car as we drove. It was pretty standard stuff – for a time bomb.

You see, after the usual: *Fragile victim Tina fought bravely for her life that dark night in Bradford when Britain's most terrifying serial killer crept up behind her as she waited for a bus in the city's notorious red-light area of Thornton Road . . . pretty teenager Tina was viciously assaulted by the evil killer now known as the Night Creeper . . . sobbing as she clutched her favourite teddy, Tina brokenly whispered the story of her nightmare – this reporter could barely hold back the tears as she described the horror of the slashing blade that has left her scarred for life . . .*

Well, after all that came the clincher.

Tina, now able to remember most of her terrible ordeal, describes the Beast, whose frenzied attack makes her Victim Number Four of the insane killer, as a tall, muscular black man with a husky voice and hideously strong hands. His dark, burning eyes will haunt her dreams forever as will the memory of the old-style cutthroat razor that he wielded. Tina broke down as she described how he seemed to appear out of the night like a terrifying shadow, dragging her into an alley where he slashed at her viciously. He only dropped her blood-soaked wounded body and fled in a sinister black van when a loving couple in search of privacy disturbed him in mid-attack. 'I'd be dead now, if it weren't for them,' sobbed the once bubbly and attractive Tina . . .

A black man. God alone knew what would be the result of that tidbit in a multicultural city like Bradford. Sure, generally it was cool racially – but there's always the racist tossers who'd leap on something like this.

I suppose I half hoped that the media would be sensible and not sensationalize all this. But that was naive – they fell on that poor, fucked-up little girl like a pack of hyenas on a dead zebra. Talk about a feeding frenzy – there was barely time to catch

231

your breath before Tina Ferris was 'exposed' as a drug addict, a teenage prostitute and the daughter of a prostitute.

Mind you, it depended on what paper you read on how it was presented. The 'quality' press did long, postmodern angsty pieces with moody, black-and-white pics of shattered, ex-industrial landscapes. Stuff like: *Sometimes, Tina seemed like a flower broken on the savage wheel of the encroaching millennium – at others, like the canny, streetwise survivor she must surely be. Her pale, ruined face, with its cruel new contours no longer the ticket to the drugs her body craves. The archetypal 'dark man' of all our modern nightmares carved his fury on her delicate, corrupted beauty. And what was she, this modern Lolita, robbed of her childhood to feed the appetites of men who will pay to plunder innocence? A victim, yes – but a victim of a society in meltdown. Now Tina must pay for all our sins, she must live with our apathy and our cowardice . . .*

The gutter press, naturally, had a field day. Only the original paper who first bought the story still defended Tina as a misunderstood victimized little girl, and ran 'interviews' with her mother who was furious at being called a whore and accusations that she had put her own child on the game aged thirteen – despite the fact it was true. The rest went ballistic with the racial angle in barely disguised rants against immigration and integration.

But I'm getting ahead of myself. When we got home that first Sunday we had other things to concern us. Firstly, Sean had been in a fight that Saturday night and was a mess. He had a black eye and the furrowed marks of scratches on the side of his neck, plus various bruises and scrapes. He was in a monster bad temper, railing about the type of scum who frequent city-centre bars and how a decent bloke couldn't go for a quiet pint without being set on by thugs, etc., etc. He threw in a few bits about how he'd never have bothered going out if *his girlfriend* hadn't been off gallivanting round the country. Jamie flew to him as if he was a wounded soldier and never even noticed that he'd not lifted a finger in the house since we'd been gone, and it was a stinky tip of greasy old washing-up and those rolls of dust and gritty fluff my ma calls 'slut's wool'. While I tried to tidy up, Sean regaled us with the details of his battle, and how only his paramilitary survival skills had gotten him out of a deadly situation. The size and number of his assailants increased as the tale progressed until you'd think he'd tackled the fucking All Blacks single-handed and won. Wah!

I ignored him and his injuries as best I could and wrestled fruitlessly with the dying Hoover which insisted on vomiting and fainting if you so much as plugged it in. It had the soul of an hysterical consumptive, that appliance.

As I coaxed it upstairs, I noticed Mojo's door was open, which was unusual, and my first thought was – that bloody Sean's been rummaging around in Moj's room while he's out. I went to shut it and

233

looking in, saw that it was totally, totally cleaned out. Nothing was left. Not his precious kilim rug, not the saris he draped over the window, not a scarf, string of beads or broken earring. The room looked as if had been *stripped*. All that remained of Mojo was a strong odour of Poison and a faint dusting of Chanel face powder. It was obvious Mojo had moved out. In a *big* way.

I was gutted. How could he have just gone without a word? I went in and searched for a note – nothing. *Nada*. Nowt. I ran downstairs and burst into the living room, where Sean and Jamie were playing Nurses and Patients.

'Sean, where's Mojo?' I blurted out.

'How the fuck should I know?' He sounded defensive to me. Had he rowed with Mojo once too often and finally driven him away? As he turned his discoloured face to mine, I again felt that disquieting ambivalence towards him; a shiver, like someone walking over my grave. I gritted my teeth and stared him out.

'Well, you've been here all weekend and Mojo was home when we left – so where is he?'

Jamie interrupted us. 'What's all this – what about Mojo? What's happened?'

'His room's totally empty – looks like he's gone. Ask Sergeant fuckin' Fury here what's happened, why don't you? Mojo wouldn't leave without a word, he just wouldn't.'

Sean's jaw started working with anger and he looked away from me, staring instead at the telly which was flickering away with the sound muted.

'I don't fuckin' see why it's got owt to do wi' me. Don't fuckin' blame *me* because that fuckin' queer's fucked off. Good fuckin' riddance, in my opinion.'

Jamie flinched. 'Sean! Don't . . . oh, pack it in, Sean. Don't talk that way about Mojo, he's our friend; it's not like him to sod off without a word . . .'

'Oh yeah? Some fuckin' friend who fucks off without a fuckin' word or any fuckin' rent money – oh yeah, great mates you got, yer?' He looked at me meaningfully. I dead-eyed him back. Come on, you fucker, I thought, just you come on then.

But he dropped his gaze again and whined to Jamie instead. 'Why blame me? It int my fault – he never liked me anyways, too straight for him, I suppose. Well, I can't help that, can I? I can't help being a proper man, it's the way I am. Look, love, he's probably gotten that . . . that boyfriend of his to get him some posh flat somewhere, eh? I mean, that's life, int it? Rich types don't bother with the likes of us when the chips are down, do they?'

Rich folks, eh? That was weird – in fact, it was always weird the way he made himself out so poor when he had a good job repping for Raptor Sports – and the firm's van to use all the time. And his family were loaded, everyone knew that. Why did he want to make himself out so skint? But that was him all over, never tell the truth if you can tell a lie. Yeah, and he believed every word of his fibs as well, you could tell. It was almost as if he literally couldn't tell the difference between true and false. If he'd given himself that black eye and those scratches as a bid for sympathy, I for one wouldn't have been a tiny bit surprised. No-siree-bob. Wanker. And, he was really pissed off about something, you could tell – I mean, it was probably his bit of a brawl, but whatever it was that was irritating him made him swear much more than usual. He only did that when he was really cross – usually he prided himself on being above using 'language'. Naturally, that made me swear like a trooper round him. Small revenges, but hey – they're the best.

Mojo gone, though – I couldn't believe he'd go without a word like that. I mean, I know he'd talked about leaving, we both had, but just to sod off like that – it wasn't like him. And the rent thing – he was always very free with his cash – almost princely in his dislike of money. He'd never dap us for the rent, never. Oh Mojo, I thought, where *are* you?

He'd ring or something, I thought. I tried his mobile over and over but it was dead, turned off. Never mind, he'd get in touch. Probably on a cruise round the Greek Islands with Someone, or sunning in Acapulco, knowing him. He would get in touch when he got back, I was sure of it.

But the time passed, filled up with the mounting revelations in the Night Creeper case, and no Mojo. Nothing. Eventually I thought – well, you just can't tell with people, can you? Even

Reena-next-door asked after him and out of guilt, I told her Mojo was not a girl, really. She was *thrilled*.

'Oooh, I read about them Drag Queens in a mag – well, no wonder she, whoops, 'e, were so bee-yootifull an' like a film star – they go in for that, they do, you know – *glamour* – it were all in the mag, wi' pictures an' everythin'.' She dropped her voice breathlessly, like she always did when she was excited, and hugged Charlene until the baby squeaked. 'Surgery, they have, it said. False boobs an' everythin'. It said they was more like a woman than a woman, if you see what I mean. An' to think, 'e was livin' next door to me – an' so gor-ge-ous. Oh, I 'ope 'e comes back, d'you think 'e will?'

I said I didn't know, and pondered on the enigma that was Reena with her massive tolerance of race and sexuality and her besotted fascination with the glamour and magic of 'celebrity' lives. I patted Charlene's downy, pointed head and sighed. At least Reena wasn't infected with the Night Creeper virus that was sweeping town.

Things were starting to get out of hand about that. The low fever of racism that usually never really peaked in Bradford was now increasing, point by point, as the papers whipped up the frenzy. Each ethnic group that could conceivably be called 'black' was issuing statements of denial like confetti. Tempers were fraying as Christmas approached and the usual gangs of piss-drunk white casuals in their 'smart' pastel shirts and

Armani jeans that roamed the streets at closing time had a new grievance to air.

Consequently, black and Asian lads, wound up and furious, banded together in their separate gangs, too. And each ethnic group blamed the other for the whole shebang. No one was immune. There was no reason, and no solidarity. As a biracial I felt like shit, thoroughly disliking both sides for being stupid, violent and so easily baited by Fleet Street. As a woman, I hated the bull-headed blokiness of it; the testosterone escalation. What about the Night Creeper's victims? What about those poor women? Everyone blamed *them* for being whores and 'dragging Bradford's name in the mud' (pull-ease!). Sara Evans's family gave countless statements separating themselves and their dead girl from the other victims.

Tina Ferris went on television. She had an agent, apparently. I saw it – she was hopped up to her eyeballs and dressed like a Spice Girl in a pink mini-suit and white platforms. Even with heavy make-up, her triangular little fox-face was a mess, most of it still splattered with black stitches and plastered. The *caring, sympathetic* Asian bloke who interviewed her *in depth*, had obviously been chosen to show the telly wasn't biased – if you shut your eyes he sounded like every other middle-class London telly-journo. He *could* have been more patronizing but I don't see how. Tina didn't seem to know quite where she was and mumbled stock phrases that stank of coaching. Sickening. The papers loved it all and interviewed both sides as town geared up for a Race-War Yuletide Spectacular.

Even Naz at the shop was jumpy. When I went in for some coriander and a bag of apples, he wasn't his usual gossipy self at all. I was reduced to making small talk about the cold, damp weather. I saw why he was so quiet when a white woman came in for a loaf of bread. She practically flung the money on his counter and stumped out muttering something that sounded suspiciously like 'bloody niggers'. I felt adrenaline leap in my blood like a hit. Naz stood miserably staring out of the window.

'Naz, what's all that about, man? Tell me it's not this stupid Creeper business, it's not, is it?'

He nodded unhappily. 'You know how it is, lovie. All this stuff int papers an' they are all thinking oh, it's me, or me mates or anyone who int white, like. It's gettin' bad for us here. My mate – him in the police, like – he says they shout stuff at him like 'bloody nigger cop' an' worse. Says they go on about him not wantin' to catch one of his own, like. But that girl, she didn't say he was Asian, did she? Or West Indian – just black. Could be anyone. My wife, she won't go out the house no more, nor my sisters an' me mam, neither.'

'Does your mate in the police think they'll get him, like?'

'Dunno. Says there's stuff don't match up with what that girl said, like. He says they don't trust 'er, like, 'cos she takes drugs an' that. Not reliable, he says. He thinks he's goin' to leave the cops anyways, after all this. Says it's not the place for an Asian lad; but I says, we gotta do these things if we live here, know what I mean? But he don't know what to do.' Naz shook his head sorrowfully and packed my stuff in a stripy plastic carrier.

'Look, Naz, if anythin' – well, if anythin' happens, like, we're with you, y'know. I mean, we think it's all crap, too, an' that.'

'Thanks, lovie.' He paused, and looked at me seriously. The shop was empty, but he looked round anyway. It was weird – he looked suddenly much older and not like cheery Naz at all. I found I was holding my breath.

'Lovie, you been looking for Mohammed, int you?'

For a moment, I didn't know who he meant – then it flashed on me, *Mojo*.

'Naz, d'you know where he is? Is he all right, what . . .'

Naz held up his hand and I stopped. 'I know Mohammed. We all know him an' his family. Lovie, he says, be careful; he says, he'll phone you on your mobile, maybe today, maybe tomorrow – sometime. But he says, *be careful.*'

'What – what . . .'

'That's it, you gotta wait. Now, 'ere, you have this bit of sugar cane, it's nice an' sweet.'

And I couldn't get anything else out of him for love or money. I shot home to Jamie through the thickening mist and nearly came a cropper on a

240

swathe of decaying leaves rotting sweetly on the corner. Panting like an old woman, I spilled the beans. We could *not* figure it out. Why would he call me an' not her? We ate potato curry that night and the house was thick with the scent of Garam Masala and the spicy green bite of the coriander.

Later on (this was a blessed Sean-free night as he was apparently delivering an order to Manchester for the firm and would stop over – with a 'mate' – yeah, right) we went over and over what Naz could have meant and what could have happened to Mojo. I could see Jamie was puzzled and a bit hurt by the idea that Mojo would contact me, and not her. I was a bit mystified, too – but as I said, I was the one with the mobile, and it was probably just that.

Jamie was very sweet that night. I mean, she could be a very sweet and loving person, as I've said – it was just that recently, all that had been expended on Sean. I realized how much I'd missed her company, just the two of us chattin' away like old times. Brewing endless pots of tea, and making plans for the future.

But even so, I felt a kind of difference in her that I hadn't noticed before. It was a sort of, well, I don't know – a kind of stillness, maybe. Or melancholy. As if some of that great fire had gone out. She'd even taken out the horrible gold creoles Sean had given her and put her old piercing rings back in. She just looked *changed*, somehow. To be honest, I was minded of that silly horoscope

– the bit about a 'great fatality' hanging over her. She seemed like a person accepting a terrible fate. I remember thinking – this is what suicides must be like before they let go finally. OK, that was a bit overdramatic, but that's how I felt at the time and I vowed to keep an eye on her and to mention it to Ben as well.

We got on so well, though, I was almost tempted to confess the awfulness that happened between Sean and I. But I just couldn't. I still didn't want to think about it myself. Sure, she might have thought differently about him after hearing that – but she would have thought differently about me, too. I was too much of a coward for that.

Instead, we talked about Moley, her little habits, her pointy velvet face, how lovable she was – had been. We wished she'd come home, we missed her so much. But that was a quicksand topic – after all, it was Sean's fault she'd gone – he'd hurt her. The conversation faltered.

The telly wittered inanely, and Jamie lay back on the old sofa, propped up on her favourite embroidered cushions – the ones Mojo had given her a couple of Christmases ago – and cradled the teacup in her long hands. There was a faint scent of sandalwood and she was wrapped in an enormous old black 'baggie' dress we'd made years ago, and which she now relaxed in. Her nails were lacquered turquoise, and it all reminded me, with a little stab, of the day we'd met.

'Lil,' she said gently.

'Yes, babby? What?'

'Lily, I'm in a mess, aren't I? I mean, like, more than usual – you know. I know I am, you know – really. I know he's messin' me up – worse, I know he's messin' us up, isn't he? Or is it me? Is it all my fault?' She paused and squinted at me over her reading specs, her grey eyes direct and guileless. 'You want to move out, don't you – like Mojo.'

As usual, she just knew what I was thinking. I felt my cheeks grow hot and I looked down.

'Honey – it's just, well, it's – I – I don't know, bab. I just feel like you don't need me any more, that I can't help you any more – oh, Jamie, please, please, get rid of him, please. We all feel the same, well, me and Ben and Lonnie, anyways. It's just the likes of that cow Jenny who think he's great, an' look what happened. I'm sorry, but he's driving everyone away – he's making you so fuckin' unhappy I can't bear it, I can't – an' neither could Moj.'

'Could you stay, d'you think – just a bit longer, just a bit? Lily, I'll try – I wanna try; I feel real strange these days, like this is *my* winter, not just the . . . weather winter, if you see what I mean. Oh Lil, I'm afraid, but I don't know what of exactly. I don't want to lay this on you – but, he's so . . . cruel. Everyday I ask myself why I put up with it, and everyday I think, no more, really. Like, he doesn't hit me or anything, but he . . . it's horrible, just – horrible. Oh, God, Lil, I don't think you could go further down than I've gone. But it's so fucked-up, it's, well, when I try to leave him he falls apart, he's like a child – he cries and begs me not to leave him like everyone else has. I know bad things happened to him as a kiddie – I don't know what, but I know something bad happened. An' – I've been there, I know what it's like so – it just gets me every time and I give in to him again. An' it's the impotence thing, an' . . . well, other stuff. He's such a mess, in his head. Christ, all I wanted when I was a kiddie was to be good-lookin' – I thought if you were good-lookin' everything just fell into place for you. But look at him – all it's gotten him is pain and bein' fucked-up. I can't help it, I still feel sorry for him, but . . . I don't know if I love him any more, or really, if I ever did. I don't think I know what love is, romantic love, that sort of love. I know I love you guys, though, I really, really do. I don't want to lose my friends – lose you – no way. Let's get through Christmas an' I'll get rid, I swear. It's not long – what? A couple of weeks? Gabriel will be home soon, he'll help. Sean won't tackle Gabe. Lily, we'll move if we have to. Sean will just go back to Lisa, I bet that's where he goes half the time anyways – he lets on he does and somehow, I don't care any more, I just don't care. He only does it to fuck my head up even more. Lily, I love you – you're more than family to me, we're like blood. No bloke's worth losin' my friends for – I won't let it happen.'

I was speechless, as usual. I knew I'd stay – she needed me, she hadn't given up on us – on her buddies. We hugged wordlessly, then I made popcorn and we ate it with honey and watched a crappy true-life drama.

It would all be all right. Gabe was coming home and me an' Her Nibs were still sisters.

The stars outside twinkled frostily through my skylight that night as I lay in my little bed. The mist had gone and the sky was velvety and deep; just those sparkling diamonds flickering. I fell asleep trying to find Orion. It would all be OK; I knew it.

CHAPTER 27

Christmas came and went in the usual way; it hardly seemed any time at all since the last one. I waited to hear from Mojo, but no word came and I quizzed Naz to no avail – he just said Mojo would get in touch. He wouldn't even tell me anything about how he knew Moj, only that everyone knew the Iqbals. It made me think of *The Godfather*, only no one was making me any offers I couldn't refuse . . . no horses' heads in my little truckle bed, thank God.

Gabe came home and despite being knackered from touring with what he called 'a bunch of needle-dicked fuckwits', the three of us went for rambles over Baildon Moor and had tea at Betty's in Ilkley, which is our totally favourite place in the world. Sean hated seeing us all so happy – he sulked, ranted and was horribly irritable by turns. OK, I didn't try to hide my enjoyment of our days out together from him – why the fuck should I? *I* wasn't goin' out with him and with any luck, neither would Jamie be soon. He just didn't seem to get the hint though. When he wasn't glooming about, he was in the cellar pumping iron until he dropped – he practically lived down there. I took to calling him the Cellar Dweller. He would come upstairs with all the veins standing out like hosepipes on his arms and dripping with sweat. I avoided him where possible – the smell of him turned my stomach. He knew, too – I think it gave him a nasty little kick because he'd always try and stand a bit too close – invading my space, like. I'd move away and he'd sort of snicker in a childish way. The thing that had happened lay unspoken between us and he must have twigged I hadn't told anyone. Although it meant nothing to him personally, I knew he enjoyed the sense of control over someone it gave him.

As to the Festive Season – hah! He didn't get anyone any presents; just packed his fuckin' Adidas bag and vanished without a word on Christmas Eve. I thought Jamie would be gutted, but she seemed full of a new, quiet determination to have done with him. She was very gentle at this time, buying a lovely toy big-foot rabbit for Charlene, and consequently winning the undying love of Reena and the grudging respect of Gary. We even babysat the Blessed Turnip (as we called Charlene), when Reena and Gary went to a New Year's Eve do at Gary's works. We just didn't seem to fancy going out in town or anything – we wanted to be quiet, and cocoon. It was sweet, and we got happily broody – until it was nappy-changing time.

Then on January the first, the world got the news

that the Night Creeper had struck again. Some start to the New Year, all right. Town went up like dry tinder – there were running battles up the Lane and the police had emergency meetings with community and religious leaders, trying to calm stuff down. There was a massive protest outside the central police station and a candlelight vigil for the latest victim, a student from the university, Lucy Allbright.

I cannot describe the way the media exploded – if we all thought it had been bad before, it was nothing to what went off after Lucy died. One paper offered a £50,000 reward for information leading to the Creeper's arrest – the others ran stories about the trouble in town and how Bradford was a *City In Meltdown – Riot-Torn Bradford Mourns Latest Victim*. The coppers were doing their tits trying to control things and I'd have given a week's wages to be a fly on the wall at Police HQ every morning when the papers came out.

Lucy Allbright had been just nineteen – a first-year student on the liberal arts course 'Modular Humanities' up at the uni. It was a notorious raver's course, with a rep for being an easy ride to a degree; people did their theses on stuff like – 'Gender and Childhood – Images Of Oppression In *The Magic Roundabout*'. You should have heard Ben rant on about it. It sounded like fun to me, but I'm not a philosopher, after all.

Well, Lucy had gone to a townie club that was hosting a touring London club night 'Sanctissima'

– all hip young DJs and crap music, costing £25 to get in. Students like Lucy weren't the poor, ragged protestors of yesteryear. The papers made a great deal of her privileged Southern background and possible Ecstasy use – like the whole world and its auntie weren't gobbling gear like Smarties. Seemed the poor little cow had decided to leave early after a row with her boyfriend and had walked off in a huff to get a cab. She never made it. She was found the next morning, hacked to shreds, apparently. It had been snowing a bit, and she had been dressed in her new silver metallic mini-slip and fluffy white fun-fur coat; presents from her family. *Death Of An Angel* was one headline. *Blonde Angel Victim Number Five, Blood In The Snow* and *Tragic Angel Slaying* were others. The 'Angel' tag stuck, though. Like, everything fashionable in one murder; clubs, Ecstasy, blonde, glitter, angel, blood – it could have been designed by Gaultier.

If I sound bitter – well, yeah. Don't get me wrong, I felt more sorry than you can imagine for the reality of that little girl's dying – but the press made me vomit. Lucy Allbright was re-created from a nice, ordinary young woman – not terrifically bright by all accounts but pleasant enough – into a sacrificial victim, the Virgin Angel Of The Snows. Just to sell papers. Just for *money*.

As for the telly – well, it was a documentary-fest *par excellence*. I know for a fact they bribed kids with cans of Special Brew and cash to throw Nazi salutes and shout 'nigger', never mind interviewing absolutely anyone even slightly connected with the killings just to fill up space. And not just the British media, either – I'm talking global, here.

It was as if the whole business had touched a strange nerve somewhere – a nerve that throbbed and screamed 'black versus white'. A black man killing white girls. The Black Devil and the Blonde Angel. The ultimate taboo come to life – or death – in our backwater city. It was hateful. I hated it, it was personal. I hated seeing our normally solid – OK, maybe a bit dull but reasonably tolerant – folk whipped up by outsiders – jumping like trained poodles through the hoops of the media. Would town ever be the same again after this? I doubted it somehow. Things were changed forever; subtly, but changed.

When I was a kiddie, someone wrote in my Motto Book, 'The word is like a sped arrow, it cannot be returned.' They should tattoo that on journalists' foreheads.

Town reeked like a dry iron pan heating on the stove – the hot metallic stink of rage and hatred. Worse, of mass hysteria. Really strange things happened, even to me. Like, at one point, I had to get the bus to a client's as the motor was in the garage, and a plump, respectable older woman sat down next to me, with her shopping. I hardly noticed her until she turned to me and said in a perfectly normal voice:

'They should cut his balls off, in my opinion.'

'Sorry?'

'This Creeper chap – they should cut his balls off. String him up. One of your lot, isn't he? You should be ashamed.'

I got off the bus. My hands were shaking. For years the whole business of being biracial hadn't bothered me one bit. Now, apparently, I was black. I was the enemy. It was unbelievable.

Then the police acted – not soon enough, in my opinion. They issued a statement to the effect that 'forensic evidence' indicated the killer of Lucy Allbright was not a black man, but a fair-haired Caucasian. That this was definitely a Night Creeper killing – as it had 'certain characteristics'. So he had a 'signature', like the murderers in the thrillers we all read so avidly. Which meant all the killings were done by the same person – and that person was a white man. To me, 'forensic evidence' meant that she'd ripped a lump of his hair out, or something, and they'd found it. That's what we all thought on account of the fact we'd seen stuff on the telly about forensics. They had a piece of him. The Night Creeper was white. White. Not *black*.

No one paid a blind bit of attention. Everyone just thought the police were trying to diffuse the race thing. Even I thought that. I didn't want to, but I did.

As to the press – hey – no one was goin' to let the truth stand in the way of a good story.

The whole media went nova, baby. This was the sexiest story of the year – race, murder,

whores and angels. We're talking big bucks, right?
Right.

Everyone knew the Night Creeper now. No one seemed to be able to remember his victims' actual names. How postmodern.

CHAPTER 28

Still, like everyone we knew, we were obsessed with the Creeper too – with living in this cauldron of media attention that was so weirdly focused on our city. We talked endlessly about why this particular case so totally obsessed the press, when it wasn't even as if he'd killed that many – not like some. If Sean managed to surface from his cellar during these debates, he got very irate – said we were gossiping about something we 'knew nowt about'. The implication was that he, as Sass Bloke Extraordinaire, was obviously more clued-up than us poor, frail girlies could ever be. He would drop hints about 'fellas he knew' who 'told him things' that the press weren't privy to. Such bollocks – nearly every bloke in town claimed to be 'in-the-know' in some way or another; you couldn't ask the time of day without being treated to some fella's personal theory on the case. Naturally though, Sean wouldn't share his particular take on things with the likes of us – too shocking for our delicate sensibilities, I suppose. Doubtless he saved them for his invisible mates. If we pressed him, he'd just look smug and enigmatic then tap the side of his nose with his finger in that really tedious knowing gesture beloved of pub bores the world over. Then we'd have a rehash of his Virgin/Whore Theory – nice girls or nasty girls – with the 'nasty' girls coming out somewhere down the scale from a cockroach. I often wondered where I came on that scale of virtue – but I supposed I was under Jamie's wing as far as that went – purity by association. If we chorused that some of the victims hadn't *been* prostitutes he'd go off on one about decent blokes not being able to tell the difference these days – like that last girl, fer instance. Oh, she might have been *posh*, but staggering about lashed in that area dressed in that type of gear – well, *anyone'd* take her for a whore, wouldn't they? Natural mistake to make. Yeah, a real Man's Man, the Creeper – you know, apart from him bein' a murderer, like. Well, he didn't actually say that last bit – but you could tell he *thought* it.

I tried to believe he was just trying to wind us up – it reduced me to stuttering fury and Jamie left the room on more than one occasion – but really, like it or not, that sort of comment was far from uncommon in town. Plenty of 'hard men' thought women had gotten far too uppity of late and well – this was the price they paid. Sean's admiration for the Creeper might have been more openly expressed than was usual, but the Robin Hood element of a lone bloke against the forces of Law, Order and Feminism was definitely there. Sick fucks.

In fact, it was one evening at Ben's when we were talking about just that subject when my mobile trilled its version of 'Jingle Bells' that I hadn't altered since Christmas. I excused myself – thinking it was a call from a promoter in Canterbury about his increasingly dodgy-looking gig – and went into the kitchen.

It was Mojo. Through the crackle of bad reception I heard his dear, familiar voice:

'Lily, Lily – can you hear me? It's Mojo.'

'Yes, yes – I can hear you – oh, Mojo, where are you, what's happened, are you all right?'

'Will you meet me, darling? Can you come to Leeds tomorrow?'

He sounded strange – not at all his usual flamboyant, careless self. I juggled my client appointments furiously, thanking God we had no gigs until the weekend, and decided I could reschedule Mr Farrer for Thursday afternoon – he'd be pissed but what the fuck, he was always pissed about something. This was a friend-in-need thing; this was *Mojo*.

'Yes, yes, no problem – where, where d'you want to meet, what time . . .'

'The Montmartre, at three – will that be all right?'

'Sure, OK – Mojo, please, what's . . .'

The line went dead.

Next day the weather was stormy, clouds blooming like ink on wet paper across the leaden sky. I decided to leave the car and catch a train as parking in Leeds was horrendous and I didn't want to be late or anything. Actually, *Leeds* is horrendous, in my opinion, but then I'm from Bradford. As far as most Bradfordians are concerned, Leeds may only be six or seven miles away, but it's Sin City, The Red-Brick Metrollops, all fur coat and no knickers.

I was musing on this and other small rantings about our beloved sister city when the train lurched to a halt and we all disgorged on to the platform. It was 2.30, so I opted to empty my pea-sized bladder and rearrange my locks before trotting off through the icy, gusting wind to the Montmartre Café, a dark, faux-Parisian gaff near the great stone beehive of the Corn Exchange. The Montmartre purported to be a copy of a famous French eatery près de la Sacré Coeur, ooh la la, Folies Bergères, etc. I couldn't imagine why Mojo had chosen it, as the only time we'd ever been in there, he'd demolished it with a wit so scorching I was surprised he didn't set the sprinklers off.

When I was blasted through the doors by a particularly savage gust, I realized why. It was very dimly lit – for 'atmosphere', I imagine. Very private. The room was divided into dark wood booths down one side and rickety little tables clustered round one of those 'real' flame gas fires on the other. A few intellectual-type students played chess and read *Le Monde*, trying not to move their lips. It was totally chocker with whatnots, knick-knacks, bits-and-bobs and absolutely anything even vaguely 'French' – except letters. A languid bloke who might, or might not, actually *be* français polished a coffee-cup in a bored way behind the counter. The odour of Gitanes wafted about like incense – it was probably a type of room-spray called 'Atmosphère de France – Une Petite Boîte de Montmartre', or something.

The thought made me giggle slightly – I was feeling a bit hysterical what with all this secrecy an' stuff – I mean, talk about 'I weel say zis onlee once' – pull-ease. I fumbled for one of the bandannas I use as hankies and wiped my snotty nose, hoping my inadvertent snicker would appear to be a sneeze, when I spotted him.

He was sitting in the furthest booth, in deep shadow – I must have missed him at first glance. That was odd, too. Why hadn't he waved his usual graceful wave to signal me over? Why wasn't he doing it now? He just sat there, wearing dark glasses, in the dark. I hurried over.

The first thing I noticed was that he was dressed as a man – like, I know that sounds odd, but he had no overt female stuff on. He was wearing a beautiful black cashmere sweater with a polo neck and, from what I could see, black baggy trousers – the expensive, tailored kind, not the funky sort. No jewellery, just tiny, discreet matte silver studs in his ears. His shining hair was in a ponytail and there were those big ol' Ray-Bans on his perfect nose. Weird.

He didn't move or speak as I slid into the booth. A studenty-girl waitress bustled over, her round, freckled face rosy with admiration for this bee-you-ti-ful fella all in black that she'd already brought an espresso for. I ordered a cappuccino – Italian coffees in this imitation Petit France. Still Mojo didn't speak; in fact, he said nothing until my coffee came. I was freaked out, totally. I tried to say 'hiya' but he just minutely gestured me to be quiet. I started to get a bit cross – what was with him, for fuck's sake?

He took the Ray-Bans off. A red, angry scar snaked through his once-exquisite eyebrow, and another couple wormed their way along his lower eye socket and up to his temple. The scars distorted his eye, pulling at the tissue-thin skin; the eye itself seemed inflamed and watery as if the wind had chilled it.

I was profoundly, horribly shocked. My heart raced and bounced in my chest – I know I gasped out loud. It was like seeing a work of art vandalized, defaced. OK, I know it would be awful for anyone to be scarred, really awful – but somehow I couldn't help it – it seemed worse for Mojo. To be so perfect and then to be – ugly. Not that *I* thought he was ugly – scars don't bother me, to be honest – but I was sure that's what he must be feeling.

Suddenly, the affected dimness of the fake café seemed oppressive, frightening. I wanted daylight, bright, normal daylight. My hand trembled and I split my coffee a bit. He saw, and looked away.

258

'What – Mojo, Christ, Moj, what the fuck happened – how . . . ?' My voice sounded thin, insubstantial – I couldn't seem to make the right words come. I cursed my stupid, brain–mouth scramble.

'Lily, Lily – little Tiger Lily.' He used his old nickname for me and I felt the blood rush to my face; I reached out my hand and grasped his fingers – so thin and delicate-seeming. His hand was icy-cold.

'So, you see, I am not as I was.' A tear trickled down the gleaming curve of his cheek; was it a real tear, or his ruined eye protesting at even this faint light? I couldn't tell. He took his hand from my grasp and dabbed at the moisture with a silk hankie.

'Don't speak, my Lily – I, I . . .' He took a deep breath and sighed. 'I didn't want to do this, to tell you anything – but I must. So listen, but please, don't speak – please.'

His voice was thick with urgency and I nodded dumbly, anxiety gripping my guts. I felt cold, and nervous, my hands still shaking. I sat on them.

'You must believe what I'm going to tell you is true; it is true and I believe you and Jamie are in danger – serious danger. There is no good way to say this, no easy way, no clever way – Lily, Sean did this to me, he tried to . . . rape me; he beat me and he cut me with a broken perfume bottle. Hush, hush – don't. Just let me say it all straight out.

'It was when you were away at a show; I came

259

home and he was there. Oh, I thought – just ignore him, go to your room, smoke a little hashish, ignore him. You see, I thought he had a crush on me – oh yes, the oh-so-macho Sean, he had made – remarks. There was body language. All when you weren't around. What did he say? It doesn't matter – mostly insults. But insults, well, in my experience, insults can be more indicative than compliments, with some men. I'd had it before – the rugby player, the cricket captain, the Real Man – it always started with those insults and then – oh, that terrible, fumbling, forbidden *fucking*. Ha! Women would be so shocked if they knew just how many of those butch pin-ups were – queer. Or maybe they wouldn't, I don't know. None of us are what we seem . . . So you see, that's what I thought. Another closet case. That would account for the impotence, the rage – that refusal to admit what he was – at least, what *I* thought he was. I was so arrogant – so proud of how I'd dealt with my own sexuality. I considered him pathetic! That's how I viewed him – as pathetic. Oh, I knew he was cruel, manipulative – I often overheard the horrible things he wanted to do to Jamie – what she let him do. Our mutual bedroom wall is very thin, you know. You have the best room for peace of mind, in *that* house. Still, I had no respect for someone I thought was so basically – weak.'

I was numb with horror. Stuff had been going on in the house where I lived that I'd had no idea about – I felt stupid and oddly – *excluded*. Why hadn't

Mojo (why hadn't *Jamie*) confided in me? Didn't they rate me enough to tell me stuff? Contradictory emotions rolled inside me like the rain clouds in the sky outside – I couldn't take it all in.

Mojo lit a cigarette, flinching his ruined eye away from the smoke as it wreathed around him. I took one from his packet and lit it from his lighter – I felt sick, freezing, I couldn't have spoken if he'd wanted me to, I think.

'So when you weren't there, when he came to my room and just opened the door and lounged in the doorframe wearing nothing but those grey joggers, flexing his muscles, *showing off*; I thought – this is it – how boring. I was debating whether to give him a blowjob just to shut him up when he began to speak. I won't trouble you with what he said. It was filth. Pure filth. If filth can be *pure*. The gist of it was that it was dangerous for me to pretend to be a woman. What did I want to be a woman for anyway; women were cattle, whores, degenerate, disgusting. Fleshbags full of vileness and gross, corrupt lust. Talking seemed to excite him, he pulled down his joggers a little and took out his cock, played with it. I remember thinking rather frivolously how very small it was – what a disappointment for his ladyfriends, such a beautiful boy – such a tiny dick. I couldn't help it, I smiled – he saw it, saw the contempt on my face. God knows I was never *tactful* about stupid people . . .

'You know how strong he is. I did try to fight him, I know I hurt him a little – I'm not as frail

261

as I look – but it was no use, he just hit me and hit me until I fainted, passed out. Then – I'm sorry – he tried to – to fuck me. It wasn't – he couldn't – well, he was impotent, totally. He went mad with fury, hissing at me, blaming me – saying it was my fault he couldn't get hard. Again, he hit me over and over – I stopped struggling at all. I thought that if I don't struggle, it will be over quickly and he'll go away. He won't hurt me any more. I remember thinking the smell of Poison was terribly strong – during the struggle he'd knocked that big bottle of it I'd got for my birthday on to the floor, and it had broken. I was gagging on the fumes of it – such a violent scent. My face was on fire from being grazed on the rug. I was in terrible pain from the beating and I felt so sick, and dizzy.

'Then, it was so quick, so quick – a split second – he picked up the broken bottle and pulling my head back – God, oh God – he stuck it in my face . . . he cut me. He was laughing like a maniac – he *was* a maniac, babbling incoherently about whores, and queers and how I'd never tempt a decent man again with my filthy lies . . . Then suddenly, he became quite still – I was crying, I think, you can't imagine the pain, it was – well . . . He was quite still and calm and he touched his fingertip into the blood on my face *and licked it*. Then he said very steadily, if I told anyone, told you girls, he'd find me and kill me. That he had ways to trace anyone, contacts, something to do with the military. I don't know. My God, he was insane, rabid, like a mad dog. Just flicking from one mood to another. And his breath as he hissed in my ear, I'll never forget it – hot and stinking; I thought, this is hell, I'm dead and this is hell and he's . . . he's the devil, Shaitan . . . I can't remember anything after that, I must have passed out. When I came to, he was gone.

'Oh, Lily – I – the horror of it. Words can't – nothing can explain the terror I felt, the cruelty of it – the pain. I managed to get hold of my phone and called – my friend – and he rushed me to a clinic, a private place he knows. They did marvels with my face, really. The top people in their field, I believe. A few more operations and *voilà*! Apparently you'll hardly be able to tell . . .'

He cried in earnest now. But not noisily, redly or snottily like I would've. The fat, crystal tears slid down from his long eyes like water flowing over marble. From the other side of the room, you wouldn't have noticed, apart from him patting his face with his hankie. He cried like Berengaria was supposed to have cried in the legends – the most beautiful woman in the world, the Lionheart's bride, cried like that because the inner corners of her eyes had been slit slightly in the Saracen manner so even weeping did not disfigure her. I remembered it from an historical novel. It went over and over in my mind like an idiot refrain as he recovered himself. Mojo. My friend. My poor, poor friend. God, Christ in heaven, how could You have let this obscenity happen? This *desecration*?

'That night, my friend took my key and had

263

my things removed from the house; even the rug, which was ruined by blood – my blood. He – he said I need never go back there, that he would protect me. It's strange, for the first time in our long relationship, I actually needed him, really needed him – and he is grateful. I'm grateful. Is that love, my Tiger Lily? I don't know, I don't know. I have to find out what I am now – to make a real life for myself, and him. Lily, I'm going away, abroad – I don't know how long for. I will have my operations done in America, or Switzerland, it doesn't matter. But Lily, please, you must leave that house – get Jamie away, both of you get away from Sean. He's like that terrible murderer, that Creeper – a man filled with rage and hatred. Twisted, deformed inside. I beg you, get the Angel to help you but please, *get away*. What he did to me, he could do to you. I know I should go to the authorities, the police – but I can't. The way they treat men like me – the humiliation, it would be – unbearable. I couldn't stand it. I just want to get away. Please promise me you'll go . . . I can't come back, I can't face Jamie. I know it's not her fault but . . . God help me, I blame her for bringing him to us. I know it's not fair, it's not right – but I can't help it. Perhaps in time . . .'

The devil on my shoulder prodded me hard with his pitchfork. I knew what Mojo meant. I felt it too. Yeah, maybe it wasn't fair – but had bringing that brute into our lives been fair? Had this appalling fucking thing that had happened to Mojo at Sean's

264

hands been *fair*? The shadowy café was intolerable now in its tacky silliness; I picked up Mojo's cold hand and kissed it, then, desperately, excused myself and went to the Ladies. In the yellow-tiled cubicle, stinking of disinfectant and sewage, the harsh light showed my haggard reflection in the cheap mirror cruelly. I didn't recognize myself. I felt a thousand years old – I felt like a corpse. What could I do? Stuff like this just didn't happen to people like us – it wasn't right, it was unnatural. My God, what the fuck could I do? What?

I went back to the café area, determined to get Mojo to go to the cops, at least – I'd support him, I'd make him see reason about it – but the booth was empty. Only his gold-tipped cigarette ends remained in the ashtray. I felt stunned, stupid.

The plump waitress waved at me and dully, I went over to her.

'Your friend said to say he was called away urgently – he paid your bill and everything. Is he an actor? Because I thought – you know, wow, he's so famous-looking, if you know what I mean . . .' She blushed. I reckon she was about nineteen. She looked like a briar rose. Fresh, innocent. Christ.

I said, Yeah, he's a famous, famous actor. Films. TV. You name it. Hollywood. Just here for a visit. Had to fly home, no doubt. Contracts. You know. She was thrilled. I almost believed it myself.

I never saw Mojo again, or heard from him. But I think of him, often, especially these days – and I miss him, I really miss him.

CHAPTER 29

The trip home seemed to take forever. The train stank of ciggies, damp and BO. Everywhere I looked people were reading newspapers with headlines that screamed things about the Night Creeper – now there was a crucify-the-coppers campaign on, saying they were stupid, incompetent plods who had been fooled by a false lead – if indeed it was a false lead and they weren't just stupid incompetent etceteras who were trying to calm the racial troubles down by lying about the Creeper's colour. One posh broadsheet paid a psychological profiling geezer from America, from the FBI, to analyse the Creeper. Said he was a white male aged between twenty and thirty, or something. That was the most dangerous age, apparently. Oh my gosh, really? Like every woman in the world didn't know blokes were at their most leary between those ages. Before twenty they were kids, after thirty they were Shed Blokes who did angling or kite-flying. I bet the FBI geezer got paid a fortune for that fascinatin' snippet.

I couldn't seem to get away from images of violence, of pain. It had never really touched me before, I think. Oh, sure, I'd been in brawls when I was younger, but nothing serious. Well, not serious to me, though I bet some precious types would shudder. This was different though. It was horrible, twisted, cruel. To deliberately disfigure someone with a broken bottle – man, that was psycho stuff. Get the profiler on Sean, I thought, let him fucking work that fucker out . . . yeah, well.

My insides were raw with hurt for Mojo; I felt so useless, so frustrated. I decided, first thing I'd do was get hold of Jamie, no – I'd ring Gabriel first and get him to come home from France, yeah. I knew that was rock n' roll heresy, coming home off tour, but he just had to, I needed him, Jamie needed him – it was serious, he'd understand. And this time, fuck it, I'd tell him how I felt. If it was cool, great. If not – at least I'd know. It was time to grow up.

What next? Right. I started organizing things in my head, like I always did when I was upset. First, get Jamie out of the house – it was Wednesday today – no gigs until Saturday and Sunday, and they were only Huddersfield and Manchester. Mr Farrer and the other clients would have to be put on hold for the week. Flu again – or food poisoning. Dreadful how sickly I am, really. No, I could do this. If Sean kicked up – threaten him with the coppers. Or get Andy and Pete to give him a major kicking. Maybe I should do that anyways. May as well. A & P owe me a favour after that bit of accounts wizardry I pulled for their 'motorcycle spares' *business*. Yeah, waste the fucker – let's see how *he* likes being a scar-face, the bastard.

I ran into the house primed an' ready to do battle.

What I found was an envelope addressed in Jamie's blocky italic hand propped on the mantel-shelf; addressed to 'Lil'. I ripped it open.

Dear Lilikins

Sean and I have gone away for a bit to sort things out. Don't worry, have not forgotten gigs, will be home definite *on Friday morning. Sorry not to have let you know but is a kind of spur-of-the-moment thing – going to deliver orders to some shops for his work, then get a B & B and try and really talk about stuff. Don't worry about me – am fine.*

Love love love *(and kisses – self-admini-stered!!!!!!!!)*

J. xxxxxx

P.S. think I might have clocked Moles this morning round by the scrapyard – keep yr. fingies crossed and put out some milk in case xxxxxxx

I shouted out loud with anger and . . . fear.

For the next five minutes or so I ran around like a headless chicken, running from room to room, tripping up the stairs, falling down them again, cursing like a trooper.

Oh Christ, oh fuck, fuck, *fuck*. What should I do, who should I – what should I – Christ, bastard, bastard, *Christ*.

Finally, breathless and sweaty, I fell over my hiking boots in the kitchen and went down heavily on my knees. It hurt and the pain sobered me up somewhat. I sat trembling at the table, my hands knotted together and white at the knuckles. Pull yourself together, girl, come on, pull yourself together. I chanted it like a mantra until my breathing slowed. Be logical. *Think*.

Right. If he – if Sean – hadn't done anything to Jamie before, he wasn't likely to immediately. I mean, he never beat her up or anything, why would he start now? He wouldn't risk it in a B & B – this was England. I could wait until they got back, pack loads of our things and on the pretext of the gigs, leg it. Yeah. Yeah. OK. No probs. Cool.

I'd break the news about Mojo as soon as possible to Jamie; God, what a job – there was no way to do it gently. Maybe she and Sean would be finished and so she would take it better – if there was a good way to take it. Gabriel would be on his way home so we'd be safe physically; we could maybe stay at Ben and Lonnie's, or Mrs Smith's, until we got a new house – wouldn't take long in Bradford. There wasn't exactly a housing shortage as long as you weren't overly fussy and had the deposit money. We could just get somewhere grotty until we found somewhere nicer. Sorted.

Not fucking sorted.

Gabriel's phone didn't respond – I later discovered he'd dropped it on to a tiled floor the day before and it had died; by the time he got a new one . . .

Ben and Lonnie's Ansaphone was on and I left a fairly hysterical message, not knowing they'd gone to visit Lonnie's mother for a week.

Mrs Smith had flu; she was really poorly and I just couldn't tell her anything, couldn't worry her – and no, it never occurred to me to tell the Popsies. This was my world, my problem, it didn't cross over into my parents' world. I felt very mature about that, I felt as if I was shielding them from unpleasantness. Very fucking grown-up; like, they were the kids and I was Mommy. They'd protected me from all that stuff about Jude and her family – now it was my turn to protect them. I felt worldly-wise and wearily experienced – I'd do what had to be done alone. I wouldn't contaminate my family by associating them with Sean. That was a total no-no.

For about an hour I just sat in the mess of a kitchen and waited for Ben to call me back on the house phone, while I incessantly redialled Gabe on my mobile. *Nada*, naturally – but I wasn't to know. I thought about leaving a message on Jamie's pager but what could I say? *Come home – Sean a monster?* I knew Sean had a mobile now that his boss had got him for work purposes, but I didn't know the number. Anyway, again, what could I say to him if he answered? *Put Jamie on and then bring her home pronto, you perverted bastard?* Great idea.

I drank about two gallons of tea and shook like a leaf; my brain raced and I couldn't seem to get a hold of myself at all. Mojo's beautiful, destroyed face kept appearing before me like a ghost image – a fetch. It made me sick to think of it happening, of his terrible ordeal happening in this house, on the floor just above where I sat now.

Then a thought occurred to me. I mean, sure, when I told Jamie the terrible thing that had been done to Mojo, she'd freak, good stylee – naturally. But hearing it second-hand, it might not have the gut-churning impact it had on me seeing and hearing it all face to face, like. What if the bastard got round her? What if – God forbid – he made it all out differently, made up some scenario that Jamie went for? He was quite capable of it, I knew that. His whole life was one huge lie after another – God, he could say *anything*. I couldn't *prove* Mojo's story – there was no hard evidence and no Mojo.

There was only one way to go. Definitely. I would prove once and for all, totally, forever and ever amen to Jamie what an out-and-out bastard Sean was. No stone left unturned – I'd get an arsenal of proof against him – nuke the fucker. I thought – what would he hate the most? You got it – to have all his lies exposed and the truth of his pathetic, nasty, *shitty* life stuffed down his throat with so much force he'd just die of it. I'd get a tidal wave of evidence that would swamp their relationship completely. No get-out, no loopholes, no fucking surrender.

I felt like a crusader riding out with the banner of righteousness clutched firmly in my mailed fist. Joan of Arc. If in doubt, go flat out, as Gabe used to say. But how? Where to start?

Right – start at the beginning. I picked up the phone directory and looked up Taylor – L.; I'd find his precious bloody Lisa and get the truth out of her about his so-called visits – yeah, and then his parents, everyone. I'd screw up his life like he'd screwed up ours. No vengeance would be too tiny, really. I was thorough at my job, well, I could be thorough at this. I was angry; really pissed – I'd fuckin' show him, I'd get some revenge for Mojo, however small – Sean wouldn't get away with this scot-free, no way.

There were about nine million Taylors.

Never mind – be persistent. It was eight o'clock, not that late to ring someone – anyhow, I didn't give a shit. I found three L. Taylors in the right postcode area and rang them – the first one was an elderly lady. I pleaded wrong number. The second was a pig-ignorant git and I just put the phone down on him.

The third was a woman. My heart banged in my chest. Softly-softly, I thought, softly-softly catchee monkey. Be cool. Be *nice*.

'Oh, hello, excuse me, but is this *Lisa* Taylor?'

272

'Yes, who's this?' Her voice sounded tired, busy. I could hear the sound of the telly and children in the background. She didn't sound anything like the young, glamorous, predatory sex-bomb Sean had made her out to be.

'Ah, I'm sorry, Miz Taylor, you don't know me, my name is Lily, Lily Carlson. Look, I'm really sorry to disturb you but – it's a bit awkward, but I'd like to talk to you about Sean Powers, I –'

The phone went dead. The trill of the dial tone echoing in my ear. *Fuck.*

I redialled and got an Ansaphone.

'Lisa, Sammy and Joe aren't here just now, but please leave a message after the beep and we'll get right back to you . . .' This was followed by children giggling.

'Uh, Miz Taylor, this is Lily Carlson. I, um, rang before. Please, I, er, have to talk to you about Sean. It's – um, it's my friend, she's, well, she's involved with him and . . . and I think she might be in danger – er, in trouble – oh, look, please ring me on my mobile which is, er, 0621 45374 and I'll ring you straight back. Please, Miz Taylor, please – it's really important. Sorry, I mean, goodbye.'

Crap, eh? Typical of my stupid, stupid mouth – words may be perfect in my brain, but the minute I open my gob – chaos. I didn't hold out any hope. I must have sounded like a right idiot, like a complete loony, not the suave, cool detective type I was always reading about. Bollocks. What a fuck-up.

I put the kettle on again. I felt totally depressed and deflated. All my grand schemes come to nothing. I dialled Gabe – zilch. I put some bread under the grill and burnt it. I tried again and slumped on the collapsing old sofa in front of the telly picking at the toast and jam and flicking through the channels. Avoiding the news, I settled for a programme about weird people's sex lives on Channel Four. Now, sex, there was another subject I didn't want to think about. I couldn't remember the last time I'd . . . on the tube, two people in alternative-style bondage gear stuck pins in their genitals and talked about how happy they were. I flipped over to wildlife. You can always rely on penguins. Not big on genital piercing, penguins.

I realized I was starting to get hysterical; I always got overly flippant when anything big happened. Someone once said to me that always being flip about everything was like a prison – once you got into it, you couldn't get out. But it was all so awful and I was all alone – I felt like my whole world was suddenly darker and nastier. I was scared, too, for all the Masked Avenger stuff.

I was so completely shaken by what had happened to Mojo – I mean, I know I've said it before, but really, things like that didn't happen to folks like us. They just didn't. They happened to people in the newspapers – to those poor women the Creeper murdered. Then I thought – this is how their families must feel. Like I was feeling. That it was just unreal, unbelievable. My mind kept refusing to believe it had happened; I had to keep telling myself what I'd seen and heard was really true. I mean, I know murder was a whole other ball game, but this business with Mojo, well, it was in that league, if you get me. It was serious. It was savage. Sean *was* a fuckin' monster, in my opinion; a weirdo, a headfuck.

I turned the gas fire up to Mach 10 and scrunched down amongst the cushions that still smelt faintly of sandalwood; Crabtree & Evelyn 'Mysore Sandalwood' – the one in the pretty bottle with the elephant on. Jamie's favourite – I always got her some for her birthday. It was unmistakable, it was so Jamie that I felt tears prickle in my eyes and I swallowed hard and watched the penguins do their underwater ballet with rigid interest.

Eventually, around half-ten, I couldn't hack it any more. I thought I'd go to my attic and write the events down in my diary, maybe pick up my e-mail, if there was any. If I couldn't sleep after that, I'd browse the tedious reaches of the highly overrated Internet. That always sent me to beddy-bye-byes.

Wearily, I trudged upstairs, avoiding looking at the dark hole that was Mojo's room. Another thought occurred – money. We'd have to find his rent as well as our own, plus the deposit for a new place. I didn't grudge him the money – how could I? But it was a problem. Also, I felt sad at having to leave our dear, shabby old nest; was there nothing that pig hadn't dirtied or ruined? It was another reason to despise Sean.

As I booted the computer up, I thought about how I'd carry out my plan of revenge – I'd find a way, somehow – only, I was so tired now. I missed Moley – you're never alone with a pet in the house. I don't care what anyone says, animals are such a comfort. Poor little velvet scrap of a cat – where were you on this freezing-cold night? Probably scarfing up someone else's Whiskas, no doubt, cats being as they are.

I was just getting into doing my diary, when my mobile played 'Jingle Bells'.

I grabbed the phone – please, please let it be Gabe!

It was Lisa Taylor.

CHAPTER 30

'Is that Lily Carlson – this is Lisa Taylor. You wanted to talk to me, yeah?'

She was drunk. Not blasted, but definitely pissed. Her voice rang with the fake confidence and aggression of booze. I was so flustered I just ummed like a fool.

'Well, din't yer? Din't yer wanna talk about *dear* Sean? Are y'there, or what?'

'Er, yeah, yeah, sorry – I didn't – I didn't think you'd ring back . . .'

'Well, int you the lucky one. Look, I int paying for this pleasure, lady, so you just ring me back, if you wanna talk about *our mutual friend*, like.'

'Right, right, no probs – I'll ring you right back, an' thanks, thanks a mill –'

Again, the line went dead. She was a wizard at the old hang-up routine, our Lise. I shot downstairs, nearly breaking my neck, banged the kitchen gas fire on and dialled the number on my scratch pad from the house phone. It picked up immediately.

'Miz Taylor?'

'Oh, don't be so formal – call me Lisa, *Lily*. God,

I mean, we've gotta lot in common, we 'ave, int we? We got Sean, for one thing . . .'

'It's not me – I mean, really, he's not going with *me* – it really is my friend he's seeing, living with. We share a house, he – he sorta moved in . . .'

'Yeah, right – if that's how you want it . . . it's no skin off my nose.'

'No, really – I mean honestly – look, hasn't he told you he's living with us?'

'Why should he? What's it to me? Look, what exactly d'you want?'

'But – haven't you seen him recently, then – only he tells us he's staying with you all the time – an', an' it really upsets my friend an' . . .'

'Oh Seanie, up to yer old tricks again, eh? Look, Lily, or whoever you are, I haven't seen Sean bloody Powers in three years, got it? Three whole years. An' I don't want to see him neither, thank you very much.'

'But he swore blind . . .'

'Well, he would, wouldn't he? Swear black was white, Sean would, if it suited him. The bastard . . . oh, pardon my French.' She paused, and I thought I'd lost her, but she went on, her voice less aggressive, less combative.

'Look, I – I had to have counselling after him. Yeah. Took all me money, ruined me life – oh, he's a cracker is our Sean . . .'

Her voice kind of sagged, and I heard the clink of bottle on glass.

'Are you all right?' Suddenly, I felt bad about

pushing myself into this woman's life. 'Look, Miz – Lisa, it doesn't matter, we don't have to do this, it's just, well, it's Sean, he's done something really awful and I'm frightened for my friend – well, for me too. But it's not your business, I just, I don't know . . .'

'You wanted to know if you were right? Yeah? That you weren't imaginin' it all, am I right? Because how could such a handsome, charmin' fella like Seanie be such a *cunt*?' The obscenity dropped like a brick; I could tell by her accent – Bradford wannabe-posh – that normally she'd have died rather than say that word. She was *really* upset.

'Well, yes – I mean . . .'

'Oh, I know what you mean, love. I know full well what yer *mean*. You can't tell me anything about Seanie. Four years. Four years outta my life he had, the bastard. Four stinkin' years. Oh yeah. Well, what did he do this time?' I heard the clink of glass again and the hiss and breath as she lit up. I was on tenterhooks, waiting for her to hang up at any moment.

'Um, you see, it's, well – he beat up a friend of ours, very badly. I'm really frightened for my friend and . . .'

She laughed. It wasn't nice to hear. 'Yeah, that's our Sean all right. I bet he had some excuse for it, eh? She provoked me, it weren't my fault – did you get the SAS stuff yet? You will. Fancies himself quite the little soldier-boy, our Sean does.

He tried to get in the Army, they wouldn't 'ave 'im – failed the psychological bit – what does that tell yer?' She laughed again. I wondered why she'd assumed I'd been talking about a woman when I'd said Sean had beaten someone up. I was about to ask her when she continued, dragging noisily at her ciggie.

'My counsellor says I should put it all behind me. Forget him. Concentrate on the kids, make a life for ourselves, like. Nice enough woman – but she don't really get it. Says, *Oh, why didn't you just leave him?* They don't know what it's like, living with a man like that. Still, you know, don't you? They get a sorta hold on yer, don't they? Put a sorta spell on yer. All the lies, the violence – it doesn't matter – they've always got an explanation, an excuse. Make you think it's all your fault . . .'

She was crying now and I felt like a complete shit. I wanted to burble an apology and get off the line, but Mojo's face wouldn't let me. I took a deep breath and went for it.

'Lisa, why would he lie about seein' you when he wasn't – like, where would he be goin' if he weren't at yours?'

'I dunno why he'd say he was at mine – he just lies all the time about everythin'. Doesn't know how to tell the truth. Prob'ly just wanted to throw you off the scent, like, 'cos – 'cos I'll tell you where 'e does go, oh yeah. He'll be off with that slag of an auntie of his – off wi' Lana Powers, up to God knows what. That's where he goes, to Lana. She's got 'im on a tight leash, that 'un, filthy bitch. Been at it together for years, nearly all his life – oh yeah, him an' Auntie Lana. Started when 'e was a kiddie. She babysat 'im and . . . you know, abused him. From the year dot, the slag. Her own nephew, she didn't care. He told me everythin' one night. I didn't know people went on like that. He said she made him – God, it's awful – he said she made him give her oral when he was *five years old*. She *trained* him, he said. I didn't know what to say, what to do. Next morning he said he'd been lying, winding me up. But I don't think he wor lyin' – for once. He used to go off for days an' come back – all marked. Bruises, burns – even proper cuts. He allus goes back to her, like a dog goin' back to eat its sick. He tried to get me to – do stuff to him, an' he wanted to tie me up an' stuff – not for a laugh, like, not . . . it hurt, I hated it. I couldn't stand it . . .'

She was sobbing, weeping – the sound was terrible. I closed my eyes against the thought of what Lana Powers had done to her own flesh and blood. I didn't want to know, but Lisa went on, like there was nothing she could do about it. It had to come out – and why not to a faceless stranger on the end of a phone line? They used to call it confession, but I was no priest. I didn't want this – but I'd asked for it.

Her voice quavered on the other end of the phone. Slurred now, as the drink took hold more.

'Has . . . has he got you – your frien' into it? Is that what the matter is? Don't let 'im, love, don't.

He's – he's a bad man – proper bad, inside. Don't listen to what 'e says, he's a stone liar. I 'ad to throw him out, I 'ad to – I 'ad the kiddies to think of. It were all too much. He went mental; absolutely *mental*. Said no one had ever finished with him before – that it wasn't right, it wasn't supposed to happen like that. All sorts of crazy stuff. Scared me stiff – but what else could I do? He's not right in the head, honest. Look, if you don' believe me, check out tha' bloody Adidas bag he always has – fulla porn mags, it will be – 'orrible stuff, real 'ardcore – an' worse. You check it, I'm not wrong.'

Hardcore porn? Violent S & M? What the fuck else had been goin' on that I didn't know about? A black tide of horrible, repulsive suspicion was crawling over me. Jamie – God, no – was that what she'd been trying to tell me?

Lisa was calmer now. I heard her light another cigarette; I wished I had one.

'Look – mebbe – mebbe I was wrong to speak to yer – that's what a bottle of plonk does for yer, right? Oh, anyways . . . Sean'll never leave Lana – it's like he's her slave or somethin'. His dad knows – oh aye, 'e knows summat's up, but 'e thinks the world of Lana an' anyhow, 'e won't do owt in case it upsets the mother – though some bloody mother she is, too busy prayin' to protect her kids. But that's why Sean's dad traits him so bad – 'e blames Sean for it all. Sean *disgusts* him, like. It's all the two lasses, the sisters, with him – not Sean.'

Her voice dropped to a hoarse whisper, I had

to strain to hear her. I huddled over the phone, with the creepy sense of being all alone in the old house.

'What I wanna know is, what went off in that hotel room, wi' Lana an' her mate that died? He was there, he was, Sean, he was there all right – that's what he said, said to me that night . . . that's why he said it was all lies next day – he'd let too much out. He were only a kid, but he were there all right an' Daddy had it all 'ushed up, like. Oh yeah . . .'

Suddenly, her voice changed, hardened – as if she'd gone too far, said too much. She became the sharp, aggressive woman who'd first called – put up her shield again. I realized that our conversation was over. I heard her take a long pull on her ciggie and then she said harshly:

'Look, I told you what I know, that's it. Take my advice, kick 'im out before he does you real harm, or robs you, or both. I . . . I don't wanna know no more, right? I don't wanna be involved. Mebbe I was wrong to talk to you . . . don't ring again, right? Not ever. I just wanna forget 'im now, OK? I don't wanna be involved.'

Click.

My stomach heaved. I just about made it to the bathroom.

CHAPTER 31

That night, sick and exhausted, I fell into sleep like I was tumbling down a well, falling through the clotted darkness into nightmares.

I dreamt I was running through landscapes covered with a clinging, thigh-high tide of congealed blood, the lead-coloured skies filled with screeching carrion birds bloated on the pallid bodies of little children. A sickly moon lit the horrible scene, silvering everything. I was filled with a terrible panic and horror, my heart pounding and my mouth stretched open in a raw, silent scream. I ran and ran from a huge, black angel – black like it had been burned. Its skin was cracked and charred, red seams of fiery blood webbing it. But I couldn't run through the thick, sticky blood and the ghastly angel gained on me no matter how hard I struggled. It had a great knife in one ruined hand and its blackened face as it loomed over me was Sean's. It pushed me down into the gelid blood and as I thrashed and screamed, its face turned into Jamie's, a beatific smile on her lips as she ran me through with the blade.

I woke up in tears, sobbing and crying into the sweat-soaked bed linen; the first time I'd cried for years, since I'd cried with happiness at coming to this house. I felt wrung out, ill.

I put joggers and two sweaters on, choked down a bowl of Sugar Puffs and cancelled all my appointments until further notice. I must have sounded dreadful, as even Mr Farrer said nothing except 'get well soon'.

Then I did housework in a maniacal, obsessive way until lunchtime. I decided it was time to stop when I found myself rearranging the spice rack into alphabetical order. Putting on my new white puffa jacket, and stuffing my locks into an old woolly hat, I walked the two miles or so into town. I didn't trust myself to drive – that would be all we needed, a car wreck. Also, I wanted some exercise and walking helps me think. I had to try and sort things out in my head, so that when they got back, I'd be calm and ready.

As I walked down the hill, I seemed unnaturally aware of my surroundings. I slowed my pace, dawdling past the great heaps of fruit an' veg piled outside the 'corner' shops – persimmons, aubergines, and knobbly green things I didn't know the name of; tangerines, apples, plums and spinach greens. Sharp, sweet and spicy smells made my queasy stomach turn. Past plumbing-supply shops crammed with turquoise plastic baths and mis-matched taps. Past luggage stores, their fronts hung all over with multicoloured handbags, daysacks and school satchels. Cloth houses, mobile-phone shops. It was all so familiar and cheerful in the icy clear light of the pale sun that hung in a faint drift of cloud above us all. I felt on the edge of tears again. All the people working in these shops had normal lives, I thought, why couldn't I? Just be normal and ordinary and potter through life.

I picked up speed again, my breath coming hard in the sharp cold. I started to run things over in my head, like I was balancing a column of figures.

1) Sean was a liar, a violent psycho and had viciously brutalized a friend of mine.
2) He was some sort of S & M pervert who was screwing his own auntie and might have drawn my best friend into his sadistic games.
3) Oh, God, the first two were enough.

It wasn't the S & M thing itself that bothered me – plenty of people played a few oooh-tie-me-up-Brian sex games with toys from Ann Summers and thought themselves dead kinky. Some went further and got more serious about it. But I knew enough to understand that consensual S & M, as they called it, had very strict rules and regs – passwords, role-play, rituals, that sort of thing. Safety nets for the players, if you like. Like the genital piercers on the telly last night, they had taken something most people thought of as negative, and for whatever reason made it positive for them. Why or how, I didn't know – I was no psychiatrist. However nasty or silly it seemed to those not into that scene, it appeared to make the participants *happy*.

Sean didn't make anyone happy. Coercion, manipulation and cruelty were his rules. I doubted his sex-games involved get-out words – or mercy, for that matter. That was the difference; his sexuality was gravid with hatred and savage violence; it boiled away in him like some thick, poisonous brew, contaminating everyone around him.

I was nearly in town now; I could see the Gothic sandstone buildings nestling in amongst the sixties cock-ups like crocus buds nosing out of winter mud. Fifteen minutes out of town, you'd be on the moors, free as a lark.

Once again, that desire to just run away came over me. I could run away and leave them all to it. I couldn't help Mojo – his friend had the time and more importantly, the huge sums of cash needed to do that.

The devil stuck his grinning mug in my face: Leg it, he said. Save yourself. Jamie's a lost cause. This is the crowning achievement of her lifelong addiction – Sean is her nemesis, her beloved torturer. *She wants this pain.* She loves this pain. You're a nice, normal girl, don't get involved – run.

'NO! NO! *She's my friend!*' I actually shouted this out loud, frightening an office girl with her paper bag of greasy-sandwich lunch. I stopped dead, realizing I'd practically been running. The sight of the startled girl's face as she bolted into her building made me jerk to a halt. Weakly, I leant against a lamppost, thinking how she'd spend the afternoon recounting her narrow escape from a unisex lunatic in a big white jacket who ran at her whilst having an argument with itself.

It was no good. I couldn't leave Jamie in the lurch. Apart from anything else, and to be totally selfish, what would Gabe think of me if I did? I had loved him too long, too much, to risk his disapproval and the loss of his respect at this stage of my one-sided courtship. I loved my Jamie, too. I really did, poor cow. She needed me. She needed saving. Saddle my charger, Knight-Girl is ready to tilt at that windmill.

I decided – tomorrow, it would all be over. As soon as they got back, I'd confront both of them, together, with what I knew. Get it all out in the open. Into the sunlight. No more scrabbling about in dark corners – disinfect things in the bright daylight. I wasn't afraid of Sean Powers. One false move and I'd have the cops on him, the wanker. Yeah, way to go, girl!

With a sense of unfounded optimism, I turned into the posh new bookshop which had taken over the old Wool Exchange and headed for the terminally trendy balcony coffee-bar for an Americano.

That night, unaccountably starving, I made some red spaghetti, heavy on the garlic – if Sean bothered me, man, I'd just *breathe* on the fucker. It was so unsettling – my mood seemed to swing alarmingly from hysterical panic to inexplicable calm. I tried Gabe again several times and left another, somewhat more coherent, message with Ben and Lonnie. I rang the Popsies and talked about their upcoming expedition to the Alhambra to see a musical – Ma wanted to meet me in town on Saturday afternoon to help her buy a new top, something evening-ey. We arranged to meet up in the bookshop café, as I told her how nice it was and she wanted to try it out.

I put the telly on after my tea and listlessly watched *Crimelines*, the shop-all-your-dodgy-mates phone-in show. It decked itself out as a 'public service' but like that other bit of telly nonsense with the big fat fella who pesters criminals, it was a load of bollocks. It was just gossip and voyeurism; as such, I quite enjoyed it. I especially liked trying to identify fuzzy grey blokes off surveillance videos, filmed while they ineptly blagged some building society. Most of them looked like Gary-next-door. But then Gary looked like Everyman, Twentieth-Century Style.

This time, they had a chunky, soft-voiced copper on asking people to ring in if they clocked the Night Creeper's 'dark van'. The plod had one of those reassuring Dales accents that make you think of lambs and heather – not some evil loony with a penchant for cutting up women in lonely ginnels. He was nice, the copper. Comforting. I liked him, but he was not allowed to talk long, as the spike-thin anchorwoman bonily elbowed him off the set and launched into a glib spiel about '*help us catch this evil killer before more terrible crimes are committed*', etc. She looked as if she'd learnt how to do 'concerned' that afternoon and was struggling with it as a concept. I lost interest.

I flipped through the channels, nibbling pensively on the back of my labret-stud – a bad habit which was chipping my front teeth. I watched a bit more of this and that, then decided to chuck it in and have a marathon diary session. That's how I remember so much stuff. Every day I'd write my life into the humming box of my computer; dissect my life ruthlessly for what – posterity? No one was ever supposed to see any of this. Funny, in a not-funny way – all that time in front of the computer thinking I really should stop writing all this – what's the point, my life's so boring.

Oh, Jamie. You were innocent of the one thing you were condemned for; and we were – no, *are* – Sean's last victims. The ones he left alive for his memorial. The only thing we were guilty of was naively believing we were safe in our own little lives. That we were freaky bohemian alternative types – how *cool* we were, how clever, how in-the-know. Liberal, open-minded, free from prejudice and unshockable. Yeah, sure – like blind children wandering through a war-zone.

I wrote in my diary that night: *I hate Sean Powers. I hate him, I hate him, I fucking hate him. I wish he was dead, dead, dead.*

Yeah.

CHAPTER 32

I slept heavily that night – worn out, I suppose. I woke very late and for a moment I felt confused as to where I was; I'd been dreaming I was at home and could hear the Popsies' voices downstairs. I woke up sharply when I realized I actually could hear voices downstairs – Jamie's and Sean's.

Flinging on my dressing gown, I bolted down the attic stairs in time to hear the front door shut. Without thinking clearly, I ran into Mojo's old room and peered out of the side window that looked out on to Hardy Street, as I'd done the night of the party. I'd been spying on Sean then, and here I was doing it again.

I saw him unlocking the door of his beat-up blue van, his bleached-blond highlights glittering in the sharp frosty light. I put my hands on the windowsill, leaning forward to get a better look as he opened the van door. Something about the scene niggled in my mind, something I couldn't put a finger on. Something to do with . . . no, it wouldn't come.

I was just about to leave when he looked up at

the window. At me. His blind, ice-blue eyes locked on to mine and my heart started to pound horribly. I realized *he'd known he was being watched.* How? How had he known?

Then I thought – he remembered I'd watched him from this window the night of the party. No, that was too weird – why would he remember something like that? But the answer was simple, if you knew Sean. He remembered stuff like that because that was the sort of thing all those paramilitary types went on about – surveillance, preparation, don't get taken by surprise. He'd gone on for hours about Sass-blokes 'reccying' the 'killzone', or doing 'deep cover operations' which depended on 'operatives' being constantly on the ball and forgetting nothing. Leaving nothing to chance. That's how he saw himself – as an operative. What did that make me, then? The enemy?

All this flashed through my mind in a jumble as we stared at each other. I must have looked like a gawping idiot, but he looked – I don't know – composed. Calm. Speculative, really. Like he was thinking on his feet, weighing something up. His blunt, feral face was deadly pale in the white winter light, his transparent eyes cold and frightening. Yeah, he frightened me. I didn't feel half so fucking brave now I was staring him in the face – even though it was through a window.

I broke the contact and drew back, away from him. He just turned back to the van, got in it and drove off. I felt incredibly relieved, glad he hadn't stormed back into the house in a rage. Nothing in his expression had suggested anger, sure – the opposite in fact. But I knew, I just knew, he was boiling with fury; bursting with it. I don't know why. Maybe because I was, too. Yeah, takes one to know one.

But he was filled with anger because he was an evil bastard, I thought. I was furious with the righteous anger of the avenger – yo! Well, I comforted myself with that thought, but if I'm honest, I was angry because he'd frightened me fuckin' stiff, the wanker.

Suddenly, I didn't want to be in that dark, hateful room any more – the room where poor Mojo had suffered. I ran upstairs and threw my clothes on, dashed in the bathroom for a cat-lick wash, and, taking a moment to calm myself, went down to tell Jamie the news – and my plans for our escape.

CHAPTER 33

Naturally, Jamie was brewing up when I got downstairs into the living room. I sat on the sofa as she bustled about with tea things and put toast under the spluttering grill. I didn't try to tell her anything until we'd eaten – better on a full stomach, I thought.

Finally, she shook the crumbs off her checked flannel shirt on to the floor and settled into the armchair by the fire, drawing her bare feet up under her for warmth. She looked – glowing. Happy. Oh shit.

'Well, Lil, it's weird.' She shook her head and then nodded in a thoughtful way. 'I mean it – weird. Like, I thought, you know – well, I said, didn't I? I said I thought it was just a waste of time with Sean, really. I was all set to jack him in, honestly. But man, what a turnaround! Unbelievable – totally a changed person. He said it himself – Jay, he said – I am a totally changed person. You've opened my eyes, he said. Really. Did this whole thing about how, you know, how immature he'd been, how he had finally seen how stupid he'd been with Lisa, how he wanted us

294

to have a proper future together – the lot. How he hadn't realized how much he felt about me until he'd thought he was losin' me. OK, OK, I know what you're thinkin' – but he was being dead honest, I could tell – no lies, just really open and straight up. A different bloke, honestly. Sure, we had differences – who doesn't? But you know, compromise, seeing the other person's point of view is the key to a mature relation –'

'He hasn't seen Lisa for years. He's shaggin' his Auntie Lana.' It just fell out of my mouth like a rock into a pond. She stopped in mid-sentence.

'He beat up Mojo, Jamie. Cut his face with a broken bottle. He's scarred for life. That's why he left. Christ, Christ, Jamie – Sean – Christ, he's a fuckin' monster – it's all lies, all lies he's telling you. Don't – it's true, it's all true. I phoned Lisa, I did, I really did an' she told me – an' Mojo, I saw Mojo, it's awful, his face, I . . .'

I told her everything as the afternoon grew golden and the gas fire hissed – but no heat could warm us up. It was a cold, awful thing I was telling her, and she took it like a child being told about dying. We were both shivering and tears stained her face as I finished my story. For want of anything else to do, I put the kettle on again.

'So it's all lies, then?' she said in a low voice. 'Just more fuckin' lies. Oh God, Mojo, no, I don't want to believe it. Where is he, Lily? Why won't he see me? I love him – he's my friend . . . Lily, why won't he see me?'

I couldn't tell her he blamed her. I just couldn't. Maybe some other time, when things were calmer. I put the teapot down beside her, but we didn't drink any of it – never even poured a cup out. I told her about what Lisa had said – about Lana Powers, the abuse, the porn and the S & M. She looked away, shut her eyes. I couldn't read her expression, her face was closed in on itself. We sat a moment in silence.

'It's upstairs,' she almost whispered.

'What . . . what is?'

'The bag – his bag. His Adidas bag, the one he always has with him. I saw him, he left it in our – in my room. When we got back, he was late for some work thing. He just chucked the bag on the bed. It's upstairs.'

I got up. 'Come on then. Let's have a look. See if she was right. Prove it. If she was makin' it up, I'll say sorry or whatever. If not – well, there you are. Come on.'

'I can't – I – he'll go mental. If he finds out he'll go mental. I promised him I'd never touch any of his stuff. He's got a thing about it – I couldn't . . .'

I swung round on her, furious. 'Fuck that, d'you hear? Fuck that stuff! Fuck *him*, too. Fuck him. Fuck his fucking mind games – Jamie! Think of Mojo! Think of your real friends! Sean's crazy, Jamie, fucked in the head – Jamie – he's *dangerous*! Come upstairs *now* and prove it once and for all!'

I was shaking with anger at her – at him. We went

slowly upstairs, while she sobbed quietly, wiping her face on her sleeve.

Jamie's double bed was tucked in behind the door, next to the window. The curtains were open and the wind, which was beginning to get up a bit, rattled the big, old wonky window frames – it was a sash window – nice, but getting past it. There was a terrible draught in that room, I always thought.

Her bed was a cheap one, put in by the landlord, with an imitation brass-type bedhead and foot; peeling semicircles of metal tubing decorated with big pearl-effect balls. I could see it reflected in her one bit of good furniture, a full-length, free-standing mirror we got at the flea market years ago.

The room was a tip – her floor, chest of drawers, mantelshelf, everywhere – littered with clothes, books, make-up, hair stuff, teddy bears, dirty teacups and toast plates. I couldn't have lived like that for a second. Still, different strokes . . .

I looked everywhere but at the bag that lay on the rucked-up mess of her bed. I didn't want to look at the bloody thing. I knew once I – we – opened it, that would be that. Everything would change, one way or the other. Our lives and our friendship would change – either for better, or worse. I didn't know which.

Reflexively, Jamie bent and lit the little gas fire – all the rooms except the attic had one – Bradford central heating, we called it.

We were delaying the moment, each in our

different way. But it had to be done. I grabbed the bag – it wasn't very heavy – and put it on the floor. I unzipped it, turning it round so we could have the light from the window. Our backs were to the door and we sat on the floor like children with a new, puzzling and not very nice toy.

What did we see? Socks. Grotty old athletic socks. My heart sank. OK, maybe I should have been relieved – but I wasn't. I could feel hope rising like a steam off Jamie as we gazed at Sean's dirty laundry. It irritated me to think she still didn't really believe me, that she wanted to believe him.

I grabbed the dirty clothes and was surprised when there weren't as many of them as I had thought – just a sort of thin layer, in fact. Underneath were – yeah, you got it – magazines. New ones, old ones, mostly small in size. And yeah, they were very nasty porn. I won't go into details – you don't need a vivid imagination to conjure up what we saw – what I made Jamie look at. I don't know, I just cannot *get* the joy of torture. These were pictures of women being horribly abused. Hurt. Beaten. Cut. Burned. They didn't look like they were having a great time, either. No amount of ridiculous costumes and cheesy sets could disguise the pain and suffering on their faces. None of them looked 'sexy' or 'hot'. They looked like junkies and victims, doin' it for some cash-money. There was some dominatrix stuff there too, from what I saw – women with bored expressions and naff outfits prodding grovelling lumps of flesh that would call themselves men, in the real world. It was all about hurting, and humiliating; pissing into mouths and shoving things up arses. I was disgusted, to be honest.

I just threw the mags on the floor and Jamie picked some up and looked at them numbly, as if she was trying to understand them – or understand Sean. I rooted about in the bag some more. There were another couple of smaller bags – one was an old sponge bag, which I opened first.

Jamie just sat crying like a Weeping Madonna statue, her lap full of those savage pictures.

In the sponge bag were a few bits and pieces of wash stuff, and contact lens solutions – odd, since Sean used daily disposables. Must be old stuff from his previous lenses, I thought. But the bottles and boxes were brand-new. As were the two phials I picked out and held to the light of the window. In the first, a pair of green lenses floated in their little plastic cage. Well, Mr Vanity, eh? Coloured contact lenses, my, my, my. Still, if I had weird eyes like Sean, I'd want a change now and again. Funny I'd never seen him wearing them though . . . The second phial held dark-brown lenses.

'Jamie – *Jamie*! Does Sean wear coloured contact lenses ever, like, green ones or brown ones?'

'What? No, no. Just those throwaway ones. He's short-sighted, like me . . . oh, Lily, I'm so sorry, you were right, you were . . .'

I wasn't listening. Something was bugging me, niggling in my mind again, like before at the window. I just couldn't put my finger on . . . I opened the inner zipped pocket of the baggie and pulled out some sticks of Leichner stage make-up, in various skin tones. One of them was a dark-brown. Dark-brown?

Things started coming together in my mind like a kaleidoscope pattern forming out of little pieces.

I went on to autopilot and opened the second bag.

There was a sort of wire hoop in it – thickish, cable-type wire fastened with a pair of snaplocks, clipped together. I held the hoop in my hand, puzzled.

It was threaded with . . . I couldn't understand – with what looked like mushrooms, dried mushrooms, only . . .

Something glinted. It was an earring. A small gold creole. These weren't mushrooms. Not mushrooms. Ears. Fuck, fuck, fuck, *ears! Threaded on to the wire – human ears!*

I suddenly felt dizzy, faint, and like I was wrapped in a cold, sweaty whiteness. Everything went slow motion. My hand holding the hideous wire started to shake violently. I heard Jamie, as if from very faraway, as if we were underwater, saying, *What's that . . .*

Brown contact lenses. Make-up. A dark-blue van. This, this *thing* in my hand. Then everything happened simultaneously. I knew what Sean was just as Jamie pulled an old cutthroat razor, then a black silk thermal balaclava and some matching glove liners out of the bag. *Camo, it was all camouflage*! Put on a cheap, black tracksuit, make the crystal eyes into brown ones, pull on the clinging, black balaclava – any skin showing could be made up brown. Sure, in a dark alley in the dead of night, a stoned girl terrified out of her mind . . . *the white man becomes a black man,* the white . . .

The razor Jamie held in a trembling hand was crusted with something. Blood. Blood. Oh Christ, oh God, oh God. I wasn't going mad. It was true.

We looked at each other horrified, dumb – and at that moment, I saw a red dot of light appear on my hand. I stared at it mindlessly – it didn't make sense. Then I heard Jamie gasp.

I twisted round to the door. Jamie was already staring at it with her face livid white. Sean stood there looking down at us, smiling. I hadn't heard him, heard *anyone* come up the stairs – not a fuckin' sound. In his hand was a huge, black gun. The red dot was its laser sight. He was pointing the gun at us. I couldn't breathe.

'Well, well, well. You have been busy lasses, haven't you? I thought you might be, when I saw the nigger staring at me outta that window. But I was distracted – mistake, mistake. Then I thought, well, my special lady wouldn't disobey me, would she? Eh? Would she? She wouldn't mess with my gear, after I told her not to. But you've been naughty, haven't you, Jay? You've been a naughty, bad girl and now . . .' His smile vanished as he saw what I was still holding. 'Put that down, you – put it down, you nosy black bitch. Mine, they are, *mine*. Proof. They'll want proof of the kills. *Put it down* . . . Christ, Christ, you stupid bitches, look what you've done, look what you've done . . . now it'll all come down, and it's your fault, you stupid . . .'

I dropped the filthy thing back into the Adidas bag. My mind was racing out of control. I heard Jamie say:

'Sean, what – Sean, please – that's not a real gun, is it? It's a replica one, isn't it? Sean, love, you frightened –'

The noise – the noise of the gun firing in that little room was unbelievable. I was instantly deafened. The acrid stink of it caught in my throat and I could feel myself coughing, but I couldn't hear it. The noise was like a blow, it knocked me senseless for a second. I saw the brass cartridge eject somehow from the gun and bounce and spin on the lino by the door. Glittering. The recoil of the gun knocked Sean backwards into the doorframe, his hands waving madly as he tried to right himself. My hearing cleared slightly and I heard Jamie screaming and screaming. Someone else was screaming too – me.

The air was full of plaster dust where the bullet had knocked a massive chunk out of the wall. Dust floating in the late afternoon sunlight. A gun – fuck, a real gun. I could hardly take it in. What I did take in, though, was that Sean didn't know what he was doing with it. He hadn't expected the recoil. He didn't know how to use the bloody thing properly.

302

Stupid, stupid, it could just go off anytime, he didn't know what he was doing . . . we were going to die, this fucker, this stupid, bastard fucker was going to kill us with a gun he didn't even know how to *use* properly.

Anger overcame fear for a second. I rose up on my knees and screamed at the top of my lungs.

'Police! Help! Help us! Police! Gary, Gary, Reena, get the police! It's Sean, he's the —

He stepped forward and kicked me in the mouth. I fell on to my hands and knees, blood pouring from my split lips. He kicked me again, in the head. I blacked out.

CHAPTER 34

They called it a siege. I don't know if it was actually that, if it lasted long enough to qualify. Sometimes, while it was going on and I fought to stay conscious, it felt more like a play I was watching. Whatever.

When I came round, I found I'd been put on the bed. I was sitting up a bit, and tied to the foot rail, my feet facing the head of the bed, and the window. I was secured by plastic cable ties. One looped tightly round each wrist, then another attaching my wrists together behind me. A kind of chain of the plastic ties fastened me closely to the bed's foot rail. Someone had put a cushion behind me. My feet were tied together in the same way, but not attached to anything as I was too short to reach the full length of the bed itself. I thought – these are what he ties her up with, plastic fuckin' cable ties. None of your black silk scarves and handmade leather love-cuffs. Cable ties. Christ.

Jamie had put the cushion behind me – and helped him tie me up. Afterwards, people asked me if I was angry about that. But what else could she have done? He would have just killed

304

me straight off. I believe that. I was meaningless to him. I guess I always had been. Like so many other people in his world, I was just a *thing*. He never, throughout the whole event, called me by name. Always 'it' or 'the nigger' or 'the bitch'. I was a piece of carrion to him, nothing, not even human – just as the women he'd killed had been nothing. That became plain enough as the hours went by. It was the worst feeling, really, to know you are completely without value, even to the point of life and death. It's like being invisible; powerless. I wasn't a person who was used to that – but Jamie was. Had been all her life until she went on-stage. She'd often tried to explain it to me, but though I'd made the right noises, I hadn't really understood. I did now. It was the worst kind of mindfuck.

But anyway – the first time I woke, man, was I in *pain*. My whole head hurt terribly; my lips and mouth were swollen, one of my top front teeth had broken off and my labret-stud was totally buried in the puffy, bloody flesh of my lower lip, the steel pin tearing slowly through the damaged tissue as it puffed up. My shoulders ached like fire and my feet had gone numb. Every part of me hurt and I could barely concentrate on what was happening, except I remember thinking the room stank, literally stank, of Sean. A sour, animal stench. It made me gag and retch.

'What, what . . . Jamie, what . . .' I started coughing and spitting blood.

Jamie started towards me from where she was

sitting on her heels by the dresser. Sean levelled the gun at her and screamed furiously:

'Stay! Stay there! Don't you fuckin' move, don't fuckin' move, d'you hear me? Leave that bitch alone! Leave it . . .'

The phone rang. The phone by the bed rang. I – we all jumped a mile and I felt my heart thudding hard. Christ – it was so silly, so banal. That little, homey noise. I prayed hard it wasn't my mother.

Sean bent down, holding the gun pointed at Jamie, and picked up the receiver. I was so terrified the fucking gun would go off, I could hardly hear what he said. I had almost forgotten about Jamie, but I realized she was back on her knees, staring at me with huge, pleading eyes. I managed to nod fractionally at her but then the phone call took my attention.

'. . . you're who? You're who? Superintendent Oates, Oa – Owen; Superintendent Owen? Well, d'you know who I am? Yeah, that's right, the Night Creeper. What? Yeah, yeah, I can see out the window – oh, very fuckin' good, sure, go nearer to the window an' have your blokes blow my fuckin' head off? D'you take me for a twat? Don't – I mean it, *don't* fuck with me or I'll kill these bitches . . . Yes, I fuckin' have. A great big fuckin' gun, how about that? For your information, Superintendent fuckin' Owen, it's a Desert Eagle point-44 magnum, with an infrared . . . yeah, hollow-point . . . loads of 'em. A cut above the toys your lads get, eh? A real man's gun,

306

yeah . . . Manchester, where'd d'you think? What? No. No. I don't give a fuck. Wait – just you wait on. Have the Sass contacted you yet? The Sass. The SAS. Yes, yes – well, they will. Then all you little boys in blue will have to fuck off home, won't you? Yes – no, right – no, that's enough, *fuck you* – I'm in fuckin' charge here.'

Sean slammed the phone down and moved over to me. Dear God, I thought, please don't let the coppers get heroic, don't let them try anything stupid, please, please. Sean stood over me. He was grinning like a maniac, the gun jittering in his hand. He stuck the muzzle hard in my temple and gestured with his free hand for Jamie to come round to the foot of the bed, behind me.

'Get on your fuckin' knees, slag. Did you hear that? Did you? Hear all that outside? This bitch got us into a siege, got us in a right mess shoutin' its fuckin' head off like that, forcin' me to – fuck, the place is crawling with coppers. You're gonna die for this, hear me? *Die.*' He yelled at Jamie and jabbed the gun at me; I could feel its cool greasy metal and smell it – acrid, burnt almost. Jamie cried out.

'Don't – Sean, please, you promised – don't hurt her – you promised me . . .'

He ignored her and continued jabbing and shouting. 'That was the coppers, that was Su-per-in-ten-dent fuckin' Owen. Top man, the bloke in charge. Oh yes. Oh yes. They fuckin' know who's in charge now, all right. They're all out there.

Snipers. Marksmen. The lot. But it's me, *me*, I'm callin' the shots now.'

I coughed out, 'No!' He pushed the gun hard into my mouth. The metal grazed the exposed nerve of my broken tooth and I choked with the pain, tears leaking from my eyes. I panicked, I thought I was suffocating, gagging.

Fear is a strange thing. I became horribly aware of how fragile my body was; just a bony cage holding my organs in, covered with a membrane to stop it all sloshing out. So easy to tear, to break. For the first time in my life, I understood mortality, that I really could die. That I would die, that I would not exist any more, just be blown away and forgotten. I felt a strange detachment creep over me, as if my mind was slipping its moorings and floating away. I realized I was more afraid of the gun going off accidentally than I was of him shooting me on purpose. I felt my body go loose and my bladder let go. Pissed myself. I could smell the urine and feel the hot wetness – but I didn't care. I felt so far away, so far . . . all I could think of was that I'd been supposed to meet Ma in that café . . . my dearest ma and pa, so good and kind . . . I'm so sorry, I . . . I heard Jamie screaming as Sean yanked the gun away.

'Christ! Dirty bitch, it's pissed itself! Fuckin' animal, Christ!' He jerked away, disgusted.

Jamie was nearly incoherent with terror – for me, not for herself. She was babbling at me, entreaties to be calm, to stay still and a flood of pet-names and endearments. I felt her touch my locks through the bars of the bed foot where she was crouching. Then she crawled round to the side of the bed.

'Sean! Sean – please, please don't hurt her, please . . . look, Sean, I'll do it, what you wanted me to do. You know, what we argued about – I didn't mean to cross you – honest, I'll do what you wanted, I will, I swear it, I swear it on my nana's grave – but don't hurt her any more, don't hurt Lily – it's Lily, Sean, Lily, *Lily* . . . don't hurt her and I'll do it, I swear . . .'

He was standing side on to the window across from us now. His head swivelled round as she said this.

'Oh yeah?' He licked his lips. His tongue was red and pointed. It was repulsive.

'Yeah, yeah, Sean, I will, I promise – only . . .'

'OK, OK – forget the nigger, forget it – go on then, go get the – careful, mind . . .'

Jamie inched across on her hands and knees to the chest of drawers. Sean watched her hungrily as she pulled open the littlest top drawer and took out a piece of paper.

I was going in and out of consciousness. All I could feel was pain, just pain and a terrible fatigue. In the papers afterwards they said, *The terrified women screamed for mercy as crazed killer Sean Powers hurled abuse from the upper-storey window at the Police Task Force officers below, threatening them with an illegal handgun* . . . He didn't. We didn't.

We listened to Jamie recite her Slave Contract to Sean.

She unfolded the crumpled paper and sat back on her heels, sobbing. Sean laughed and pointed the gun at her.

'Go on – go on then . . .' He was like a wire, his once-handsome face skeletal, his skin curdled like bad milk in the bluish light from the window.

She choked and sniffed, wiping the back of her hand across her face. Outside, I could hear muffled sounds of radio chatter, and cars, and voices . . . The only light in the room was from the gas fire, but sometimes, sweeps of light from outside arced across the ceiling. Jamie read aloud in a slow, hoarse voice.

'I, Jemima Olivia Gerrard, also known as Jamie Gee, do solemnly swear by all I hold sacred and of my own free will, declare that I am now and henceforth the slave and sole property of . . .' Her voice faltered and she looked at me. I shut my eyes. '. . . of Sean Powers, now called and known as my rightful master and owner. I will do whatever he wants now and always. I will submit to him in everything and cut off all ties to my former life, friends and family as he so desires. All my property is his to do what he wants with, and I will have only what he gives me. My body is his to do what he wants with. I have no soul, no mind, no spirit of my own, only what my master allows now and forever. I will make the mark of a true slave upon my own body as a token of my submission. Signed . . .'

'Do it, do it – you know what to do, *do it* – then sign it – in blood, it's gotta be done in blood, like I said . . .' His voice was thick and urgent. I opened my eyes again as Jamie unbuttoned her shirt, took it off and then took off her bra. She wasn't crying any more. I was.

I looked at her poor breasts. They were laced with marks – mostly bite marks, and half-healed cuts. Bruises bloomed purple under the thin, fragile skin.

Sean handed her the dreadful straight razor. 'Do it!' he hissed.

She took the blade and putting it to her breast, started to cut. She cut the letter 'S' in straight, rune-type lines. I realized she was going to cut the word 'slave' into her own flesh, to save me. I couldn't bear it. I struggled against the cable ties and shouted out, 'No! No! Jamie, no!'

Sean stepped over to me like a snake striking and slapped me hard round the face. My head snapped back and my vision blurred as I fought to stay conscious while pain filled my world with white fire.

Jamie stopped cutting. Blood ran down her belly and soaked into her jeans. Sean was laughing mirthlessly and going, '*Yeah, yeah, do it – go on, do it . . .*' over and over. He was rubbing himself and laughing, so engrossed in his fantasy-come-true he didn't notice she'd stopped cutting and was looking at me with her face full of sorrow, and shame. I looked back at her and tried to show her, somehow, that I loved her. That I forgave her. We shut Sean out, in that moment, we shut that fucker out.

And he felt it. His rage burst like an explosion, his whole body rigid and twisted with fury. He grabbed her arm and dragged her to the window, throwing it up and open, leaning out with her and howling abuse at the police.

Shoot him, I thought desperately, shoot him, shoot him . . . but they couldn't, because of Jamie. Jamie forced half out of the window, her body naked and bloody, hell in her eyes.

Evil funnygirl Jamie bared her breasts at policemen as she hung laughing out of the bedroom window at the siege house last night. The failed celeb had carved her killer boyfriend's initial into her own flesh and she flaunted her naked body at the officers below . . .

Have you seen that photo? The window one? It was everywhere. Usually under a headline like *Creeper Hostage Drama*, or *Evil Killer Siege Horror*. My poor girl. It only took a second and then he flung her back into the room. But that photograph destroyed her.

The phone rang again and Sean picked it up; he looked fatigued now, drained – as if he was waking up from a nightmare. His skin was waxy and his hands blotched with Jamie's blood. The gun trembled. It was huge, ugly and angular. It must have been heavy and awkward, especially with the laser thing strapped on it – I wondered how long he could hold on to it for. I didn't know how long we'd been there – hours? He was getting tired.

As for me, I knew that I hadn't understood what pain was until that day. I tried to move around a bit, to sit up more as he spoke irritably into the phone.

'. . . what the fuck are you on about? Yeah, she's all right, what's it matter? No, you can't – you don't need to speak to them. I call the shots here, geddit? And – look, have they called yet? You know – you know, the Sass? Well, why don't you know? Do I have to kill these bitches – no, all right, all right – it's proof, isn't it – it's proof they want – well, here . . .'

He put the gun down on the floor and reached into the Adidas bag. My heart leaped wildly. *Get it Jamie, get the gun, get it, get it, get it* . . . I twisted my head round, ignoring the sickening starburst of pain and our eyes met. She left off buttoning her shirt and slowly began to move towards it.

Sean flung the loop of wire with its terrible burden out of the window, bent down and retrieved the weapon and the phone. I wept silently with frustration.

'. . . there, there you are, give 'em that, give 'em . . . proof of my kills, you know, like they did in 'Nam with the Gooks, like in them films about 'Nam . . . they'll be beggin' to take me now, beggin' – no! no! Not my family – don't fuckin' bring them here, don't! No fuckin' way, no fuckin' – I'll off these bitches, I swear, I swear I'll . . .' He slammed the phone down again.

He began to pace around the little room talking to himself furiously about what he would do, how he would deal with all of this. The window was still open and I could hear the sounds of the police and kept hoping to God they wouldn't do anything to force Sean's hand. It was cold, too, despite the gas fire. I found myself shaking violently in spasms. I kept thinking – if I ever get out of this – *if* – I'll never be the same again. I could hear Sean shouting at Jamie, accusing her of disobeying him by putting her shirt back on; saying she was worthless, stupid, ugly. That this was all her fault, and she'd pay for it. He kept kicking her in the hip and thigh as he stalked back and forth past her, lashing out with his boot as she knelt on the floor shivering.

Then suddenly, the fight seemed to go out of him. Like a puppet with its wires cut he slumped into the bentwood chair next to the big mirror, the gun dangling from his hand.

Jamie lifted her head up and looked at him. I strained against my ties to watch them.

'Sean, Sean – let us go. Let us go now, it's no good; you don't want to hurt us, love. Everyone knows you're the Man, now – show how strong you are, let us go. Look, just let Lily go – I'll stay with you, I still love you, Sean. Be strong, let Lily . . .'

He hit her hard across the face, and she fell sideways, blood pouring from her nose.

'Shut it! Shut it, you slag!' he screamed, spit flying from his lips like a dog. 'I know what you're doin'! I know! I'm not stupid! Tryin' to get round me, trying to fuckin' manipulate me! You whores are all alike! Dirty, dirty – allus trying to get a bloke to do what you want! Allus wheedlin', crawlin' around me! All my fuckin' life! One after another, just like Lana said! Just 'cos I'm good-looking – you just wanna fuck me, use me up and get what you want outta me, dirty, dirty bitches, sniffin' after me like you was in heat – fuckin' animals.'

Jamie pulled herself up and leant on one elbow, trying to wipe the blood off her face. He kicked her arm from under her and she hit the floor hard. I cried out:

'Sean! Sean! Stop it! Listen, man – listen – it's the police chopper, outside – it's the Sass fellas, they've come . . .'

Jamie looked at me and shook her head, blood flying like strings of red beads. But I had to do something, anything, just to distract him. I knew it was dangerous – stupid, even – but I had to do *something*. To fight back somehow. Not just die snivelling. It was my last gasp, really – I fell back again, trembling and exhausted.

He stood sideways to the window and peered out, gun raised, pointing at the ceiling.

'It's them, it's them, isn't it, Sean – they've come . . .' Jamie spoke to him quietly, reasonably, taking up where I'd left off – behaving as if this bizarre fantasy was real and the SAS really were arriving to whisk Sean away to whatever destiny he thought was his.

'Shut up – shhh!' he said, like a cross child. 'I can't see – it's gotta be them, they've had plenty of time to mobilize . . .'

'What will you do if it is them, Sean?' said Jamie, still apparently calm and cool. She always had been a good actor – her voice was dead steady. It was as if she was suddenly on-stage – she seemed to have gone into her stage persona; in control, focused. I struggled to see her properly, it was eerie, the way she had become her stage-self – like this awful pressure had created the same effect in her that stage fright did. It had gone into her blood like the adrenaline rush she got before she went on-stage and without thinking, she'd become the other Jamie – the Jamie all the punters thought was so strong, so together. I didn't understand why it had happened, I just prayed she could keep it up – for both our sakes.

'I'll go wi' 'em.' He spoke to her as if she was being particularly dense. 'They look for blokes like me. What d'you think 'appens to all the really great killers? Prison? Hah! Bollocks, that is. Government smoke screen, like. To keep the public quiet. No, they train them up as an elite cadre, special combat corps, assassins. Oh yeah, I read about it in some literature I got – dead secret stuff, I 'ad to send off for it an' everything – but see, I knew then it were just a matter of provin' myself to 'em an' bingo! No one would give me the fuckin' runaround ever again. She – they'd 'ave to take me serious, then. That's why I did those targets like I did. Stealth. Oh aye. Hand to hand – ninja style. They look for that sorta stuff, they do.'

He sat down again and cradled the huge gun to

his chest as if it were a baby. He looked totally blank and vacant for a moment, as if he were in a trance. His moods seemed to alter constantly; they rippled across his face like the wind disturbing the surface of water. As I watched him, he seemed to be – I don't know how to put it – but he seemed to be *dwindling*. As if the enormous mental energy he was expending was eating him up, dissolving him from inside. It was weird, like watching those things on wildlife programmes where an insect lays its eggs inside a captive grub, then the larvae eat the grub up slowly – it's still living, but it's being hollowed out by the ravenous parasites.

He came to, as if he'd been a long, long way away. 'See this?' He waved the gun at Jamie. 'Five hundred quid I paid for this, offa bloke – got fifty rounds with it for nothin'. He knew a real mover when he saw one, that fella did. Yeah . . . I shoulda got it sooner, done those targets with it but . . . Lana wouldn't have liked that, she likes cuttin' . . . she – she . . . I had to make her pay attention, pay me respect, I'm not a kid any more . . . I did Simone, you know. We were doin' a scene, I were only sixteen – in that hotel, doin' a scene . . . we had her beggin' for it, the fat whore, beggin' – she liked bein' strangled when she came, did Simone – so I – I just didn't stop, made like I didn't hear her safe word and she – she died. It wasn't my fault, it wasn't. Simone just pissed me off – allus creepin' round Lana, trying to shove me out, get rid of me like I was rubbish or summat. Slag. Lana said I shouldn't have done it, though, on account of it was her in control, she was topping, not me. She were bloody furious. She don't care about me, really – you know? She don't – she says I'm too old for her now – it's not fair, it's . . . I did everythin' for *her*, it's not fair . . .'

He sagged in the chair, tears rolling down his cheeks, silvery strands of mucus sliding down his chin. The moment spun out longer and longer. The whole ruin of his life lay before us and crumbled into dust.

I felt sorry for him – only for a second, but I did. Then my pity was instantly dissolved in a terrible fear – not like the fear I felt before, but a cold, overwhelming terror. *He was going to sacrifice us to Lana.* To his fantasy of winning her love back and impressing her as a real, potent, adult *man*. A strong, successful man, like his father – a proper soldier, recruited for important, Real Men's business by his imagined covert operators, his 'Sass Blokes'. The whole, sad, sick dream fed by those stupid, idiot paramilitary films and books and the cruel pornography he was addicted to. It was insane. It was – how could you – God, how could you *ever* get through to him?

You couldn't. Because inside that perfect, killer's body was the emotional heart of a desecrated five-year-old. The five-year-old Lana Powers froze in time with her obscene *training*. This whole thing, this siege, the murders – were his temper tantrums, his attention-seeking. He was a *child*.

Jamie crawled over to him and laid her bloody hand on his knee. I tensed involuntarily, willing her to be careful.

'I love you, Sean, it's all right, I love you.' Maybe she was still acting – stringing him along. Maybe, for this instant, she wasn't. I don't know. I felt myself drifting again; that strange, dreamlike detachment. I couldn't help it – my mind flashed back to that instant in the pub, the night we first met Sean and I'd thought: *They look like a pair.* Only this time it wasn't their physical appearance, it was their moods, the both of them – their moods changed so swiftly. Then I thought – well, yeah. They had a lot in common. But at some point in their lives, he'd gone down one path, and she'd gone down another. Then I thought of her horoscope – *a terrible fatality* – and I felt that sickening terror wash over me again and I snapped back into reality. I willed her to be careful, not to push it too far. I heard her speaking to him – just murmuring over and over that she loved him, it would all be all right. Her ruined voice was tender, full of compassion as she gazed – her grey eyes lustrous with pity – into the ravaged face of this murderous, destroyed creature.

I was too frightened for compassion. *Get the fuckin' gun and shoot him*, I screamed inside. *Waste the fucker, kill him, Jamie, kill him . . .*

He bent his head, and she put her long, gentle hand on his blond hair. Outside, I could hear another world; a sane world where people didn't murder girls in order to show off to a vicious, depraved old woman. Where people had children, loved each other, worried about bills and schooling – not whether this lunatic was going to blow their heads off out of spite. I groaned out loud.

Sean's head came up, his strange, blind-seeming eyes looked at me, but didn't see me. Jamie froze.

He put his head back like a wolf and screamed out loud – it was terrible, inhuman. It echoed around the room and sliced into my throbbing head like a razor. It seemed to go on and on and on. His throat bulged with the raw, brutal effort and the veins on his neck stood out like thick worms. It was like a black hole had opened up and we were all being sucked into its icy void by that tearing, unbearable cry. It was like nothing I'd ever heard before, that awful, awful noise. I can't forget it.

Then suddenly, he stopped and stood up, dragging Jamie to her feet. This is it, I thought. Dear God in heaven, it's going to happen, he's going to kill us now. He shoved Jamie, who was rigid with fear, in front of him – I could see her face over his shoulder and his face in the mirror. I struggled again against the unyielding plastic of the ties, feeling the raw scrape as they bit into my flesh. I would have torn my own hands off to escape this trap, if I could have; I would have done anything, *anything*. Panic boiled through my blood, uncontrollable and bestial.

I saw him take Jamie's face in his free hand,

pinching her cheeks between his thumb and fingers. His eyes reflected in the glass looked like a dead man's; gelid, congealed. He raised the gun and I started to pray convulsively, the half-remembered prayers of my childhood: *Our Father, Who art in heaven blessed be thy . . . oh Jesus, Jesus . . . Matthew, Mark, Luke and John . . . if I should die before . . . oh Christ, oh Christ . . .*

He pulled Jamie to him by her face, then let go and gripped the back of her neck, forcing her to him. Then he ground his mouth on hers in a brutal kiss. Her hands flew up and she slapped at him, frantically, struggling to breathe. Then he pushed her away and stepped back until he was nearly stood against the bed, but still facing her – and she fell back against the mirror, her lips swollen and bruised, her face like a Greek mask of tragedy, from some ancient, terrible play.

I saw him smile. His beautiful face was smooth again, he looked very young and calm. He said, steady and quiet, like: *'It's all bollocks, isn't it?'* Then he put the muzzle of the great gun in his mouth and Jamie screamed:

'Lily, shut your eyes!'

And he pulled the trigger.

CHAPTER 35

The sound seemed even more huge and deafening than before, and I felt a stinking, hot rain fall over my head and face, and a stinging cut below my left eye. My ears were ringing and when I tried to open my eyes they were thick and gluey with what I knew was Sean's blood. I vomited helplessly, choking and spitting, desperate not to swallow any of the blood that coated my face. I felt Jamie tugging at the ties, and saw her slashing at them with the straight razor. The murder weapon, as they called it afterwards. It didn't seem to matter; nothing seemed to matter. I didn't look at – Sean. I shut my eyes again, only the appalling pain of the feeling coming back into my feet and hands and the uncontrollable shaking of my body seemed real. I felt someone heaving me over the bed foot but I couldn't seem to help them, or move.

It was Jamie. She carried me bodily into the bathroom next door and wiped my face with a towel, then wrapped my dreadlocks in it, like we'd just played shampooing. Then she left me and answered the telephone that I was just beginning to hear through the noise in my ears. I was crying, but helplessly, not sobbing but just unable to stop the tears.

Jamie didn't cry. Funny, she'd always cried at everything – telly adverts, films, broken hearts. Me, I only cried a few times in my whole life – now I couldn't stop.

Then the little house was full of coppers in riot outfits, smelling of outdoors. Bigwigs in uniforms and plain-clothes detectives strode about barking orders. The ambulance crew bundled up the stairs at full tilt. All these big blokes looming over us, shouting. Oh, not at us especially, just shouting like blokes do when they're worked up. A nice woman copper with a soft voice talked at us for a bit, but I couldn't seem to understand what she said. She went into the ambulance with us and we went to the Infirmary – it seemed to take hours, or maybe just minutes – like that teacher said, Time is just a mode of thought. It was a dark blur prickled with lights and snatches of noise, talking, people asking questions. I said, *Don't separate us, don't separate us* – but they did. Then I asked for Ma and Pa and they said they were on their way. I asked for Jamie again but they shhh'ed me.

It made me angry; I felt anger rising like bile in my throat and I struggled off the hospital bed in a formless, irrational way, wanting to find Jamie, to find my friend. I stumbled out into the treatment room, shaking off nurses like a dog shaking off water. I couldn't find . . . where was she? I felt dizzy, faint. The white hard light bouncing off the white surfaces hurt my eyes. The hospital reek of disinfectant masking human body smells sickened me. I was confused, and panicking again. The towel-turban Jamie had wrapped so tightly round my head fell off and my locks tumbled over my face.

I stopped, and took my dreadlocks in my hand, staring at them. Everything in the room seemed to recede, as a wave is sucked back into the sea. All I could hear was the roaring in my ears. A nurse grabbed me but I threw her off. My locks. I squeezed them, and then looked at my hand. The palm was red and thick with sticky, coagulating blood – flecked with gritty-feeling granules.

My locks were soaked with Sean's blood, with his shattered bone, with fluid and *tissue* . . .

I started screaming and screaming while they tried to bundle me back into the cubicle.

Cut them off cut them off cut them off cut my fucking locks off cut them oh God cut them cut them off Jamie Jamie . . .

All at once, Jamie was there; like a lioness defending a cub she yelled at them to crop my head, to get that stuff off of me. They said they wouldn't, unless I signed a release form because people had complained when they'd done that sort of thing before. It was more than their jobs were worth, and who was she to give orders and was she a relative? And, *I'm sorry but* . . .

She said, deadly quiet, her voice cold, slicing

through their chatter; 'Get the fuckin' form *now*.' They did. I wept as they cut the bloody mass off my head, shoving the foul, soaking matted hair into a blue plastic bag in case the coppers wanted it.

They tried to stop us, but we staggered to the toilets and Jamie washed my shorn head with dispenser soap and gently rinsed it over and over under the tap, patting me dry with paper towels while I cried and wouldn't let go of her waist. There was a three-centimetre cut under my eye where a piece of bone had sliced me, and despite their best efforts to prevent it, she sat with me while they sorted it. She sat with me until Ma and Pa came, and all the nattering and jabbering was done. She sat with me while the whole idiot circus swirled and eddied around us and we sat silent, because there was nothing for us to say.

They wanted to keep us in overnight, especially me because of my head. But the X-ray showed no fractures or anything so we discharged ourselves after signing more forms and pocketing slips of paper about the symptoms of concussion. Yeah, yeah, yeah. Oh, just to get *out* of there, to get away from the people – the medics and the coppers and the gathering press with their lumbering, uncomprehending prying. We had each other, that was all that mattered; we didn't want anyone else. No one. We didn't want to talk about it. We didn't want their *help*. We wanted it all not to have ever happened; to press rewind and erase. We didn't want the platitudes, the soothing bullshit, society's pacifiers. We wanted everything to be normal again. Normal. Like before – before we ever met Sean Powers. Normal.

And it never could be, never again – I knew it. Oh, we'd get on with our lives, sure – what the fuck else could we do? But it would always be there, that heavy, stony lump in our bellies, that bloody weight of guilt – guilt that we didn't suss what Sean was, guilt that our ignorance cost those women's lives. It was like we were pregnant with that brutal, hideous guilt but we'd never be able to bring it to birth – it'd just stay there forever, we'd carry it *forever*.

My head ached and churned with a spinning mass of half-made thoughts and I felt feverish and totally shit – Jamie did too, but she was livid-white with exhaustion and couldn't talk. As we lay together in Ma and Pa's saggy old spare bed I could hear her crying – she wasn't, like, sobbing out loud, but I could hear her anyway, and feel the rigid tension of her body curled up at my back.

I wanted to comfort her – but I couldn't. Eventually, I felt her twitch into sleep and I tried to make myself sleep too, but I just couldn't, so I lay there, breathing in time with my poor big girl and praying over and over a prayer that I knew could never be answered.

Normal. I want it all to be normal again – God, God, God, let it all be a dream, let everything all just be normal again; please, please . . . give us our lives back . . . give us our lives back . . . please . . .